T0163452

THE DARK SISTER

Library of American Fiction

The University of Wisconsin Press Fiction Series

REBECCA GOLDSTEIN

The

Dark

Sister

NEW AFTERWORD

THE UNIVERSITY OF WISCONSIN PRESS

The University of Wisconsin Press
1930 Monroe Street
Madison, Wisconsin 53711

www.wisc.edu/wisconsinpress/

3 Henrietta Street
London WC2E 8LU, England

Copyright © 1991, 2004 Rebecca Goldstein
All rights reserved

Lines from "Planetarium" from *Poems, Selected and New, 1950–1974* by Adrienne Rich. Reprinted by permission of the author and W. W. Norton & Company, Inc. Copyright © 1975, 1973, 1971, 1969, 1966 by W. W. Norton & Company, Inc. Copyright © 1967, 1963, 1962, 1961, 1960, 1959, 1958, 1957, 1956, 1955, 1954, 1953, 1952, 1951 by Adrienne Rich.

Selections from *Diagnostic and Statistical Manual of Mental Disorders, Third Edition, Revised,* American Psychiatric Association, Washington, D.C., 1987.

5   4   3   2   1

Printed in the United States of America

Library of Congress Cataloging-in-Publication Data

Goldstein, Rebecca, 1950–
The dark sister / Rebecca Goldstein.
p. cm.
ISBN 0-299-19994-0 (pbk. : alk. paper)
1. Fiction—Authorship—Fiction.   2. James, William, 1842–1910—
Influence—Fiction.   3. Women—New England—Fiction.   4. Women
novelists—Fiction.   5. New England—Fiction.   6. Solitude—
Fiction.   7. Sisters—Fiction.   I. Title.
PS3557.O398D37   2004
813'.54—dc22   2003064500

This book is for my daughters—

Yael and Danielle—

who have and give me light

ACKNOWLEDGMENTS

Hedda's appetite for the nineteenth-century novel at times makes her reproduce in her own writing the prose of her betters. In most instances her liberties amount to no more than a phrase or two; in several places they are more substantive. Among the sources of which I am aware are

Wilkie Collins: *The Woman in White*

Dr. Charles Fayette Taylor: *Theory and Practice of the Movement Cure*

Thomas Hardy: *Two on a Tower*

Nathaniel Hawthorne: *The Blithedale Romance*

Alice James: *The Diary*

Henry James: *Letters, Roderick Hudson, Washington Square, The Bostonians, The Portrait of a Lady, The Author of Beltrafio, The Wings of the Dove*

ACKNOWLEDGMENTS

William James: *Letters, The Principles of
                   Psychology, The Varieties of
                   Religious Experience, Final
                   Impressions of a Psychical
                   Researcher*

Edgar Allan Poe: "For Annie"

                                            R.G.

CONTENTS

[xi]

CONTENTS

THE DARK SISTER

I

*

Prologue

The pull of the family is irresistible. Even when oceans and years—even when death—intercede.

Action at a distance. Passion at a distance.

Like a closed astronomical system, only many-sunned. The women: dark moons, silently circling.

The cork-legged father, Henry James, Senior, dazzlingly eccentric; a disciple of Swedenborg, the mystic Swede, whose visions of good and evil overlay, too, the sights of Blake and Balzac, Yeats and Strindberg.

Tell them I'm a Lover of Books, a Student. Better yet, tell them I'm a Seeker of the Truth,

Henry Senior instructs his boys, when they are asked by their school chums what it is their father does for a living.

The study of Swedenborg ends, finally, the two years of psychic terror that were unloosed by what the family dubs his "vastation":

Suddenly and inexplicably seized with a perfectly insane and helpless terror, without ostensible cause, and only to be accounted for, to my perplexed imagination, by some damned shape squatting invisible to me within the precincts of the room, and raying out from this fetid personality influences fatal to life.

Henry Senior innocently regards the foul specter as a real external presence. His children, when their own vastations come, know better.

That shape am I. That shape am I, potentially. Nothing that I possess can defend me against that fate, if the hour for it should strike for me as it struck for him.

William James, declining the term favored by his younger colleague in Vienna, speaks not of the Unconscious, but of the Hidden, or Subliminal, Self.

The mother is Mary. She doesn't emerge very clearly within the starry constellation of the family. Others' words, not her own, provide her traces. She is deified as Virtuous Woman by the father. But that, of course, is how he sees Woman. He himself is in an infinitely more complicated, demanding, and altogether more fascinating position— being, in short:

. . . the arena of a hot conflict between heaven and hell engineered principally with a view to universal issues, as he writes a similarly afflicted son. This is, of course, trying in the extreme; and yet—how could one deny it?—cosmically gratifying.

> I should be however sometimes terribly tossed and wrenched between the combatants, if I were not a married man; that is if I were not able when the celestial powers were in force to lavish my infinite and exquisite interior tenderness and peace upon my wife and children, and when they were in flight to run to the bosom of your mother, the home of all truth and purity, and deafen my ears to everything but her spotless worth 'til the inflowing infamy has spent itself.

Was the mother as insipid as all that? A vapor, a fume? Noxious or life-supporting?

There are five children. Mary has charge of their prattling infancy, but they are their father's ever after.

William James, the eldest, is the strongest attractor. A shimmering orb, spilling light; phosphorescent, but burning with intensely human colors.

Henry James, Jr., is eighteen months younger, with an obscure hurt that keeps him out of the Civil War; an obscure hurt that keeps him out of life.

There are two brothers after Henry: Garth Wilkinson James (Wilkie) and Robertson James (Bob); shooting stars, leaving trails—like their mother's—of only others' words to indicate that they once had lived.

Henry Junior, writing from England to Edward Emerson, a boyhood friend and son of the Concord seer, mourns:

Poor Wilkie himself becomes to me, with the increase of the gulf, the most pathetic of dim ghosts. . . . I rejoice that you sometimes see William. He deals in ghosts, but is blessedly not one.

Ghosts. William is an active member of the American branch of the Society for Psychical Research, conscientiously attending séances, most especially those that feature the "manifestations" of a Mrs. Piper of Boston.

Henry too has a great affinity for the ghostly tale, gracefully ambiguous.

And the youngest child is a girl: Alice James. She too has the Jamesian heightened consciousness, its gift for making itself known to itself. But her gift does not show itself to that outside world, which her two eldest brothers transform into their own.

It is a short life, stunted by mysterious nervous ailments.

In some sense, she is the most haunting of them all, her pale face in the outside darkness pressed up against the lighted window.

I have seen so little that my memory is packed with little bits which have not been wiped out by great ones, so that it all seems like a reminiscence; and as I go along the childish impressions of lights and colors come crowding back into my mind, and with them the expectant, which then palpitated within me, lives for a ghostly moment.

FROM THE JOURNAL OF ALICE JAMES

When I am gone pray don't simply think of me as a creature who might have been something else, had neurotic science been born.

ALICE JAMES, IN A LETTER TO WILLIAM JAMES

The extraordinary intensity of her will and personality really would have made the equal, the reciprocal life of a "well" person—in the usual world—almost impossible to her—so that her disastrous, her tragic health was in a manner the only solution for her of the practical problem of life.

HENRY JAMES, IN A LETTER TO WILLIAM JAMES

Hedda

"Alice," whispered Hedda into the mirror.

It had become a sort of ritual lately: she would write for one or two hours and then stand for another one or two, staring into the full-length mirror that stood on her floor and slanted unmounted against her bedroom wall.

In this way, the ideas came. Reluctant characters were coaxed forth from the preverbal murk, skewered on language, and forced to speak their lines. Her reflection, the lower half elongated by the angle at which the glass met the wall, was her conduit, for the time being, to the shadowy realm, metamorphosing the vapors into words.

Sometimes her own image held her attention, and the words she sought was for it.

She slipped easily out of her identity. It was, in a sense, her profession. She so rarely occupied her given self, these days, that were she altogether to misplace it, the loss would probably go unnoticed for some time. Perhaps this had already happened.

Her body, however, would be immediately missed.

Hedda could view her body as remotely as any other, but this in no way diminished its fascination. She was an astonishing creature. She, no less than others, stood in awe before that form that went beyond itself, signifying a content commanding interpretation, disturbing and deep.

In short, she was not merely unattractive. She was mysteriously, mythologically, grim.

Or was she deluding herself? Was it vanity, cunning and sthenic, that made her think her want of beauty as evocative, in its own way, as a more common comeliness? What, precisely, she evoked was forever fluid—more fluid, she believed, than all but the rarest shapes of loveliness.

There is a kind of haunted beauty, destined for an *interesting* unhappiness. There were times when she saw her homeliness as similarly haunted. A gossamer veil of tragedy seemed eloquently draped before it, woven of sighs, studded with tears. One could not help but be touched.

Nothing to wonder about there, the Ubiquitous Voice sneered. *That an ugly woman should be fated to suffer!*

Ah, but not necessarily to suffer interestingly.

And is your suffering so very interesting?

On other, fiercer, days she saw herself in more heroic terms. She wore her ugliness as a coat of mail. Armed against the insidious enslavement of her sex, she resisted (easily) the seductions of a sweetly deadly submission.

It was a supreme gesture of defiance, the prognathic jut of the jaw. She could almost bring herself to believe it the result of an active assertion of her vengeful will.

In short, she was not merely pissed. She was convulsively, orgastically, unappeased. She felt, at times, that her anger could not be contained within the precincts of her person, capacious as these were. She felt herself the repository of all the unowned anger of all the gently smiling females of all the unenlightened (that is, of all) times. And as she sopped up this floating feminine fury, it seemed to her that she grew still huger (for what else was it that had deformed her in the first place if not the unowned fury of her own grotesque mother, the Saint of West End Avenue?), until it seemed to her that, should she choose—and why not?—her shape might blot out the entire world.

Getting delusional, are we? put in the Ubiquitous Voice, who rarely let anything pass.

She had been a beautiful child, with glittering dark eyes; further proof of the maternal perfection; another charm dangling on the sterling chain of an ostentatiously displayed martyrdom. And just look at those two daughters of hers, Hedda and Stella. Did you ever see such girls? Jewels! Diamonds! How does she do it? And all by herself! Never complaining! A woman of valor! A paragon!

A monster.

"A woman in the shape of a monster / a monster in the shape of a woman / the skies are full of them," as in a poem by Adrienne Rich.

That shape am I, potentially.

Did she glorify the situation? Was it vanity?

She stood six feet two. There was nothing vaingloriously induced in that perception. It was a fact—by anybody's standard of factuality. Even a scientist couldn't quibble with the measurable. Also measurable: she weighed one hundred and forty-two pounds. Can't-pinch-an-inch gaunt. She was thirty-eight years old and was still waiting to need a bra.

Was that funny or sad? It varied with her mood. She was losing her grasp of the distinction.

Her voice deepened the visual ambiguity; it was so at odds with her oddness. It was a little voice, randomly halting, fading into uneasy pauses . . . from which it emerged even further reduced. It had the female tendency to end its statements in the upward curve of a question . . . soliciting contradiction?

She had recently, in her predatory forages through Henry James, come upon the word *osseous*: "And Mrs. Ambient, who had seated herself again, held out her long slender slightly too osseous hands." Hedda scooped up the word and deposited it in her own account. She wished to appropriate the entire sentence, find a place for it somewhere in the book she now wrote. Perhaps she would. She was appropriating right and left. She had a huge hunger within her for a certain sort of prose, easier to ingest than to manufacture.

Her style of writing was undergoing a wrenching transformation. Her protagonists had always been articulately angry women, who, though beautiful—and, strangely, they invariably were, making good on the exquisite promise of Hedda's own childhood—were never duped into seeing their purpose in terms of the adornment of some Rigid Prick. Her women strode out to do battle impregnably armored in irony, with brilliant flashes of polished polemics. Deftly, they thrust their spears into the soft underbelly of the Pig.

These books had sold well. There was a lot of female fierceness out there.

But the voice of her present narrator was embarrassingly

nineteenth century and unironic. He was male and a prig;
roast prig, done to a turn. He was sounding increasingly like
Henry James himself; and this was becoming something of
a trial. The demands were becoming excessive, and there
was precious little assurance that these demands, peremptorily as they presented themselves to her, were going to
add up to anything at all.

There never are any assurances, intoned the Ubiquitous Voice
portentously. *Especially never in Art. That's the Woman in you,
whining for your assurances.*

Hedda decided to ignore this.

The craftiest way she knew to meet the rigor of these
demands would be to lift as much as possible straight from
the incomparable prose of that prissy old virgin who wrote
like an angel. If possible, she would narrate the entire story
in this way, like a kidnapper clipping and pasting together
the dark words of his message.

Ah, but would that be Art? sneered the Ubiquitous Fart.

She returned his sneer. Hedda's sneers were perfection.
Her face tended in that direction anyway.

Her face was all jaw—which meant it lacked a certain
versatility. There were expressions—any, notably, making
reference to the softer or more contemplative affections—
that she was unable to execute with any conviction. She was
grand, however, when it came to the more combative array
of facial orientation. Contempt, rancor, rage. She did them
extremely well. The jut of the jaw, the glittering dark eyes:
they suggested the permanently adversarial.

Of all the unspeakable lies nonetheless spoken of women
of genius, Hedda found most hideous the claim that someone
(George Smith, Brontë's very own publisher?) had made of

Charlotte Brontë; that she would have given all her talent
to be pretty.

Hedda, we have said, had been a beautiful child; but her
bones had continued to grow. They had missed, somehow,
the cue to cease—or the cue had been mislaid, fatefully
delayed. The Mother said she was overcalcified and ordered
her to stop drinking milk. Hedda guzzled it on the sly,
furiously pleased by the Mother's furious displeasure. Nothing could have embarrassed the Mother more than this open
and *huge* failure that was become her daughter. A more natural, less inspired response to the Mother's mothering—
neurosis, say, or even, more ambitiously, psychosis—would
have mattered not a whit to the Mother, just as long as no
one would ever have seen it. (Her Greek chorus of approbation—the women of West End Avenue, the members of
her synagogue—for whose praise she lived, apart from
whose words she had no sense of her self at all. And the
words they spoke were good words: A woman of valor! A
paragon! And those two daughters! Jewels! Diamonds! What
a scoundrel the man must have been!)

In those days, too, Hedda used to stand before the mirror,
a witness to the transformation, in that pink and ruffled little
girl's room, purchased complete from a showroom at Macy's,
now made grotesque by Hedda's grotesquerie.

Of course, she hadn't grown from an exquisitely framed
child into a monstrously proportioned young woman over-
night. And yet the span of time in which her form became—
fleetingly—something stunning, and then, that something
exaggerated, passed into freakishness (not for her to mince
words), seemed in retrospect quite brief. It had all transpired
in her sixteenth year. (At the end of which had come men-

arche, the glut of womanhood that curtailed the year of wondrous growth. Otherwise, where might it not all have ended?)

Hedda had found recently, in her literary looting, a passage in Thomas Hardy's *Two on a Tower* that had stirred her, the fine dorsal hairs raising themselves, on Nabokovian command, in the presence of an aesthetic moment. A greater tribute than this hirsute salute was her immediate determination to find a way to plagiarize the passage. (She'd plunder any nineteenth-century writer. It didn't have to be a James. She'd never had any patience for academic niceties.)

There is a size at which dignity begins, a young astronomer explains to his lady love. *Further on, there is a size at which grandeur begins, further on, there is a size at which solemnity begins, further on, a size at which awfulness begins, further on, a size at which ghastliness begins. That size faintly approaches the size of the stellar universe. So am I not right in saying that those minds who exert their imaginative powers to bring themselves into the depths of that universe merely strain their faculties to gain a new horror?*

For a time—the span traversing Hedda's dignity, grandeur, and on into the greater part of her solemnity—she had been unearthly in her beauty. Marty Factor, the lingerie wholesaler for whom the Mother worked as bookkeeper, had pestered the Mother to allow Hedda to model the goods to the salesmen.

"I guarantee her girlhood. I *guarantee* it. Not one man will even exchange a word with her. I *guarantee* it."

But the Mother was the bookkeeper. She knew all about Marty's guarantees.

"Okay, Marty. Agreed. But only granny nightgowns and housedusters. She may look like she's twenty-five and knows a thing or two, but she's just an ignorant child who drinks too much milk. She gets too much attention as it is, the *lange lukshun.*"

(A *lange lukshun* is a long noodle. The Mother often called her this, her eyes narrowing in good (bad) fun. Sometimes she varied it with *dunkele,* little dark one, a name Hedda recalled from primeval infancy. Sometimes it was *dunkele lukshun.* Her sister Stella (who, as second born, tended to get less), was almost invariably *knaidle,* i.e. matzo ball.)

In any case, long before the year was out, Marty had had his way with Hedda; and she was modeling his peekaboo teddies and camisoles—all of pure silk and satin; he sold to Bloomingdale's, Saks Fifth Avenue, and Bergdorf's—which she displayed with a precocious stance of bored indifference. (She *had* been indifferently bored.) Where Hedda went, eyes had followed, as an anonymous poem, addressed to her when she was twelve, had promised. Tourists, in their eagerness for significant sights, quickly leaped to conclusions and came shyly seeking her autograph.

Hedda was still unearthly. The eyes still invariably followed.

The Mother had tried to hide Hedda. Try hiding a six-foot-two-inch prognathic daughter.

At the time of Hedda's own metamorphosis she had experienced the reversal mostly through the Mother's un-quiet desperation. On this level, it was a deeply gratifying process. The Mother's horror was so great as to shield Hedda from much of the trauma that would be expected to attend the arrival of "a size at which awfulness begins; further on, a size at which ghastliness begins."

Because, of course, people, especially the vilely adolescent contemporaries with whom she was forced to rub shoulders—or would, if their shoulders were up to it—were true-to-kind unkind. The boys, and many of the girls (with whom she had never been on chatty terms—always, always, she had felt the finger of Destiny goosing her from behind), called her Bones and, anticipating Spielberg by a decade, Jaws. Her sister, Stella, called her Stick.

Hedda shrugged her osseous shoulders and trudged on.

Hedda always dressed in black, which accentuated the gauntness of her breadth and the redundancy of her length. A pair of man's baggy trousers and a sweater or, sometimes, a T-shirt. (This last only on the doggiest of days, for her body temperature was subnormal, her massive hands and feet perpetually icy. Another anatomical anomaly: she menstruated only once every six months. Her oddness was more than skin deep.)

She had her dark hair cropped short so that the contours of her skull were clearly visible. She had a habit of running her hand through her hair, unconsciously feeling for the bumps.

Hedda had a superbly expressive cranium, with well-articulated swellings in the regions of Sublimity, Secretiveness, and Language. Phrenology was one of her skills. She had pathetically few, despite the fact that she had not been to college. Phrenology and phrasemongering. She might put out a shingle, open a cottage industry. *Skulls read.* That ought to draw them. Why *had* this refined nineteenth-century pseudoscience not made a glamorous comeback? Why, when astrology, tarot cards, and all those varieties of psychotherapy have lived to thrive in the soft rich loam of simplemindedness? Phrenology could boast claims equally reductive. It was an idea. The extra money would be very welcome at this stage in her life. (There was still the rent on the Manhattan apartment she had fled. Bella—who was her editor, but much, much more—saw to it, subtracting the monthly sum from Hedda's royalties.)

Of course business would not be brisk, she reminded herself briskly. The house she rented was a few miles beyond the village—not even standing on the poorly traveled road, but set, inhospitably, on a pile of boulders a few hundred feet above the churning sea.

She had come to be here entirely by accident, though the place was so superbly suited to her present purpose that it was possible, at times—when the blue light of the dusk wrapped itself around her tower and she looked up from her writing to hear the sea advancing upon the rocks—to think she detected the pale, ghostly tracery of a hidden design.

Her intention had been to go to Canada. She was fleeing Manhattan in a rented car, with little more—in addition to the word processor, upon which she was hooked like a preemie on its life support—than she had been able to stuff hastily into a few grimy pillowcases. She was on her way to the ferry that connected Maine with Nova Scotia when she spotted the weathered brown shingled house, with its strangely watching tower, about a quarter mile off the road.

In retrospect she doubted that she could have seen— even, as they say (she was squeamish of their jargon) "sub- liminally"—the FOR SALE sign stuck in the dirt before the sagging porch. She had simply and immediately known that the place was available; that it was quietly biding its time. Something—perhaps the empty stare of the windows—gave it the air of a deserted house.

> I have always thought of the impression made upon me at first sight, by that grey colonial dwelling, as a proof that induction may sometimes be near akin to divination; for after all, there was nothing on the face of the matter to warrant the very serious induction that I made. I fell back and crossed the road. The last red light of the sunset disengaged itself, as it was about to vanish, and rested faintly for a moment on the time-silvered front of the old house. It touched, with perfect regularity, the series of small panes in the fan-shaped window above the door, and twinkled there fantastically. Then it died away, and left the place more intensely somber. At this moment, I said to myself with the accent of profound conviction— "The house is haunted."

That, of course, is the inimitable voice of Henry James, in one of his minor spook tales, "A Ghostly Rental."

(*Hedda* sometimes made up ghost stories. It must have been for her own private amusement and terror—since she never intended them for publication. She was, in fact, rather ashamed of them. Stylistically, they were contemptible things. But they occurred to her with that peremptory presence that compelled her complicity. And she did happen to find them chillingly effective. There were certain images— faces in the dark outside pressed up against the window; faces staring out of mirrors, their colorless lips shaping inaudible words—that invariably occurred in Hedda's spook tales, sending an icy spasm up the formidable length of Hedda's spine. Her ghosts stared with mournful longing: they could not quit their lives because they had so little lived them. They had never known their due—till dead. Quite often they were children.

Sometimes Hedda succeeded in frightening herself so badly she had to flee her lonely tower, perhaps even walk into the dreary, unpicturesque village, staring into the few shop windows. Her favorite was the fish store: those poignantly beautiful carcasses laid out on the chipped ice. And what a test for their regional lack of detectable affect she had presented the villagers when first she had appeared upon the scene! The children, of course, had stared and pointed and sniggered; but the grown-ups—the mothers calmly exerting a slight admonitory tug to the sticky little hands in their keeping—had managed the obligatory nod and murmured greeting, as impassively blank as to any stranger in their midst. Hedda, who was used to being noticed even within the condensed chaos of a New York City subway, was significantly impressed.)

Hedda had known immediately—with that groundless quickening of belief which was the only sort she trusted—that the house with the empty eyes and the watching tower would be made available to her; and knew too that this was a place she could inhabit in relative safety.

She had stopped the car, pulling over to the shoulder to have a look. She didn't see any road leading to it. The place seemed accessible only by foot. Better and better.

It was the wooden tower, the windows facing out to sea, that made her feel, with the nervy instincts of a novelist, the peremptory presence of a story. It would be a story unlike any of her own. A different place, a different time, an altogether different voice.

Later, the schoolmarmish real estate agent who rented the house to her—quite reluctantly, it seemed; or was it merely New England reticence, potent enough to neutralize even a realtor's killer instinct—had submitted herself to answering Hedda's question about the history of the house and tower with that same expression of politely subdued wonder (I don't know why you should want to know this) with which she responded to Hedda's final announcement that she would indeed and immediately accept the terms offered. Will you now?

The house consisted of three rooms on the first floor and three on the second. (There was also a damp and mildewed-smelling basement Hedda preferred to ignore.) An entire seven rooms—counting the tower—*and* for less than she had been paying for her two-room, roach-infested walk-up on Second Avenue. The windows throughout were small paned affairs—designed to keep out the northeasterlies blowing off the sea—and very scarce in number, which gave the house an acceptable level of gloom. Hedda required an interior that didn't respond too readily to the out-of-doors.

The house had been built by a sea captain in the mid-nineteenth century as a wedding gift to his young bride. It was the wife who, some years later (so the legend went) added the wooden tower, all its windows facing out to sea, after her husband had not returned from his last whaling voyage. Whaling! The dorsal hairs began to tingle and rise, as Hedda's imagination swooped down on the phrase, alive with its call-me-Ishmael associations: Man out forging his

Destiny with the Awesome, so that Woman might have whalebones stitched into her corset and farthingale.

The entrance to the tower was from the "master" bedroom: twisting wooden stairs, worn smooth by the widow's ceaseless tread, growing heavier and more halting by the year. (Hedda had heard her step, the rustle of her widow weeds, faintly on the stair.)

Hedda had known that the room in that tower would be her own immediate Destiny. She would appropriate this tower. She would appropriate this New England, this politely subdued startle that was at most a hiccup and never a burp; this winter-heart of Christendom that was as unlike the crucible-chaos of her family of origin as anything she (even she) could have imagined.

I defy you!—accidents of precedents. It shall be mine!

Despite the heroic stance, her writing was proceeding poorly, plagued by a discouraging dyspepsia. She continued to play with the idea of a little cottage industry, reading skulls. It would be a diversion, if nothing else.

Of course, the contemplated enterprise might shift her into a position of intolerable risk and exposure. She mistrusted her New England neighbors with a transplanted New Yorker's sensibility. She tried to keep—so to speak—a low profile. Who knew of what acts of uninnocence these sober citizens might be capable, the ancient superstitions hoarded as sacred heirlooms? In Hedda's narrowed eyes, these placid folk were the direct descendents of the Reverend Cotton Mather, the fiery judge who had, three centuries before, made it his holy business to go after the witches of Massachusetts with a maniacal single-mindedness. Mather too had been of the opinion that there was something unhealthy in the prevailing influence of New England, leading to morbid Psychology and damnable Religion.

> The Vitiated Humours in many Persons, yield the streams where into Satan does insinuate himself, till he has gained a sort of Possession in them, or at least an Opportunity to shoot into the Mind as many Fiery Darts as may cause a sad life unto them; yea, 'tis well if Self-Murder be not the sad end into which these hurried people are thus precipitated. New England, a country where splenetic Maladies are prevailing and pernicious, perhaps above any other, hath afforded Numberless Instances, of even pious People, who have contracted these Melancholy Indispositions which have unhinged them from all Service or Comfort; yea, not a few Persons have been hurried thereby to lay Violent Hands upon themselves at the last. These are among the unsearchable Judgements of God.

Hedda's oddness made her especially vulnerable to hostile eyes. Uncommon women are natural objects of suspicion. It is a truism that woman is more conventional than man, and a truism must always be saved the embarrassment of refutation. Hedda had no faith whatsoever in the authenticity of the enlightened era.

Already some town children had hurled a dangerous name at her. They had been snooping about the property, peering into the windows and rattling the cellar door, making eerie, frightening noises.

Hedda was queasily phobic of children and, by extension, of short people in general. They were too condensed, like undiluted cans of soup—too intensely human and, therefore, too intensely not to be trusted. The mistakes in the basic ingredients—the stupidity, the cruelty—were overpoweringly present. Her own fiendishly potent mother had stood no more than five feet four.

She decided to venture out and approach the trespassing children. Perhaps she might disarm them—charm, alarm, or palm them. Three boys they were, maybe eight or nine years old, a very terrifying age.

Nervously she rummaged the kitchen, looking for some cookies or chewing gum to throw propitiatingly before them.

She found only an apple. In retrospect she realized the mistake in her judgment; the picture she must have presented to these primitive minds, against the backdrop of the rocks and sea, the weak chill wintry light; her severe and awesome shape striding quickly toward them in the billowing black Victorian funeral cloak, which was her only outdoor garment, found in a secondhand clothing shop in Manhattan many years before; the only spot of color the deep red of the apple, shiny with supermarket wax. The association would not be lost to the juvenile imagination. They had scattered over the rocks, shrieking with altogether convincing conviction, "The witch! the witch!"

Hedda gave up the idea of her cozy little cottage industry, lest the baleful accusation be taken up in voices more menacingly mature.

Sometimes, for her own amusement and edification, she constructed phrenological charts for her characters. She hadn't yet done so for Alice and Vivianna, though it might prove very revealing. What would have been William James's opinion of phrenology? (For, very strange to say, Hedda's work-in-progress was doubly Jamesian: Henry was dictating the style, while William was emerging as a major protagonist.) Could not a man who took altogether seriously the "mediumistic manifestations" of a Mrs. Leonora Piper—had William James been *a flake?*—be made to take the phrenological measure of Alice and Vivianna? He wouldn't want to touch them, though; that would be distasteful to him—he, who in his *Principles of Psychology* measured the force of the sexual instinct by its ability to overcome our innate disinclination to touch one another; a disinclination so marked that most of us, he said, even found it unpleasant to sit down on a seat still warm from another. Physical contact—even of the pseudoscientific sort—would be unnatural to him, then—*unless* he could be made to feel the overtaking inclination. . . .

Hedda hadn't yet progressed to any degree of intimacy with her characters, especially not with the two sisters whose story mostly occupied her imagination these days. She could see Alice quite plainly. The prim New England spinster had stepped out firmly enough—no coy nonsense in that one. But Vivianna, the more elusive and intriguing of the two, still hung back in the shadowed recesses of the tower. Hedda could not yet see her, though she did feel—reassuringly—the reality of her. But she wondered—anxiously—whether she would be able to appropriate this felt reality, to skewer it pitilessly on the lances of her language.

Downstairs, in the kitchen, the phone was ringing. It must be Stella, her sister. It was four o'clock in the afternoon.

Stella had just finished her daily session with Dr. Seymour, her psychoanalyst.

Her sister Stella romanticized her childhood traumas the way Hedda (maybe) overestimated her own ugliness. Such vanity. Her sister Stella nursed, in analytic session after analytic session, her engorged sense of personal grievance, that that dancing dust mote, happiness, should forever flee before her clutching grasp. What more-than-vanity! Wherever had it been written that anyone—much less Hedda and Stella!—should be happy?

> I tell thee, blockheads, it all comes of thy vanity, of what thou fanciest those same desserts of thine to be. Fancy that thou deservest to be hanged (as is most likely), thou wilt feel it happiness to be only shot. . . . What act of legislature was there that thou shouldst be happy? A little while ago thou hadst no right to be at all.

Thomas Carlyle. Adorable misanthrope.

Hedda let the phone ring.

Hedda was considering having the phone removed. It was a barbarous intrusion, really. It was a lesion in the sacred body of her solitude. Not that its noise was a common occurrence. But lately Stella had been calling. Dr. Seymour was asking questions, factual questions, the sort that Stella could never answer, especially if they involved anyone but Stella.

Hedda wondered about Dr. Seymour's motives here. Was there malice, as there always was on Hedda's part when she asked her sister something she knew she couldn't answer?

Looking back, Hedda couldn't really understand why she had contacted Stella in the first place. It had been a temporary weakness, a desperate impulse born of a moment of panic, when she had realized that she could die here, among this alien race of Anglo-Saxons, and no one from her other life would ever know. The sober citizens would trash her bones in that little churchyard of theirs (Presbyterian, Episcopalian, Unitarian—what the hell did *she* know?), where, she had a feeling, they would not be made to feel very welcome. (Hedda happened to believe in ghosts, which is what gave her ghost stories a certain oomph, at least to her, their only reader.)

Nobody here even knew her last name. She had bought the house under her nom de plume, Hedda Dunkele, which was the name she used for her bank accounts, here and in New York. Only Stella now knew her real identity. This gave the two sisters an intimacy Hedda didn't altogether trust.

Hedda might just as well have answered the phone. The sound of its ring had already done its damage, evoking Stella's image, her voice, the clammy substance of the narcissistic mist she inhabited. Hedda always imagined her sister as befogged in an iridescent cloud, through which the world entered but dimly filtered. It was clear that her surrounding medium had a strong reflective capacity; Stella so often wore the expression of a vain woman poised before the mirror, her eyes glazed over into goofy self-absorption. Enclosed in her own solipsistic steam bath, Stella possessed a dewy complexion, like an Englishwoman's.

Stella was the fair sister: fair and fleshy and bedecked. As a little girl she had used to love to dress up as royalty by draping the bedclothes about her, accessorizing her costume with long strands of plastic pop-'em beads, a silvery ponytail clasper balanced on her head as a crown. Clutching the quilt, she would parade back and forth on top of the bed, playing grandly to the dresser mirror. (There was no full-length mirror in the apartment.) Both girls were feverishly given to fantasizing, but Hedda went about the business of hers quietly, and sitting still.

The grown-up Stella had evolved a style of dress that was still highly suggestive of the pretend princess traipsing about in the bedclothes. She adored clothes that trailed: capes, cloaks, scarves—any and all, and worn in the most unlikely combinations. Such drapery made certain tasks—for example, cooking—highly perilous, which didn't much matter, as neither sister was very domestic.

Stella favored voluminous high-waisted dresses of vaguely medieval cut, with elaborate stand-up collars and ballooning sleeves, dyed in rich Elizabethan colors and made of velvet, when the season allowed. As a child she had wanted terribly to be allowed to let her hair grow long, like a princess's. But the Mother couldn't be bothered combing out a child's fine tangles, and both girls had worn their hair cropped almost boy short. Through all her adult life Stella's hair grew past her waist, though she usually wore it elaborately coiled at the back of her head. She was always leaving a trail of hairpins. The pop-'em beads had been replaced by heavy brooches, which Stella herself made—and also sold to a few select Manhattan stores—by scavenging antique jewelry, which she then took apart and reassembled into even bulkier pieces—an activity that occupied a very great part of her time and which she certainly regarded in the light of High Art. She was an excellent saleswoman and did quite well for herself in her enterprise.

Stella too was large, though she stood comfortably within the range of normality, a good two inches below six feet. She was a big-boned, fleshy woman who had developed the stature that allowed her to carry off, however improbably, her eccentric fashion statement. She was too big to be pretty, but she was certainly handsome, with pleasantly regular features, that dewy complexion, and all that wonderful hair. Men had always seemed to like her well enough. She had a certain presence, a certain, even, majesty. Her voice—unlike Hedda's—was commensurate with her size. It was self-assured and even—younger sister though she was—bossy. She seemed a far more serious person than she in fact—Hedda knew—was.

Hedda was the older by three years. As children, their relationship had been one of uncomplicated hate, the natural enmity of siblings who have to grab for every scattered morsel of parental affection. And yet always there had been a certain restraint in their dealings. In recent years, though each delighted in the failures of the other (Stella saved only the unfavorable reviews of Hedda's books, hooting while she circled the acid in red; Hedda retained all the details of Stella's four failed marriages and numerous failed affairs—always sympathizing with the men), these restraints had become more self-conscious. Each possessed, but would never use, a certain power against her sister.

There were words they might say to one another, un-intonable, unatonable:

You know, you're just like she was really. You're really just like the Mother.

Each felt, her finger above the button, the full vulnerability of the other. With this capacity for mutual annihilation, an emotion almost like tenderness had crept into their relationship. Was this, then, the secret bonding seal of families?

The pull of the family is irresistible. Action at a distance. Passion at a distance.

I could destroy her with a few words. She'd never recover. Dr. Seymour could try every trick in his little black psychoanalytic bag; her ego would have vaporized out of existence, leaving a dull smudge on the sidewalk.

You know, you remind me of someone. You're just like someone we both know.

They hadn't seen each other in many years, even though, until quite recently, they had both lived on the East Side of Manhattan. Stella had sent Hedda a picture after each of her marriage ceremonies. She had changed little from one picture to the next—in each the look of self-enchantment perhaps a little goofier—but the men had gotten progressively younger. So much for Stella's seriousness. The last— Steve, Hedda thought it was—had looked barely out of puberty.

Now Stella was off men—for good, she said. She had Dr. Seymour. Dr. Seymour was everything Stella had ever wanted. Dr. Seymour understood. Dr. Seymour really listened.

Hedda listened, too—when she chose to answer the phone. The calls had only really begun with psychoanalysis and Dr. Seymour's questions.

Sometimes, when Hedda got a good strong whiff of what reality was like for Stella, it sent her reeling. Should she correct her? She was reluctant to stick her finger into the pot and give its contents a stir. It was all such a goo. (Use one's own experience and family as the raw material of one's fiction? But the whole point of the thing was to get as far away from *that* as was humanly possible—to slough off one's past as the snake its dead skin.) Anyway, what would it come to? Her corrections would themselves be churned up and transmuted into the oneiric vapors of Stella's sick psyche. Stella didn't want to be corrected. Seymour or no Seymour, she didn't want to see more. It was really the very *last* thing that she wanted. If Dr. Seymour had any integrity at all, he would simply tell Stella she was . . . Oh, what was the point? Hedda didn't want to think about Stella. She must see about ridding her house of the telephone's intrusive presence. She'd get in touch with Ma Bell. By mail.

"Alice," whispered Hedda into the mirror.

III

Alice

"Though we are sisters, we are nothing alike. We are to one another as the high noon is to midnight."

Doctor Sloper raised his habitually skeptical eyes from the small leather-bound red book in which he was taking down his notes to peer at the gentlewoman who had just delivered herself of her simile, holding out her long, slender, slightly too osseous hands.

The barest suggestion of unmeditated expression disturbed the stolid mask of professional noncommittal in which his heavy, handsome features were arranged. He had not anticipated any metaphorical turns, any strains of poesy, deriving from the utterly prosaic little figure who sat across the desk from him, in his consulting rooms on Washington Square. And it was perhaps even more remarkable that this diminutive spinster, with her drawn and pinched white face and gold-rimmed spectacles, the lenses so thick as to be nearly opaque, should possess the capacity to startle him, in no matter how small a way; for it was a given fact that

Austin Sloper very rarely found himself faced with the inconvenience of an event he could not, in the principle of the thing, have foreseen.

On the brisk and bright September morning that brought him his first sight of Alice Bonnet, of Willow Groves, Connecticut, he did not suspect any untoward unexpectancies hovering in his well-set-up vicinity. The Doctor's consulting rooms were in the house he had built himself, a handsome, modern, wide-fronted structure, with a big balcony before the drawing room windows and a flight of marble steps ascending to a portal that was also faced with white marble. This structure, and many of its neighbors, which it exactly resembled, were supposed, at the time of the Doctor's residence, to embody the last results of architectural science, and they remain to this day very solid and honorable dwellings. In front of them was the square, containing a considerable quantity of inexpensive vegetation, enclosed by a wooden paling, which increased its rural and accessible appearance; and round the corner was the more august precinct of the Fifth Avenue, taking its origin at this point with a spacious and confident air that already marked it for high destinies. I know not whether it is owing to the tenderness of early associations, but this portion of New York appears to many persons the most delectable. It has a kind of established repose that is not of frequent occurrence in other quarters of the long, shrill city; it has a riper, richer, more honorable look than any of the upper ramifications of the great longitudinal thoroughfare—the look of having had something of a social history.

Such, in any case, was the setting in which Doctor Sloper regarded the unprepossessing figure of Alice Bonnet. It was a setting of which he had long been master. He was all but supplied with her diagnosis before she even delivered herself of her symptoms, which were almost certain to include lethargy, insomnia, and lack of appetite as well as some combination selected from the list of sick headaches, palpitations, fainting spells, muscle spasms, neuralgias, laughing or crying fits, cold hands and feet, and dyspepsia. There was nothing in the aspect that she presented over the magnificent gleaming expanse of the Doctor's inlaid *chinois* desk—a wedding gift of his late wife—that he had not seen duplicated in the scores of females who had drooped their way before his prognosticating gaze. The narrow chest and long thin limbs and ungainly back, the almost transparent fairness, the deeply shadowed eyes, and the brittle, nervous posture.

This last, the brittleness of the women he saw, was the most telling of their symptoms. It was as if all the suppleness had literally leaked out from their tissues; so that where the healthy human female is a relatively flexible manner of creature, the depleted specimens constituting his clientele looked as if, were one to tap them, they should give out a sound like glass shattering.

Doctor Sloper was to a certain extent what is called a ladies' doctor, though his private opinion of the more complicated sex was not exalted. He regarded its complications as more complicated than edifying, and he had an idea of the beauty of *reason*, which was on the whole meagerly gratified by what he observed in his female patients.

As a ladies' doctor, Doctor Sloper had ministered to scores of women who were, from the clinical view, interchangeable with the Miss Bonnet who sat now before him, the morning sun bouncing off her spectacles and contrib-

uting its share to the impression of the telling brittleness.
She was, observably, a nervous invalid, suffering either from
neurasthenia, a disease whose hold had greatly strengthened
in the years following the War Between the States; or, even
more likely, hysteria, whose very name (from the Greek
hysterikós, for womb) bespoke its feminine affinity. Indeed,
he sometimes suspected that the overwhelming majority of
his female patients were, at bottom, hysterics. This was
almost certainly true in those cases where no organic dis-
ruptions could be detected. But even when there were organic concomitants, Doctor Sloper believed that, more times
than not, the original impetus to female disease was neurotic.
There were times when, in the privacy of his own unvoiced
opinion, and most especially when moved to impatience by
the seemingly willful recalcitrance to cure of so many of his
patients, he had found himself theorizing whether the female
state was not in itself a morbid deviation, so that the difference between it and its male opposite was very much like
the difference between being well and being sick.

In his calmer and more sanguine moments the Doctor
was prepared to concede that the, so to speak, unnaturalness
of women lay not so much with their womanhood proper,
but rather with that state when set within the topsy-turvy
of the times, which had gone so far toward effeminizing
men and masculinizing women, to the mutual, and profound,
undoing of both sexes. While it was true that women, as
individuals, were giving up their feminine essence, this did
not imply that the feminine element was passing from the
world. Quite the contrary, it appeared to be escaping into
the general atmosphere, where it perniciously lingered, cor-
roding the manly stuff of a generation. It was the masculine

tone that was passing away, to the utter ruination of civilization. It was a feminine, nervous, hysterical, chattering, canting age. For, though a man's nature was capable of sopping up, as it were, the released femininity, there was no place for the masculine substance to go, once gone from men. Men could, observably, sink to the lower state, but women could not aspire to the higher. They could be "unladied" quickly enough, but they could not be turned into the vessels of a sacred virility.

What the Doctor saw, of course, were the cracked vessels, like the pale New England spinster now aflutter before him; and those utterly shattered. The race had devised a deucedly effective method for "imperfecting" itself. And the little motor, setting the whole thing to running, as it were, went by the name of "higher education for women."

Women are emotional as a class of human beings, which is all to the good in their intended roles as wives and mothers. But subject such an unstable organization to the rigors of an education—which in the male of the species serves to strengthen and steady—and the emotional ingredient becomes concentrated to the hysterical degree, until the woman of the modern age is the bundle of nerves that she is, almost incapable of reasoning under the tyranny of paramount emotions; most are wholly incapable of becoming the mothers of rightly organized children.

You must not imagine, for it would be quite contrary to the fact, that the attitude with which the Doctor apprehended the general state of things had anything in the way of regret, remorse, or disapproval. He was content forever to observe, to connect; divinely, to comprehend. The play of forces between the individual and his social setting, especially as these concerned the etiology of disease, was his Great Subject. And as he had a sort of gluttony for theoretic sustenance, the more numerous the elements, and the greater the complexity of the relations between them, the more savory and satisfying a meal did it concoct for his mental delectation.

He had, of course, his obligations to his patients, which went so far as they went. As for the rest, he had quite lost the urge to stick his finger into the pot and give it a stir. He attended with great interest and was not overly troubled that, in the end, something quite nasty and indigestible would be left sticking to the interior—just so long as nothing of the mess found its way into the balanced order of his own diet.

As Doctor Sloper came to Miss Bonnet with his diagnosis all but firmly set into place, so too had he a pretty good idea of the prescription he would ultimately pronounce. He would begin, first of all, by requiring the cessation of all mental excess—forbid her, for example, those novels that his experience quite confidently counted among her quotidian abuses (it was a given that it was not by studious application to the pages of Aristotle and Euclid that her ocular muscles had suffered their impairment). He would be willing to wager a box of his very best Havanas that she was quite a little tippler when it came to that light literature that, intellectually insipid though it might be, was yet sentimentally, so to speak, one hundred proof, and wreaked havoc on the nervous constitutions of those who wantonly imbibed, setting weak hearts to tremble and weaker minds to brood. The doctor would also institute a regimen of massage, stretching, and light exercise, designed to redirect the flow of energy from the overstimulated brain and nervous system back to the bodily tissues, which might then be revitalized and made soft and supple once more. The very essence of the process was the plumpening—the refeminizing, as it were—of the tissues.

And of course a clever Doctor always knew to leave behind a hieroglyphic inscription, to be filled at the local apothecary—in this case, no doubt, either valerian or asafetida. The Doctor was not hindered by his knowledge that the medicine he would prescribe had no demonstrable benefits, but were rather relics from the dark days that had seen mental disease as the product of demoniacal possession. Upon that theory, all manner of weirdly assembled, foul-smelling, and evil-tasting concoctions were administered, with the notion that the Devil himself could not withstand them and would—hell-bent, as it were—be off. Patients rarely felt they had gotten their dollar's worth if one did not require of them the ingestion of some substance peculiarly nasty and nauseant.

Such was Doctor Sloper's knowledge—a priori, so to speak. It must be said, however, that in the course of the a posteriori interview, the patient went about most assiduously to thwart the Doctor's assembled preknowledge.

"Miss Bonnet," he had greeted her in his rounded, baritone voice, bestowing the smile in which were pharmaceutically mixed the precisely measured proportions of professional attentiveness, reassurance, and authority. "I am Doctor Sloper."

"How do you do, Doctor Sloper. And I am Alice *Bonnet*."

She had a strange flat way of speaking her words, together with a slight tendency to sibilate, resulting in what could only be called a mild hiss. She had repeated her name with a pronunciation different from the frenchified version by which the Doctor had just spoken it. She put the accent on the first syllable and pronounced the final t.

He was amused, if slightly taken aback. "Excuse me, Miss Bonnet. I had assumed . . ."

"Yes, yes," she murmured hurriedly. "It is a common mistake. My sister says that the mispronunciation is a kindness strangers bestow, all unconsciously, for the purpose of giving to the name a borrowed dignity. It is, as it is, rather an absurd appellation; but it is ours."

"Perhaps it is an element of the exotic which hovers round your personage, beguiling the uninitiated into presuming a foreign derivation."

You would have surprised him if you had told him so; but it was a literal fact that Doctor Sloper often chose to address his female patients in the ironical form.

For retort, the remark produced an entire jangling array of nervous symptoms. Miss Bonnet blinked furiously behind the polished lenses of her spectacles and rustled her black silk skirts in her agitated shifting. She opened her mouth, as if to make response, and then closed it; opened it and closed it; in fact, repeated this piscine procedure to the full count of four. Finally, the emotional borborygmus subsiding, she produced, at last, the words:

"It is said 'Bonnet.' As the hat which is tied beneath the chin."

This was not, then, a specimen of the clever woman. So much the better, so far as any hope of a cure was concerned.

You would have been surprised how many of the female patients the Doctor saw reminded him of some species of fowl. Perhaps it was by reason of the thin scraggly necks of so many of those who had reason to consult with him; perhaps their nervously pecking mannerisms, the little chirps and twitters. He had seen rooks and robins, chickens and geese, scolding jays, demurely cooing doves (these his personal choice, if only it *were* a matter for choosing), drab wrens and the occasional dreaded vulture. The little lady before him was, most decidedly, a sparrow. He could imagine the shudders beneath a steady, cupping palm.

The small flap over the pronunciation of her name was but the first, and the least, of the contretemps of the succeeding session. What was assuredly the greatest of the turnarounds followed quickly enough and consisted in the revelation that the Miss Bonnet whose diagnosis was, as it were, all but completed, awaiting only the actual examination, was not to be his patient at all but had rather made the trying journey from New England to New York City for the sole purpose of seeking medical advice concerning her sister's declining state of health.

"Your *sister?*" The Doctor's rounded tones elongated themselves, becoming flatter and more stentorian.

"Yes." She again stared him down coldly. None but she could have said what those lenses did for her vision of the world. But to those looking back through them at her, her eyes were made huge and blurry. "My younger sister, Vivianna. We have lived alone together, since the death of our parents, which occurred when Vivianna was but thirteen."

"Of what did your parents die?" asked the Doctor, insisting on his methods.

"They died in Italy, of the Roman fever."

"Malaria, you mean."

"Yes. Malaria."

She had then gone on to produce for the Doctor a tale that was most—yes, he really could not deny the applicability of the term, for which he had but rarely found a use; the story was most *extraordinary*, rivaling in its twistingness of plot and flamboyant disregard for the normal notes of narrative, the contents of some tawdry contemporary novel or a story in the three-penny papers. Had the little lady's imaginative sphere suffered such grievous overstimulation that her tale was but the ravings of this enfevered faculty?

Miss Bonnet's father, one Roderick Bonnet, had been a sculptor, so she reported, who had enjoyed, for a time (she was vague as to the precise temporal dimension), a certain amount of ovation: "Though he was ultimately, I suppose, rather a fizzle.

"His success came quite early, soon after he and Mother were married. The piece which brought him his first acclaim was a small statue—quite exquisite in its way—of a youth drinking from a gourd, which my father named for the Greek word for thirst. It was cast in bronze and was a product of their wedding trip, which they had spent in Italy. They remained there, that first time, for some nine or ten months. Father had wished to stay on there indefinitely, but Mother was pining away for her New England. She was, you see"—and here the sensibility of the New England spinster again made itself known in all its blushings and falterings—"already in the way of carrying me, and was in mortal dread that her child be born on the other side. At last, under her increasingly piteous entreaties, and in such a condition as she was, Father agreed to cross the Atlantic, and they returned to Willow Groves in time for the event of my birth.

"However, Father found the going in Willow Groves very little to his liking. He referred to his native New England soil as the frozen wastes of exile, the solstice of the soul. My father"—and here she produced a rather good likeness of a smile—"was seldom at a loss for words. His periods of ill humor rarely assumed the sullen form.

"He blamed on the transatlantic move the fact that the inspiring springs, which once had fed the well of his artistic imagination, had gone stone dry. Mother had given him, as her wedding gift, a studio, built atop a rounded wooden tower, with windows all about. The tower studio was, I suppose, designed to keep him content in her New England, to stop his ears to the song of his siren Italy. But it failed of its purpose, and it never did house any of the promised masterpieces. My father was an exuberant, even pleasure-loving man, who knew well how to grasp the varieties of life's offering; but he could be a great trial when he was unhappy, and I imagine that he was very unhappy in Willow Groves. At last, my father took himself off again for Italy, and my mother and I followed him several months later. Vivianna was born in Rome, when I was three.

"Vivianna was an extremely clever and high-spirited child, inclined, one might even say, to displays of naughtiness. My mother was entirely unprepared for such mischief, as I had been such an inordinately and consistently *good* child. She had quite taken it for granted that girls are naturally good, requiring only the benefit of example and none of the harsher pressures of discipline designed according to the demands of a boy's more rambunctious nature.

"Vivianna and I were opposites in every way—she quick

and impetuous, where I was always careful and methodical. We look nothing alike, so that people have always marveled that we are sisters. She is as dark as I am fair."

Then she is not so very dark, observed the Doctor, to himself; for the lady before him was not what he would have described as fair. Her hair was hidden by her prim poke bonnet, which was in the fashion of the generation before, the sides descending and closing in upon her face. But, judging by her complexion, which was distinctly sallow, he would guess the hair to be a darkish brown. Fair indeed! There was no maiden so plain as to go forth into the world unadorned with a dab from the pot of self-beguiling vanity.

"She shows, somehow, her foreign birth, reminding me always of those deeply perfumed wild roses that grow in the highest reaches of the Roman Coliseum. When she was, oh, perhaps seven or eight years old, she actually, prodigiously, climbed the treacherous wall, for the sole purpose of picking just such a rose for our father." She paused, her eyes going vague and dreamy with the reminiscence. She then recollected herself, continuing, rather brusquely. "I, of course, have always been a bit of good and hardy New England moss. Not unlike our mother, who was also Alice.

"Though only three years the elder, I was always a second mother to Vivianna, even then, when our parents were alive. It was often I who succeeded in quieting her boisterous spiritedness and inducing in her a behavior less willful and reckless. It was her cleverness, of course, that made her so bad, though Father would never see it. He doted on her quickness, teaching her all variety of things that little girls ought never to learn. The contrast between her clambering spirit and her exquisitely framed outer aspect—for she was an extraordinarily beautiful child, whom our father used as a model for one of his last pieces—this very contrast, that is, which so alarmed and appalled my mother and myself, found the antagonistic response in our father, redoubling, for him, the charm of the entire effect she produced, as objet d'art, as it were. It was my mother who, in her deep quiet calm, took the truer measure of her daughter.

"You might wonder that I, who was a child myself, should know so much of what my parents thought. But you must understand that my mother and I were extremely close to one another, and, because of what I presume were the differences between herself and our father, I became, in effect, her trusted confidante.

"My mother hated Rome, never finding her place in the little colony of expatriate Americans, whose darling our father long remained, even after the precious elixir of his genius had been quaffed, in one quick gulp, as it were. Perhaps they continued to adore him for the heartiness with which he raised his glass to others. I myself do not know.

"What was hardest for my mother, I think, was seeing little Vivianna thriving upon the tainted, baleful atmosphere. She made *me* feel the unnaturalness—my mother, I mean— the poison, as it were, about me. It was a wicked, infectious, heathenish place. And, though Rome was what I *knew*, I thought of little Willow Groves as my rightful, if unrecollected, home.

"After our parents' death, Vivianna and I returned to that home. She felt their death acutely, horribly—especially, of course, the loss of her father, whose darling she had been; whereas, it was our mother whose death left me the more bereft.

"I, who was myself of tender years—though, in a certain sense, I had never enjoyed the privilege of being a child—had now, of course, to assume the full duties of parent to Vivianna. However, this task of rearing my younger sister was lightened by the remarkable metamorphosis which she underwent in the time immediately following our return to New England. She lost, in its entirety, the capricious and often quite heartless high spirits which had hitherto deformed her character. She turned sharply inward, softening and sweetening in the turning, so that I often hoped that our mother's spirit might be hovering nearby, to see her daughter and rejoice in the sight; for she had often grieved that the child's nature would be forever corrupted by the infected influences that had worked upon her infancy.

"Vivianna did, however, retain her exaggerated bent toward cleverness. In fact, as her outward mien mellowed, her inward life became that much more intensified in its devotion to intellectual pursuits, most especially to the sundry scientific experiments that she and our father had engaged in together. For I ought to mention that our father, though his reputation was made by his artistic pretensions, had a keen scientific interest, partly connected with the artist in him, as in his study of human anatomy, but also quite separate and, so to speak, for its own sake. It is this scientific side of his intelligence which Vivianna has inherited.

"I now judge myself to have been reprehensibly remiss. But the truth of the matter is, the general amelioration of her humor so pleased me that I did not greatly alarm myself over her increasingly morbid cerebrations. In any case, it would have gone very hard with her, poor parentless child, to have to break with those labors connecting her yet with

the departed father. And the force of her nature is so great—
and you may believe me that I feel it most acutely—that I
think even my most vigorous efforts at suppressing her studies would have proved, in the end, entirely futile, effective
only of a mutually painful distancing between us.

"As she has matured her intellectual interests have narrowed, until, in her womanhood, there is only one subject
remaining to her, but remaining with a concentration absolutely undeflected and undilute. And that is astronomy."

It was here that our good Doctor—who, having been
deprived of all his standing presumptions, had also thereby
suffered a loss of his methods of examination, and had been
forced into the activity or rather, to his mind, inactivity of
listening (a procedure but rarely, and always incompletely,
engaged in within those consulting rooms)—emitted a noise,
which, though conveying no very precise sense, had nothing
of the ironical about it.

A pause of several moments ensued, during which the
Doctor attempted, with but little success, to picture the
female figure poised before the Astronomical Immensities.

"But has she astronomical instruments, then?" he at long
last asked. "Has she a telescope, an observatory?"

"She has our father's telescope, which was—for its time,
she tells me—rather a good one, though she complains of
its deficiencies when it is compared with those that are now
produced. It is I who have the responsibility of the household
matters, and it is clear to me, if not to her, that we cannot
presently find it within our means to make the purchase of
a good telescope."

She delivered this last statement of limitations with such
an overall stiffening of her pose and compressing of her thin,

bloodless lips that an even less facile reader of human nature than Doctor Sloper would have been able to infer that here was a question that had sorely vexed the relations of the pair.

"As for observatory, she has made over for this purpose the tower studio which my mother had constructed for our father as a wedding gift. She is to be found there nightly, the entire night through."

She paused here, her face turned meditatively toward the Oriental carpet, whose rich and brilliant pattern lay beneath her sensible spinster boots; and the Doctor took the meditative stance to signify that she had said what she had come to him to say and was now awaiting his professional pronouncement. He cleared his throat portentously and prepared himself to give her his drawn conclusion:

"The story you tell is most unusual. However, I may frankly assure you that I hear nothing in your sister's pronounced eccentricity that can definitively—clinically, as it were—be termed morbid. Has she nervous symptoms?"

She raised her eyes from the carpet and stared unflickeringly at the Doctor.

"My story, Doctor Sloper, is not yet completed. I come directly to my sister's symptoms.

"I have said that my sister turned quiet and inward after the death of our parents; and that, on the whole, I regarded the change as salubrious. However, as her preoccupation with the starry domain has intensified—and especially in the last several months when she has been brooding over some theory, I believe of her own invention—her inwardness has become so pronounced as to appear absolutely alarming. She is perversely, morbidly, as it were, inward.

"She works, of course, through the night. I make no complaint of this, since it is in the nature of the study of the stars. She sleeps through the daylight hours, while I go about all the household duties, and awakens shortly before twilight.

"I have never concerned myself in her larger topic; and even had I an interest, I have not the turn of mind to follow distances measured out in light-years. The very thought of vastness quite sickens me. In the past, however, my sister and I have enjoyed topics enough in common.

"But now my sister no longer speaks with me. My comments drop unnoticed into the cold deep of her solitude. She sometimes looks at me as if she did not know who I am. Days can go by without her uttering a single syllable.

"And then she will speak. Doctor Sloper, she will look at me with a sweet angelic smile playing upon the beautiful curve of her lips, and speak to me, in a commonplace manner of voice, of things that are not only apropos of nothing, but are completely, that are chillingly, lacking in all rhyme and reason.

"I have tried to remember examples so that I might tell them to you. However, since they are so without a pattern by which to comprehend and thus retain them, the great majority of them are lost to my recollection. I did, however, on the evening in which I decided at last to seek medical assistance, copy down a few sentences she spoke just as she was making ready to depart the house for her tower."

Miss Bonnet then removed from her little black-beaded draw-stringed reticule a small piece of paper, which she carefully unfolded—her fingers trembling—and from which she now read in her slightly hissing manner:

"A woman in the shape of a monster. A monster in the shape of a woman. The skies are full of them."

She closed her eyes, her narrow frame giving way to a visible shudder.

"I see," said the Doctor.

"Do you, Doctor? Do you indeed?" And, to the Doctor's astonished perception, her manner seemed, for a fleeting moment, almost dry. "Then my prayers shall indeed have been answered. But I have not yet finished. Do you know, Doctor Sloper, the name Giordano Bruno?"

The Doctor's notions of rightful order had undergone by this time so profound a sense of personal damage that he would have judged himself by now incapable of surprise. However, the last question was an *experimentum crucis* of his remaining composure, from which he did not emerge triumphant.

"Do you mean, Miss Bonnet . . ." He faltered, cleared his voice, and began again: "Are you, Miss Bonnet, referring to the Italian astronomer of the sixteenth century, who was burned at the stake by the papist fanatics of the Inquisition?"

"I am, Doctor. I am relieved that you are in possession of the germane historical facts. I had not the means myself for ascertaining whether the reference would be an obscure one, even to a man of your learning, as I had never myself heard the name before the last evening but one. It was my introduction to it that decided me at last to seek medical advice. For I believe that my sister is perilously near—if not yet already fallen within—the frightful abyss of madness!"

The staring gaze of this strange woman as she flatly spoke these last words; the hissing sound of the words themselves there in the rooms on Washington Square: what was there in these that set the fine dorsal hairs to their ascent?

"Two evenings ago my sister broke her dreadful silence with a yet more dreadful revelation.

"I could see that she was in an unnatural state of excitement as soon as she descended the stairs at dusk. I had heard her moving about her room earlier in the day, in the late afternoon, when she is usually still abed.

"Her cheeks were flushed, and there was a strange cold glitter in her eyes. She frightened me even more than I have become, in a sense, accustomed to, these last bitter weeks that I have been witness to her degeneration.

"As we sat over dinner—not a morsel of which was tasted by either my sister or myself—she went so far in breaking the silence between us as to become just as unnaturally voluble. She talked unceasingly, the words pouring out from her as from a just unblocked passage through which the water emerges white with rushing.

"Of all she said to me I can give you very little. I simply tell you that it was of this man, this Giordano Bruno. Of an infinite universe and innumerable worlds, innumerable worlds moving like great wild beasts with a life of their own; of the magical art of memory, of Christ our Lord as magus . . . oh, of terrible, terrible things! I could not catch the smallest part of the full horror of it all!

"I am used to her excesses, when once a subject has seized upon her; but never had I heard anything like the passion with which she spoke the ideas of this dead man.

"But there was something far more terrible still, though I could not immediately put my finger to it. There was

something in her telling that was inexpressibly peculiar and
. . . sinister. It was the perspective she took upon the life
she was relating.

"Doctor, she was speaking of this man *as from the inside!*

"When she spoke of Bruno's being burned alive on the
Campo dei Fiori, she laughed and said how he thought to
himself that he was yet outwitting his witless persecutors;
for where they meant to be turning him to ashes, he was
becoming icy cold.

"I stopped her then: 'How do you know that? How do
you know how he felt as he was burning at the stake?'

"She looked at me, smiling, the words ceasing abruptly
in their flow. Doctor, there was something unspeakably hideous in that smile and in that silence!"

There was a slight pause, during which the woman
looked into the Doctor's face with a stare almost imploring.
And there was that element, too, in her voice, when again
she spoke.

"My sister suffers the awful burden of her genius, which
her female frame cannot possibly support. Yes, I dare to
make use of that most frightful word, genius. I use it with
the tragic sensibility of its rightness, and yet its entire, its
overwhelming *wrongness*. You must acknowledge with me that
woman was not meant to be so. We are pitiful, frail creatures,
held together by the staying supports of human conventions.
There is no place in the great scheme of things for such a
creature as is my poor sister!

"We are not meant to be so; and yet she is so. It is not
her fault, it is not her choice. She was made so and encouraged so by our father, in his very great error.

"She is—I know it!—a woman in the shape of a monster,

a monster in the shape of a woman. I feel it, I know it, I have always known the terrifying blackness of those spaces she carries within her, the cold vast void in which she wanders alone.

"She is becoming lost! Lost to me—and to the world I know, if not to herself.

"I am losing her—and seem sometimes to be losing myself in the agony of it.

"She is my sister, Doctor—my dark, beloved sister. And she is going mad. Help me to save her!"

I V

William

Did the Victorian woman ever gaze naked at herself in the mirror? wondered Hedda, gazing naked at herself in the mirror.

Her disrobed self would have seemed not a little strange, a disturbingly different Other. Curved where her clothed body was straight. Straight where her clothed body was curved.

That shape am I. That shape am I, actually.

You've come a long way baby, applauds the cigarette ad Hedda had clipped from a magazine. Then why are you still calling us "baby," *buster?*

The ad pictures two young women. One is shown in Victorian underwear, obligingly, if undaintily, raising her petticoats, under the caption: "Back then, you didn't look through your closet for something to wear. You wore your closet." The ad enumerates the raiments of the hapless creature: her chemise, and corset and corset covering or camisole; her wire bustle tied around the waist, five petticoats, and a crinoline; her underdrawers (joined, uselessly, only at the waist so as not, immodestly, to imitate male clothing), her hose, and her boots. Behind her await her long trimmed dress, of yards and yards of wool or silk, an enormous hat with a sweeping feather, a shawl, a handkerchief, and gloves. Her hair is puffed out over a horsehair frame.

The contrasting picture shows a young woman in a slinky, backless long dress, supported, no doubt, by nothing more onerous than a pair of cotton-crotched pantyhose. And yet, interestingly, Madison Avenue has precariously perched the liberated babe on a pair of incapacitatingly high-heeled shoes, silver-toned, no less. How far, indeed?

But the point the ad makes is an important one. Victorian women did wear an unprecedented abundance of clothing. The net weight of the fashionable little lady's costume was anywhere between ten and thirty pounds. Thirty pounds! It was no wonder Doctor Sloper's patients were invariably exhausted. Even those reformers who advocated changes in dress were talking of lightening the load to about ten pounds maximum. The issue of the Victorian woman's clothing and, most especially, of her underwear, lies very close to the matter. Had Hedda any taste for acquiring academic decorations, she would have written a dissertation on the history of the female corset, about which she possessed a great wealth of material, a very small portion of which will now be set forth:

From the fourteenth century well into the middle of the twentieth, a woman's flesh was rigorously reshaped by machinery forged of canvas and steel, whalebones and padding. Breasts, belly,

buttocks were pushed up and out, down and in, depending on
the erotic sensibility of the day.

Hedda and Stella's own mother had remained a firm
believer in the benefits of the modern girdle, an elasticized
affair with optional bones and dangling garters. Hedda was
always waiting for one of these contraptions to show up in
one of the secondhand clothing stores she frequented. Fair
and fleshy Stella, in particular, had been constantly exhorted
to place herself within the confines of such a device, for the
purpose of restraining the rippling wavelets and puckering
dimples of her nacreous, rubenesque rump. Hedda always
waxed eloquent on this Great Subject, in honor of which
she had created, in their shared girlhood, many a descriptive
title, as well as several poetic efforts:

> *It's a quarter past eight*
> *And sister Stella is late*
> *Though her face got here on time*
> *Her butt lags several blocks behind.*

Stella had fought off her mother's girdles with her peculiar sense of fashion, the drapery vaguely of medieval cut,
beneath which could proceed the subversive anarchy of
jiggling female flesh.

During the early Renaissance, when a bulging female belly was
the central erotic focus, with all other parts looking almost
vestigial, the constrictions of female underclothes ended high up.
In other times, for example in the mid-sixteenth century, a tubular
corset, made of leather and whalebone and designed to make a

woman's upper body resemble a roll of paper towels, reached from above her flattened bust down to her midthigh, and so squeezed together her hips as to make it impossible for them to offer sufficient support for the heavy gathers of the skirt, which therefore had to be padded and stiffened so that it would stand up by itself.

Catherine de Médici (1519–1589), who was, among other things, the wife of Henry II of France (1519–1559) and the undisputed fashion arbiter of her day, frowned upon a thick waist as intolerably uncouth, and is said to have dictated a circumference of thirteen inches as ideal. She is also said to have introduced a particularly rigid and forceful "corps," ascending almost to the throat, resulting in an innovative drainpipe shape for Woman.

Tradition states that Catherine was the originator of the much discussed iron corset, an item of fashion that looked very much like a piece of armor. It was made in an openwork design over which silk or velvet could be stretched, and was hinged at one side and closed at the other with a hasp or a pin. A few examples still exist.

Even without such royal extremes, the woman of that period was formidably stayed, a fact which was satirically treated by Philip Gosson in his 1591 "Pleasant Quippes for Upstart Newfangled Gentlewomen":

> These privie coates by art made strong
> With bones, with paste and suchlike ware
> Whereby their backe and sides grew long
> And now they harnest gallants are
> Were they for use against the foe
> Our dames for Amazons might goe.

> *But seeing they doe only stay*
> *The course that nature doth intend,*
> *And mothers often by them slay*
> *Their daughters yoong, and work their end,*
> *What are they els but armours stout,*
> *Wherein like gyants Jove they flout?*

It must be stated that the reference here to a fatal maternal attention is not mere poetic license.

Of course, Hedda would seize upon this.

There are written records of mothers who were all too zealous in their obligation to work their daughters into the sanctioned shape, resulting in the occasional cracked rib or serious internal injury.

It was in the seventeenth century that the term "stays" came into English usage. The century began with rather short stays and a comparatively "natural" female shape. But as the century progressed, emphasis on the slim waist was again introduced, along with the tight lacing which would now continue almost uninterrupted among women of fashion for the next two centuries. This became extreme, leading to the epithets "strait-laced" and "staid," during the Puritan era of the midcentury, which did not condemn the practice as injurious and vainglorious, but instead commended it on the grounds that it disciplined the body—a theory which had little connection with its original purpose of allure.

The corset attained an unprecedented degree of serious intent by the Victorian age, at which time it became not just an item of fashion, but a point of morality, though, rather like the

*famous "Iron Maiden" of the Spanish Inquisition, it was squeez-
ing the very breath out of those it would save.*

Surely, even the most pedantic of prose could allow itself
its occasional polemical metaphor?

*Girl children of three years old wore modified corsets, which
were gradually tightened, so that by around the age of thirteen
they were wearing the full adult version.*

*The elaborateness of the later Victorian and Edwardian corset
was required by the shape of Woman then in demand, which
was an exaggerated serpentine, with an outward-thrusted, over-
hanging "mono bosom" equipoised against an outward-thrusted,
slightly ascending "mono buttock." (The famous "Gibson girl.")
This shape was by no means easy for a woman to achieve,
and the corseting it required had severe effects on its wearer's
life. She couldn't take a deep breath. Her lacing induced the
tendencies to blush and to faint, made it difficult to eat, and
impossible to move quickly. It often deformed the internal organs
and led to complaints of the digestive order. Even when she
unlaced and unhooked herself, her ribs had been so compressed
that they retained their uncomfortable position. (As women today
carry inwardly the distortions induced by previous years of
cruel convention.)*

*And yet, with all this, it was felt to be quite dangerous to
her physical (not to speak of her moral) well-being were the
Victorian woman ever to dare to venture forth without her corset.
A woman's frame was thought to be too delicate, its musculature
too undeveloped, for it to be expected to hold her up unassisted.
(As was her spiritual equipment too meagre to permit her to
withstand assaults on her virtue, had it been made any easier*

to get to. Of course, those useless unjoined lacy drawers left
her dangerously open to assaults from behind, not to mention
possible embarrassment were she to trip on her trailing hems or
billowing crinolines, while alighting, for example, from a street-
car.) And the truth is that the severity of her girding wrought
such atrophy in the muscles of her back and stomach that a
woman did indeed experience extreme discomfort when she took
it off for long.

Alice, of course, would be vigorously committed to the
necessity of female corseting. Osseous as she was, she would
be ruthlessly straitlaced and hooked. Had Catherine's iron
corset been available, it would have found a waiting customer
in Alice Bonnet. (At least Hedda's sister, Stella, had not had
to fight off a mother brandishing one of those.) The serious
literary question now facing Hedda was: Could Vivianna be
allowed to move about unstayed? Also: How would William
James feel about this? Would he notice? Of course he would.
His painter's eye would immediately espy the detail—so to
speak. Would he be charmed, alarmed? Think her a slattern?
a slut? An hysteric?

Hedda contemplated the fluidity of the conception of
the ideal female form, the mobility of the image of the female
nude, as she gazed at the angles and lines of her own radically
nonideal nude self.

No, she wasn't nude, already a term of idealization. She
was naked. There was no age that would have celebrated
her shape. Not even the Gothic sensibility, with its appre-
ciation of a consumptive pallor and a morbid thinness, would
have taken pleasure in the contemplation of such as she.

Thirty-eight years old and still waiting to need a bra.

Did Hedda dream then of beauty? Even she?

When she was twelve she had been a poet. Briefly, for less than a year, their father had returned to them, bringing back into their lives his ambiguous silence, his irascible blue eyes, and the thin gray smoke of his endless cigarettes. They moved, with him, out of Manhattan to a semiposh suburb of New York, the Mother even temporarily giving up her job as bookkeeper for Marty Factor. They leased—or, perhaps, they had even bought, though it seemed in retrospect unlikely—a tidy little split-level, as unlike their family as the half-hour television shows she took to watching in the paneled den of that house. There must have been money. The Mother had furnished the place by purchasing whole showrooms at Macy's: lamps, vases, ashtrays, even the pictures on the wall of the living room. The den had a small bookcase, and, for all Hedda knew, the few books scattered within it might have come from a Macy's showroom.

All of which had conduced to Hedda's brief career as a poet.

The local newspaper ran, every Saturday, on its back page, a junior page, in which selected items from the submitted literary efforts of the area's schoolchildren were printed. Hedda had been, for the few months of her parents' reconciliation, a frequent contributor.

One of her twelve-year-old efforts had been titled "I Dreamt":

> *I dreamt I was a goddess*
> *Who walked in grace demure*
> *Whose beauty was beyond compare*
> *Whose heart was good and pure.*

I dreamt I was a genius
Whose mind was a thing so great
As to only think of bookish things
But never want or hate.

I dreamt I was a tree
Whose boughs were great and strong
For surely in a thing of strength
There cannot be a wrong.

Alas, I dreamt all night
Of things I wished to be
But morning brought the light of day
For I am only me.

The piece had been printed. The next week an answer had arrived, addressed to her at her junior high school.

Hedda, you will be a goddess
Draped in grace and gossamer
Someone's eyes will follow closely
As you glide across the floor
Every woman is a goddess
To the man who worships her.

Hedda, you will be a genius
Not a bookish devotee
You will be the kind of genius
Skilled in drying tears away
Every woman is a genius
When there's sorrow to allay.

Hedda, you will be a tree
Strong of bough, and full of right
You will someone's refuge be
On a dark and stormy night
Every woman is a tree
To her child lost in fright.

Hedda, you are only you.
That is enough; dreams will come true.

The poem had arrived unsigned. Over the years she had come to think of it as yet another projection of the Ubiquitous Voice—who, she knew, was altogether capable of throwing his voice, as gracefully ambiguous as any of Henry's ghosts.

Though she had thought of herself, even in those vaguish days of prematurity, as a feminist, she had not yet the cultivated anger to take offense at the poem's unregenerate message. (Skilled in drying tears away indeed!) She had taken its message very seriously, startled by its suggestion of a reversal in the imagined Scheme of Things. Her own poem had voiced her belief that if only she could be prettier, smarter, better, and altogether *more*, love would appear; or, more to the point, it—*he*—would remain in situ. The unbidden response had suggested that she had gotten it backward. If he were in that state of mind that would have disposed him to stay, if, that is to say, he *loved* her, she would already have seemed the prettier, smarter, better, and altogether more she dreamt of being. She puzzled at the time over which of the two possibilities was the more disheartening: his not loving her enough because she wasn't being enough; or her not being enough because he wasn't loving enough.

Because of course she knew that he would, in the end, disappear, abandoning her and Stella to the despair of having the Mother all to themselves. Which he did, when Hedda was thirteen, Stella ten; going off one Sunday morning to purchase the ethnic delicacy of bagels and Nova Scotia salmon, never to return.

The reconciliation had been a failure. The ambiguous silences had said it all.

For a woman who spent so many hours of the day staring into the mirror, Hedda mused, she really had little idea how she looked. This was partly, with her as with everyone, due to anomalies inherent in the reflecting medium itself. Only consider the phenomenon of right-left reversal. Just imagine the result on our sense of ourselves were mirrors to reverse up and down, as well as right and left. From just such accidents of the laws of physics are we made.

That part in her hair, for example, was really on the other side of her head. That mole she saw on the left cheek of her ass, she thought, turning around and craning her neck backward, was in actuality on the right. To get any truth at all, one had to set up a little system of two mirrors.

A parallel plot! What she required at this point was a parallel plot, a favored ploy among the artifices cultivated by the nineteenth-century novel. It was often the means by which moral points were made, the two stories played off against each other, so that the import of each emerges in the crack in between, as it were.

The demand came to her peremptorily, in the form in

which she was used to receiving and obeying. It came to her there in the inverted image of her sadly sunken rump.

A parallel plot, she whispered to that image.

The long thin shadow of late afternoon stretches itself out before the traveler. He stands on the hill, his hand screening the sun from his eyes, which are directed toward the village below, held snug in the soft folds of its valley like a small child in the bend of an arm.

He has always been partial to the native landscape—a partiality that is shaded with vague longings by the great spans of time passed in Europe; and he is particularly susceptible to the charms of his New England. He would rather be, of an afternoon, taking in the American scene before him than to be, by moonlight, and beneath the deep recesses of the vaulted Roman sky, beholding the bloodied grandeur and moldy antiquity of the vast and awesome Coliseum. Indeed, the last time he had stood within the great circumference of that celebrated ruin, he had felt—despite the hot breath of the sirocco and the comparably heated sentiments of the Europe-proud brother beside him—a morbid horror spread its grim chill through him, prompted by the tableaux of ancient violence his imagination imposed against the backdrop of those pagan stones. He had had to rush away from that place, so deeply stained in Christian blood.

Before him now, like a cameo upon the blooming bosoms of the hills, lies a perfect little specimen of the New England brand of grandeur. There the cluster of white clapboard houses centered round the long rectangle of green, nestled beneath the clean reaching spire of the simple white church, which is, in the Presbyterian style, poetically spare. The younger brother would no doubt dismiss it as "too thin" for description; but such scenes as these register a powerful appeal upon the sensibility of the gazer. The town seems to him, quite simply, exquisite in its insularity, the snug warmth that is generated beneath the thick, soft quilt of New England provinciality. Even the long thin finger of the church is, in the lambent glow of late afternoon, an extension of the cozy suggestion, erected for the purpose of carrying man, not away from his companions, but rather toward the Great Companion, who is, for all eternity, prepared to bestow the "benefit of the doubt" and place the best, that is to say, the petitioner's own, interpretation upon his less than unambiguous actions. The innermost self of a man is a self of the social sort, and those reaching spires of his faith are meant to deliver him up to be in the most perfect socius.

Taken altogether, the elements of the view arrange themselves into the very portrait of *Gemütlichkeit*, if it is not too jarring a breach of consistency to apply a term of foreign derivation to a sight so intensely domestic; and such compositions arouse a response almost too stingingly poignant within those whose inmost souls are—even in a life crowded full of family and friends, students and colleagues—dyed in the tones of solitude.

The service of the Connecticut Western Railway has deposited him in the town of Litchfield, some five miles distant of his destination. He declines the expediency of the horsecar waiting there for hire, for he relishes the opportunity to exercise both his eyes and his legs on the lone country road winding its leisurely way along the lush curves and crevices of the gently rounded mountains of north-western Connecticut.

He gives himself up to the occupation of these few hours with a manly vigor of purpose, as is his wont. His step is decidedly jaunty. Indeed, the heels of his walking boots touch down upon the sod with an observable bounce. This enthusiastic nether locomotion is in agreeable contrast with the "portrait of the professor" that holds its ground above his waist, and whose characteristics include the highly dig-nified cast of features, the gray-streaked beard, spread full and fair and lustrous upon a well-presented chest, and the high hairline which recedes to reveal a cranial dome prom-inently intellectual, with well-developed swellings in the regions of Sublimity, Secretiveness, and Language.

Yet his gait is not so vigorous as to impede his powers of observation. And, his senses being raised to a high pitch of receptivity, he has several times interrupted his long strides to stoop and examine a bit of vegetation, to sniff and, in one or two cases, to taste cautiously of the chosen specimen from a probing index finger. In his youth he had cherished hopes of an artistic career and had broken off his scientific studies abroad in order to spend a year painting under the tutelage of Mr. William Morris Hunt of Newport, Rhode Island. It had turned out to be a false start (neither the alpha nor the omega in the sadly stretching series strung across his wasted youth), an erratum the beloved Father had omnisciently, yet uninsistingly, predicted. Still, it remains with the combined sensibilities of the man of science he now is and the artistic identity abandoned in youth, that the traveler takes in the heaped-up varieties of his experi-ences—which are laid out in such profusion, such a blooming, buzzing confusion, on the vast and groaning banquet board of Nature. Experience is what we choose to attend to. He has chosen to attend to much.

He has an eye now for all, as he strides through white villages and past orchards of ruddy apples, and fields of ripening maize, and patches of woodland, and all such sweet scenery as looks the fairest, a little beyond the suburbs of a town. There are little rivulets, chill, clear, and bright, that murmur beneath the road, through subterranean rocks, and deepen into mossy pools, where tiny fish dart to and fro and within which lurks the hermit frog. And everywhere, tufted barberry bushes, with their small clusters of scarlet fruit; and the toadstools, likewise—some spotlessly white, others yellow or blood red—mysterious growths, springing suddenly from no root or seed and growing nobody can tell how or wherefore. In the deep, damp mosses overspreading the roots of an ancient beech he spots a close cluster of that chanterelle—black and funnel-shaped—which the French ominously call by the name *trompette de mort* and abundantly consume; while in these native parts, though the mushroom is more salubriously dubbed the "horn of plenty," it goes largely untouched. Perniciously intermingled in the grouping are a few specimens of a similarly formed, though paler and less virtuous—in fact, quite poisonous—variety.

He had allotted himself a parsimonious two hours in which to complete the trek from train depot to Willow Groves. He had computed upon the average rate of twenty minutes for the mile, a velocity by no means that of the unhurried stroll, especially as undertaken by a man of his five and fifty years. Pulling his heavy gold watch (which bears the inscription *WJ from AJ*) from his worsted-wool vest pocket, he notes, with a faint suggestion of self-congratulation fleetingly lifting his mouth, that he has exceeded his rate by approximately three minutes for the mile.

It is well that this is so. For the moment that brings this minor revelation delivers also a somewhat peremptory desire to partake in the rich luxury of inaction, for which indulgence no remorse falls due, the extravagance having already been purchased by the portion of the hour gained upon the path. And so it is with a sweetly rounded sense of rightful faineance that he seats himself—his legs pulled up to his chest and hugged round by his arms—upon the thick carpet of grass and wildflowers sprouting beside that homely little road, which, having consorted almost the entire way on the ledges rimming the lanuginous mountains, is now about to begin its gentle slope into the valley.

The mood with which he had left Boston earlier this day had been brushed over with a familiar shade of sadness, the effect of the muddied pigments of self-dissatisfaction, of a moral sense of failure. But the brisk walk through the summer-rich Connecticut country, in the mellowing light of the advancing day, has brought on a sort of deep enthusiastic bliss, which translates itself physically by a kind of stinging pain inside his breastbone. (The sting is to him an essential element of the whole thing.) He is, for the moment, unmindful even of the circumstances that have brought him here, though it had been primarily with the thought of these, and kindred matters, that he had sat out the journey from Boston in his railway carriage.

Filling his lungs with the sharply clean air, he gives himself up to the moment, reveling in the processes of the animal organization. The circulatory migrations—com-

pleted a million times in the day! *there's* activity for you!—
of the vital crimson liquor. The agreeably regular thumping
of the four-chambered muscle directing the whole affair.
And the equally gratifying, and blissfully mechanical, exchange of the atmospheric ingredients, which happen at this
spot to be besottingly scented with the thick spice of bay-
berries mingled with pine, and a damp divine earthiness.

Is it not at once humbling and heartening to acknowledge
how tethered to the gross material substance of us is the
exalted res cogitans, all of whose world systems and tran-
scendental philosophies are as mere ghostly emanations hovering above the heated "doings" of the cephalic region?
Extract the philosopher from his everyday locality in lecture
hall and office; set him, for a few hours, in the vigorous use
of his neglected bifurcated nether regions, through a country
lush and lovely with ripened Indian summer; and, quite spontaneously, he has shed, like a serpent sloughing off old skin,
his laboriously grounded depiction of a gloom-infested cosmos. At such moments of energetic living, among the most
salubrious that we can know, we feel as if there were something diseased and contemptible in theoretic grubbing and
brooding. In the eyes of healthy sense the philosopher is,
at best, a learned fool.

Absorbed as our sitter is in his present cerebration, a
certain quantity of time elapses, during which same we shall
place a few telling brush strokes to the surface of our portrait.

His age has already been set down. We have only to
add that the viewer would not have been able to guess at
it by way of direct scrutiny. Whatever the element that gives
the aspect of volatile youth to a face and form—and there
are men and women not much more than twenty who have

already relinquished it—clings tenaciously still to him. The abundance of the cinereous shade in the chestnut of his beard does not cancel out the youthful impression, but rather suggests the thought: Here is a man gone prematurely to gray. The vivacity of his face is very much the effect of his eyes, once described by a student as "irascibly blue." They are indeed a lively variety of that color, and their stare is inclined to be alternately focused and dreamy. They are the eyes of one who merges his external perceptions with dense visions having no source outside, and of a dimension and a content not to be replicated in another's sight. That is to say, they are the eyes of either a madman or a genius.

But then it is a poor sitter that does not yield his portraitists very dissimilar pictures.

His voice, when he shall speak, shall be heard to be manly and low-pitched, rather halting, for he is not the man to offer out his ideas chilled from the mold. The dialect is difficult to decide upon—upon a first hearing, you might be tempted to say that here is an English quite unaccented, a consequence, no doubt, of the extravagantly cosmopolitan upbringing, what the adorable parent had called his children's "sensuous education." Further attention, however, will reveal our sitter to be, though subtly, a Bostonian. It is not in our power to reproduce by any combination of characters the precise enunciations and intonations, which in the present instance is to be associated with nothing vulgar or vain. The gentleman before us is, most truly, *a gentleman*, as that term is to be understood in all the variety of its unfolding nuances, in this the closing decade of our nineteenth century.

We ought, en passant, to give a glance at the attire of

our man. For, as the old adage has it, a man is the unity of three parts: his body, his mind, and his clothes. The specimens before us are, of course, rather rumpled, and, we might say, not scrupulously clean—consequences of the hours passed cross-legged in the confines of the railway compartment and then spent tramping, and occasionally kneeling, upon the rude rural affair of whose existence we already wot. But the suggestion of unconventionality, subdued but unsubmitting, that might already have fallen faintly upon the attending viewer's perception, is given an added substance by such sartorial details as the quite startlingly bright, indeed sky blue, neckcloth and the belted green-plaid Norfolk jacket, which is to remain for many years hence an invariable feature of his person.

The portion of the hour purchased upon the path has by now quite gone, while we have been at our description of William James of Harvard College—a name that I shall presume you to approach in possession of an already enacted acquaintance and forging of association. (I give you my warning, gentle Reader: there is much that I shall presume upon you.)

That quarter hour, I say, having already elapsed, we can anticipate, from one whose steely discipline of self has already been established, a momentary return to the posture of ambulatory intention. And yet Professor James continues to sit on his own small piece of claimed sod. It is my knowledge to give that, the fragile mood of exaltation now dispersing, his thoughts are once again settling themselves down upon the circumstances of his impending visit to Willow Groves, which visit has been prompted by a letter received two weeks prior to this date.

The letter came from a longtime associate, Doctor Austin Sloper of New York City. The acquaintance between the two men reached far back, into their student days at the School of Medicine at Harvard University, that seat of learning on the banks of the Charles River, which has taken to giving steady employment to some of the most distinguished minds in the land. William James had himself found his place on the Harvard College faculty some twenty-five years before, from which perch he has been able to launch his jagged flights into the fields of physiology and anatomy, psychology and philosophy.

Austin Sloper had gone on, as James had not, to a more direct, and lucrative, application of his acquired medical education; and over the years he had constructed a most flourishing practice among the best society of that metropolis, which, even as we speak, continues to swallow the grassy upper reaches of Manhattan, so that one envisions a day, all too soon, when the gasping little island will be entirely inhumed in paving stones, sagging slowly into its bay beneath the bulk of those hideous edifices. Indeed, already there prevails in that place, to my ears, at least, the howl of unholy Babel; and how anyone can lead a virtuous and reputable life amidst the tawdry architecture, the ash barrels, and the Jews escapes my scope of comprehension. However, I speak as a Bostonian.

These shabby circumstances, however, did not affect, at least at the personal level, which is the level of our concern, the fate of Austin Sloper. His patients were to be found among the island's "best people," whose symptoms were, if not more interesting in themselves than those of the lower orders, at least more consistently displayed. It is true that fortune had favored Sloper, and that he had found the path to prosperity very soft to his tread. But I hasten to add, to anticipate possible misconception, that he was not the least a charlatan. He was an observer; he was, even, a philosopher.

James's opinion of Sloper's ability at school had been high and had continued on that same plane as they progressed along the tracks of their manhood (of which Sloper's had been far the straighter). They kept in touch through the years, though it could not be said that the touch attained to the state of intimacy. Their association had always consisted of the mutuality of their scientific interests and was strictly circumscribed by these. This had been the case even at school. For, while James admired the thinking qualities of his colleague, there was a something about him too forcefully depictive, to James's taste, of the phrase *cool reason* for the warmer affections to be aroused. He seemed, to James, to maintain—but too naturally, without the benefit of a moral struggle—a position of universal cold detachment, effortlessly viewing even the events entangled in the very nerve fibers of his own life with a look of immobile dispassion, as laudable for its philosophic objectivity as it was vaguely abhorrent from the softer and more human point of view. The tragedies life had dealt him—and he had certainly not escaped unscathed from the blind and random distribution of misfortune—had done nothing in the way of making him less the philosopher and more the man.

And yet a philosopher is no mean and common commodity, to be left unreached for on the shelf—especially in this day which belongs unreservedly to vulgarity and sees the ascendancy of the likes of Mr. P. T. Barnum. James was quite prepared to take the coolish doctor as he was. Sloper's letters came studded with sound insights as to character and situation and, most interestingly, the lines of force sketched, latticelike, between them, like an electrical diagram by Mr. Faraday. He had developed into a rather competent critic of James's own publications. He had a mind more analytic than synthetic; which is to say, better at taking apart the ideas of others than at putting together his own. Yet it must be said that, if his critical faculty showed a greater bulk and dexterity than the corresponding organ of receptivity, still he withstood that tendency, so forcefully representing itself in intellectual organizations such as his, to dismiss out of hand. He attended, he considered, he probed; and *then*, and only then, more times than not, did he dismiss.

It will be seen that I am describing a clever man; a man not given to easy enthusiasms or a breathless alacrity to believe. And this is the reason why James was not disposed to be indifferent when he received a letter from this clever colleague urging before him the consideration of a certain case, presented in the person of a Miss Alice Bonnet, of the town of Willow Groves in Connecticut; a spinster, age thirty-eight, soft-spoken and genteel, clearly of "good people."

Miss Bonnet—whose name is not to be "frenchified," as I was most pointedly informed by the designee after I made the mistake of doing so—presents, prima facie, rather too classic a picture of neurasthenia to be deemed interesting. Her complexion is consumptive and her eyes deeply shadowed, with the expected dilated pupils. This last symptom was perhaps exaggerated by the unusually thick lenses of her spectacles. (Upon being questioned, she admitted to having suffered from trouble with her eyes since about the age of thirteen, including, most tellingly, episodes of hemianopsia, that blindness to one-half the field of view which is, of course, not uncommon to cases of hysteria.) However, she was most reluctant to discuss any of her own "trifling" complaints. The cause of her visit, it transpired, was not her own state of ill-health, but rather the extreme anxiety she suffered over the alarmingly deteriorating situation of her sister, one Vivianna Bonnet, also a spinster, three years the younger, with whom she has lived alone since the death of both parents from malaria, some five and twenty years ago. Her own case of "nerves" she dismissed as the result of protracted concern over her younger sister's plight, which she confessed herself as being entirely incapable of grasping. "For, though sisters, we are by nature to one another as high noon is to midnight hour." (You must not take such whimsy to be her characteristic mode of expression. Indeed it was by reason of the exact opposite that the sentence made itself to stick in my mind.)

There then ensued a most extraordinary conversation, whose details I sketch anon. . . .

I think you will agree with me that the case seems to hold out some interesting possibilities. You're the man for it, James. I pass it along to you. I know your predilection for the more exotic specimens in the garden of abnormal personality, most especially if the rare bloom should carry a faintly metaphysical tint to it.

The sun now is setting. The mountains are losing their detail, turning to flat dark planes, imposed in stark contrast to the drama being played out above—where the light of the western sky is shrieking away: vermilion and carmine; madder crimson, madder yellow, madder orange: an entire upper spectrum gone to madness. The colors look as if they had been squeezed straight from the tubes and smeared across the great canvas in a frenzy of expressivity. Thus dies the day.

The twilight deepens. The low broad orioles glance duskily from the foliage, the ravens wheel and clamor in the glowing sky; the shadows now are thick upon the valley; and still James sits, his alerted sensibility altering itself apace with the shifting scene. The village, so turned in upon itself, seems now, with darkness gathering, to show a face deliberately blank, and as if to say: I yield you nothing . . . outsider!

A last dying ray falls upon the steeple of the church, which now seems less the arm of protection and more the admonishing finger of the grim old Calvinist faith. How the extravagantly affectionate parent had hated that dogma of predestination and damnation, which had so oppressed and saddened his own tender years, in the personage of the paterfamilias, the forger of the family fortune, Mr. William James of Albany. The younger William had quite forgotten, in the afternoon light and the euphoric sweep of the earlier moment, the other side, the night side, of these New England villages. The sickness of soul so often sheltered within; lying low and huddled, confined in layers of isolation and enforced silence; but breaking out, now and then, leaping up with wildly distorted features and barely human utterance. It is one with the ferocity with which, two centuries before, the plague of "witchcraft" had swept over this rugged countryside. The stories linger over such places, in hushed, lugubrious legends: of eccentric maiden aunts; recluses, never glimpsed but as a fleeting frightened face behind a moved curtain; remembered but unmentioned when the weeping is heard in the night, or the cornfield is set on fire.

You must stand outside the mood, James tells himself, his fine lips moving. Fight clear of the reaching fingers of the tenebrous temper! It is mere crepuscular melancholia, the morbid vapors released by twilight hour.

"The blue hour," he remembers it being called, from his days as a fledgling artist; when the light takes on, but briefly, an eerie tinge of blue, which will reveal aspects of a painting lain hidden in brightness. Friends too, James knows, are apt to speak at blue hour of matters unsaid at midday. Mr. William Morris Hunt had been a great believer in the revealing powers of this fine, fleeting dimness.

And indeed, it had been at just this time of the day that James had once taken out to examine a self-portrait he had completed but the morning before, in a rare sunlit mood of self-approbation; and had found himself gasping aloud to see a cruel cold intelligence that had stared out from the eyes and a predatory hardness working itself over the mouth. It was not the face he had wanted to paint, had believed himself to have painted. The extreme repugnance he had felt toward what he encountered on that canvass in blue twilight stayed with him for some time, lingering like an ugly stain and blighting his earlier enthusiasm. It had not been *the* determining experience behind his decision to turn his back on the artistic chance for which he had argued so unquittingly the year previous. And yet, it had not been altogether unrelated to that event, either.

Stand outside the mood, he admonishes himself again. Apprehend it, and take pity—above all, take pity! But do not share in that sorrow which he now knows, with every fiber of him vibrating to it, to lie in the valley below. And yet he feels the shadow of it mounting, taking on dark substance within that damnably responsive self, with its exaggerated sensibility for suffering.

An affinity for sadness is not, in itself, a symptom of morbidity. Rather, one might say, it is a product of a well-functioning faculty of realism. Let sanguine healthy-mindedness do its best with its strange power of living in the moment and ignoring and forgetting; still the evil background is really there to be thought of, and the skull will grin in at the banquet.

And yet: one must take care to keep the apperception of sadness from transmuting into the *Ding-an-sich*. If one despairs with all one's heart at the fact of human sorrow, what *does* it alleviate the general situation (not to speak of one's own small personal plight) to allow one's self to merge into that vast and seamless swell of suffering? All one then shall have accomplished is one's own undoing and a further increase of the general level of misery. Rather, to do any good at all, one must withstand the melting urge. If truth be a matter of its pragmatic issue, leap! Leap with all the stored resources of faith, across the bottomless abyss forever opening up before your feet. If you be of such a mind to be blind to the abyss, so much the better—for you and for everyone else concerned. As for we others, what can we do but cultivate our blindness or, failing this, cultivate its pretense?

The words of his friend Robert Louis Stevenson come back to him, here on this lone road, as on many occasions before: "Whatever else we are intended to do, we are not intended to succeed; failure is the fate allotted."

Failure, then, failure! Breathing its foulness over all our efforts, so that we turn from the stink in disgust. The book that had seemed, in the delusions attending its parturition, to move with a boisterous life and cry out in lusty truth—now seen for stillborn, cold and blue. And those phrases, which seemed once to cast the aura of infinitude before them, now sounding in one's ear with a lisping, mocking hollowness. He has long since made it a principle never to reread what he has written, lest he be washed away by the cruel vision of the unending bleak futility; to correct no proofs, nor approve others' translations of his writings; but to hurry from these "ever not quite" attempts as from the final critique hurled down from the Chill Intelligence above.

How he has hurried on, these many years past, forcibly refusing to cast a glance behind. For he has been running from a far more horrible thing than the dingy fact of his own failure. Dragging itself pitifully after him, now a few steps closer, now a few steps farther, but always, hideously, *there*, has been the figure of a ghastly youth, with barely human countenance, James's demented doppelgänger!

This wretched phantom has been a fixture in James's inner life for almost thirty years now. James had been twenty-six years old when he had first encountered the specter, during one of those nightmare seasons to which he was prone: incapacitated by indecision, pressed down into nauseating inaction beneath the weight of melancholia. In such a mood, he had gone, one evening at twilight, into the dressing room to procure some article that was there. Suddenly, there fell upon him without any warning, just as if it had come out of the darkness, a horrible fear of his own existence. And there arose in his mind, at this same moment, the image of an epileptic patient he had seen that day in the asylum: a black-haired youth with greenish skin, entirely idiotic, who used to sit all day on one of the benches, or rather shelves against the wall, with his knees drawn up against his chin and the coarse gray undershirt, which was his only garment, drawn over them, enclosing his entire figure. He sat there like a sort of sculptured Egyptian cat or Peruvian mummy, moving nothing but his black eyes and looking absolutely nonhuman.

That shape am I. That shape am I, potentially. Nothing that I possess can defend me against that fate, if the hour for it should strike for me as it struck for him.

He had felt such a horror of the boy, and such a perception of his own merely momentary discrepancy from him, that it was as if something hitherto solid within his breast gave way entirely, and he became a mass of quivering fear.

After this the universe was altogether changed. He awoke morning after morning with a horrible dread at the pit of his stomach and with a sense of the insecurity of life that he had never known before. It was like a revelation. He had dreaded to be left alone and had wondered how other people could live, how he himself had ever lived, so unconscious of that pit of insecurity beneath the surface of life. His mother, in particular, a very cheerful person, seemed a perfect paradox in her unconsciousness of danger, which you may well believe he was very careful not to disturb by revelation of his own state of mind.

For months he had been unable to go out in the dark alone, mortally terrified of the visions the night might throw up before him. The experience had gradually faded. But it had left him forever open to the morbid feelings of others.

The church bell, now striking the hour, carries him back to the present moment, though with no very cheerful sound.

Stand aside! Keep the saving distance of memory between the madness of that time and now! You are not one with those lost souls, their pale faces pressed up hard against the lighted window. Their haunted visions and twisted identities are their own, and not yours.

He had clung to scripturelike texts: "The eternal God is my refuge." "Come unto me, all ye that labour and are heavy-laden." "I am the resurrection and the life." If not for these, it had always been his belief, he should have grown really insane.

The bell has long since ceased to vibrate with the call to evening prayer, and a sort of profound stillness falls now on the valley, as if the place has somehow been stricken with death. The crows, so vociferously conversational a half hour before, have now settled noiselessly into the spreading branches overhead, of copper beech and elm. James sits here, still on the edge, staring out into the blackening scene before him.

We could, of course, follow him yet. It falls easily within the powers of narration to trace him still, to stalk his receding form as it moves soundlessly into that hideous forest, where the obscene bird of night chatters.

And yet, would it not be, somehow, a desecration—to proceed beyond this point and deprive the man—for he is, withal, a man—of the thin consolation of solitude in which to enwrap his trembling form and live out the hell-sent hours of the soul? Let us rather leave the inner scene for now and look about us at the lonesome night, listen to the hush in which something crouches or gathers. There are stars coldly glittering in those distant, undomesticated heavens; and just as chillingly remote, glow the lights from the dwellings below. But see! how the language of subjectivity penetrates even now the transcribed scenery.

For how long we should have been forced to keep our solemn session through the watches of the night I cannot say, were there not come, at this very moment, a most monstrous discontinuity. It is a cry—but from where? Oh God, what a cry is this! Beginning low, as almost a moan, it rises swiftly, so that it fills horribly the ears, the head, the entire animal frame. It is a wail, of unknowable pain, coming from the farthest reaches of unprotected terror; the most mournful sound that can be imagined; breaking off—abruptly—and now continuing again, if just as unearthly, also somehow more ungodly: fierce and fell, like the howl of unpitying passion at the moment of cruelest murder. And yet it is, with that, *the same cry both times*, shattering the night into broken shards, letting loose all the shrieking demons of hell.

It lasts . . . but how long *does* it last? Long enough for James to question, while it still blasts within his ears, whether the cry proceeds from animal or human—and if human, whether male or, as it more likely seems, in its high-pitched hysteria, female; from the raven-haunted woods behind or beyond or, again, as it more appallingly seems, from the tiny hamlet below?

It ceases, abruptly; broken off in mid–high note as it had before, but, blessedly, not to be taken up again.

Our figure sits unmoving, his entire structure frozen into deathly stillness. The anguished terror, the savage hatred, held in that unchecked sound, still roils within him, gradually fading, but only in the shadow of the more terrible question that is looming ever huger before him, transforming all the world about him into the eddying blackness of that icy pit he knows too well.

The question he asks himself is: Was that most hideous shriek . . . *his own?*

V

Vivianna

"I am not partial to infinitude."

She made her murmur as one would decline the offer of a cream cake at teatime. Her interlocutor, however, showed her nothing of the oddity of her remark in the response he made her. He seemed, in his affably comprehending nod, to imply that he heard such statements of metaphysical preferences, uttered in just so matter-of-fact a tone, every day of his life—which, in point of fact of the manner of his employment, might very well have been the case.

"I myself"—he matched the matter-of-factness of her tone exactly—"have always found the infinite very much to my pluralistic liking. Just as I prefer the South American jungles to arid desertscapes, or, for that matter would betimes, and in a certain mood, choose the densely spiraling complexities of my younger brother's prose to the thinner efforts of some of his literary contemporaries."

"Ah yes, your brother." She peered at him coldly through

the glass of her pince-nez. "I confess I have never been able to read him to the end."

He remarked to himself the slight defect of her speech that gave it its strange low hiss. But he laughed aloud at her comment, his eyes crinkling into traces worn deep by previous motions of mirth.

"I could confess sometimes to almost the same—and have told him something like it on numerous occasions—were it not for the great accumulated fraternal affection charging me from behind with its great heave-ho! over those parts that are frozen thick with overrefinement and those maddening French phrases. My brother, by the by, would—I am certain of it—share with you a great long shudder at the sight of the infinite dimension stretching itself off into the boundless murk. Left to his choice, he will always deposit his affectionate and adipose person in some good leather chair in a brown old room, glowing softly with shaded candlelight, and smelling vaguely of pipe tobacco and the well-worn morocco of valuable old books."

"I am glad to hear it." She said it as one who, suspecting her neighbor of dangerous opinions, discovers him to be a churchgoing Christian and best friend to the parson to boot. "Perhaps I shall attempt to read him again."

"Yes, do. Some of his works are, in their peculiar way, supremely great. Your sister, I can presume, does not share your finitary fastidiousness?"

"My sister revels in infinitude."

"Brava!" He gave sound to a short burst of rich-toned laughter. "Revels in infinitude! I relish the phraseology as I admire the outlook. I cannot tell you how much I look forward to meeting her this evening."

"Do you?" She gave him a tightly wrapped-up smile, though it was the most extravagantly joyful she had yet exposed to his eye. "I can tell you, Professor James, that she too awaits the occasion with the quickest sentiment of anticipation."

"Yet not sufficiently quick, I may presume, so as to disrupt the established routine." He smiled briefly.

Alice, ignoring the implied query, brought out: "Would you like, in the meanwhile, to pay a visit to her observatory?"

"She would not mind our trespassing in her absence?"

"The premises," she said with that visible increase in stiffness she had found occasion to display before, "are as much mine as hers."

She is most decidedly eccentric, James thought with appreciative amusement as he followed her excessively erect person out the front door. His clever colleague had of course oversimplified in his estimation of the elder Miss Bonnet. There is that learning which is employed the better to bring the world in; and there is that which is deployed to keep it out. James already felt quite certain that the spare figure of Alice Bonnet comprised a complexity that substantially escaped the doctor's neat and narrow classification, as well as her own noontime self-comparison. The world exists to confound all such tidy schematisms.

He had already noticed the tower as he approached the home of the sisters earlier that day, well ahead of the hour of his appointment. Their property must have extended across a considerable acreage, for the tower was a good ten minutes' brisk walk from the house. The house itself was set far back from the shady road, a sprawling brown wooden mansion, in which the two Miss Bonnets must have fairly rattled around. There were three full floors, and the top story was fancifully bedecked by slated gables and peaks. The front of the house was thickly scrimmed by an arbor of the most suggestively christened "weeping willows," whose profusion in the area had given to the village its name.

The man and woman walked, talking little, toward an oddly symmetrical, double-mounded hill of no great elevation. The incline placed itself in strong chromatic contrast with the wide acreage of surrounding land by being covered with fir trees. The trees were all one size and age, so that their tips assumed the precise curve of the hill they grew upon. This pine-clad protuberance was yet further marked out from the general landscape by having at its center a tower in the form of a classical column, which, though partly immersed in the trees, rose above them to a considerable height. Upon this object the eyes of Alice and James were bent.

"Then there is no road leading near it?"

"Nothing nearer than the road off of which the house stands."

The tower now showed itself as a much more important erection than it had appeared from farther away. Soon they stood immediately at the foot of the shaft, which had been built in the Tuscan order of classic architecture and was hollow with steps inside. The gloom and solitude that prevailed around the base were remarkable. The sob of the environing trees deepened the mood; and moved by the light breeze, their thin straight stems rocked in seconds, like inverted pendulums; while some boughs and twigs rubbed the pillars' sides or occasionally clicked in catching each other. Below the level of their summits the masonry was lichen-stained and mildewed, for the sun never pierced that moaning cloud of blue-black vegetation. Pads of moss grew in the joints of the stonework, and here and there shade-loving insects had engraved on the mortar patterns of no human style or meaning, but curious and suggestive. Above the trees the case was different; the pillar rose into the sky a bright and cheerful thing, unimpeded, clean, and flushed with the sunlight.

They walked round the tower to the other side, where stood the door through which the interior was reached. The paint, if it had ever had any, was all washed from the wood, and down the decaying surface of the boards liquid rust from the nails and hinges had run in red stains.

Alice placed her small white hand upon the blistered, red-brown latch, and pushed down. The door did not give. Again, James saw that exaggerated stiffening, and even in the dense duskiness that there shrouded them, he could see how all the color drained quickly from her face, leaving only two deeply crimson spots upon her cheeks.

"She goes too far!"

Her voice was barely that of a hissed whisper; and yet it is impossible to convey the quantity of passion that was compressed therein. He could but dimly wonder at the relation joining the two Miss Bonnets; but he had already the idea that it was of a complexity and intensity such as to make of it their world entire.

It was abundantly manifest that her state was of a sort to preclude even the illusion of conversation. She did not ask him back to the house, and he took his leave soon after, human compassion this time winning out over scientific curiosity (these heavyweights of his psyche were habitually wresting within him), and having arranged to return at that hour when Vivianna should have awoken. He left Alice, by her wishes, behind, still frozen at the base of the tower, over which it appeared Vivianna had made to claim her possession.

The hour of his next appointment was dusk. But when he returned then he was greeted by Alice's prompt emergence from the door, to meet him upon her wide wooden porch, where he was informed, in cool tones of apology, that Vivianna had been taken by one of her sick headaches, of so acute an intensity as to make of the promised interview an impossibility.

He gently pressed, proffering to doff the hat of psychological investigator and put in its stead the plume of medical practitioner. Should he not—all the more!—be permitted to see the sufferer? He might have the means at his disposal—he was, for example, thoroughly accomplished at hypnotism—for easing her in her distress. But the clipped severity of the decline convinced him that the prickly spinster planted firmly before him would be quite impossible to budge in any direction.

He observed—in her eyes, which were dull and remote, and her color, which was ashen—that the glowing embers of her afternoon's ire had cooled, leaving her in a state of desolate weariness.

He retraced his steps back to the inn that sat on the edge of the willowed commons, not far from the spare white church. He would have to take the train out of Litchfield in the morn. There were obligations awaiting him in Cambridge—not so much on Irving Street, for his own Alice left him very free to come and go as he would, but rather at the college. He had in fact to deliver a lecture tomorrow evening at the Harvard Philosophical Club, which he had spent the afternoon in polishing up—torturing and poking and scraping and patting it till it offended him no more. So there was no question of his staying the extra day on the chance of encountering the more elusive of the two Miss Bonnets.

Impatient as his nature was wont to be, he yet did not feel himself put out by what now took on the goading aspect of the wild goose chase. Though failing of its purpose, the trip to Willow Groves had not gone squandered but had yielded up its own distinctive and unanticipated experience, which had been, in its own singular way, all that one could wish it. Besides, he had gotten in a very good afternoon's work, a full five hours straight of continuous, undistracted cerebration, and therefore did not find himself in a mood to make complaint. For he suffered greatly from that constitutional disease that the Germans call *Zerrissenheit*, or "torn-to-pieces-hood," and asked only for the optimal twelve hours of work on *one* occupation for his happiness.

The evening was extremely fine, and he decided upon a last stroll through the beautiful country of the surrounding hills. He could not afford the luxury of the hike tomorrow morning and had already made his arrangements at the inn for the horsecar that was to take him to the Litchfield railway station.

He walked straight upon the road leading back out of the town. The splendid evening was darkening into an equally worthy night. The stars were emerging with brilliant clarity to take their places in the great constellations etched out against the cloudless sky, and it was upon their sight that his head was raised as he climbed the slope away from the village.

When he had gained the crest he paused, very nearly at the spot where he had spent a long night's solemn meditation. He looked back down upon the valley, seeing if he could not make out the mound upon which the sisters' tower ascended. This proved to be easy, the reason for which facility he discovered with a voiced expression of surprise; for the head of the tower proclaimed itself with the muted radiance by which it was illumined above the thick black undergrowth of trees!

It was a mere quarter of an hour that found him back again at the tower's door. He had made his way quickly and surely, the light at the tower's tip his summoning beacon.

Some instinct, more scientific than genteel, made him to dispense with a knock. He unhesitatingly put his hand to the iron latch and pushed down, the door giving way to an interior of cylindrical steps winding steeply upward, murkily lit from the glow of the single candle that was coming from the story above and upon which he now noiselessly ascended.

He saw her from behind, as she sat writing at a little oaken table on the opposite point of the lead flat that formed the summit of the tower. There at a point halfway between herself and him, arranged upon a tripod and reaching its shaft halfway out the window, was poised the long, rigid instrument of her astronomical observations.

His eyes returned to the seated figure. She was dressed in something dark and soft, which fell in loose folds about her and onto the leaden floor. There was a long cape of velvet stuff that had fallen from her shoulders as she bent to her work, so that the sight of the graceful slope of her neck and back was given to him.

His artist's eye took in the natural curves in which she was arranged, which had none of the artfulness of the current strictures of fashion. Her waist filled out its natural circle. It was visibly and delightfully undeformed by stays.

Her hair, unlike her sister's, was not hidden beneath the prim New England bonnet but was tied back with a simply knotted thin black velvet ribbon, to fall in thick tresses toward her waist, catching in its descent the gleam from the candle attending to the side of her right hand resting on the table—for it was—as he, who was himself left-handed, noted—with her left that she wrote.

All of these observations were registered in the space of some fifteen or twenty seconds, before she—without changing her posture in the slightest degree—spoke:

"I have just to finish this one computation, Professor James. It shall not take but a minute."

Her voice was low and full; a deliciously feminine instrument!

A space of a minute more and she stood and turned toward him, but without coming nearer him.

"Forgive my intrusion," he began.

"It is a thing most welcome," she stopped him, her voice calm and expectant. He sensed her smile—grave, but friendly—more than saw it. The flame of the candle was low, the gloom in the tower deucedly thick.

"How did you know it was I without turning your head?"

"But who else could it have been?" she returned with homely logic.

"Your sister, perhaps?"

She smiled.

"It is not her hour. And, in any case, it was not Alice's tread I heard on my stair."

"Her hour," he repeated. "It is true, then, as your sister avers, that you have halved between you the diurnal revolution, and that she has been given the day and you the night?"

"Yes. The night is when I do my work," she said simply.

"And do you never then see the light? It seems a hard thing."

"I see the dawn, and then I retire. For my part, I am sorry for those who sleep through the night. But you must know that it is due to Alice that my twelve hours' occupation is succeeded by a full twelve hours in which to recover myself."

"Have you no freedom, then, in the matter of the hours you keep?"

"Do you truly believe, Professor James," she returned, her voice gently laughing, "in that phantom . . . freedom?"

"I do! I do indeed! My first act of free will was to believe in free will!"

"Ah . . . then perhaps I too have freely chosen—only to be unfree." She made her thrust with a light, deft hand, accompanying it with what seemed to James a queer, distant smile and a slight jutting of her chin. He was charmed, in both his philosophical and his manly parts.

Her face could not be made out altogether clearly in the dim soft flickering light of the short wax candle; and James's eyesight had been blighted since youth. She seemed, however, to be in point of individual features extremely like her sister; only, somehow, the entire impression they cast was so contrary in its effect. For where the other presented an overall look of strainedness, of Doctor Sloper's "telling brittleness"—showing itself most acutely in her face, which was perpetually pinched with deep lines of worry drawn perpendicular to her brow—the woman before him seemed the very soul of serenity, suggesting, if in the shadows, the beauty of an ideal stillness and perfect solitude, to which that something in James that was so essentially alone most deeply responded.

The brow she turned to him was smooth, and she seemed to be separated from her sister by a span more lengthy than the three years that had been cited.

The windows of the tower-observatory were opened to the night, which entered warm and still. There seemed something in its breath of Rome's sirocco, and of the perfume of the small white rose growing in perilously high places.

"It was by a most happy chance that I espied your tower's light. It had been reported to me that you were laid low by a sick headache."

"No manner of ache would have kept me away from my tower on this night. I am expecting, round midnight, an event."

"Is the night's event not then this which is now transpiring?" he smilingly offered her.

"Ah yes." Her calm voice met his. "But it is of an *astronomical* event that I speak."

"Which shall outshine our own?"

"As the astronomical must of necessity outshine the terrestrial."

She finished her declaration with one of those infinitely

expressive little shrugs by which the peoples of Italy speak their elegant volumes. Taken altogether, as a statement of absolute preference, it was complete.

"Tell me then," he said, "of that other event!"

"Are you acquainted with the delta-Celphei?"

And with that question she leaped, with graceful celerity, into her chosen theme.

She spoke, at first, in terms largely mathematical; but when he showed her, with a question, his unabashed ignorance with the ways of numbers and equations—a student had recently delighted him by speaking of algebra as a low form of cunning—she quickly changed her mode of expression, so that it was wondrously clean of the obscuring dust of mathematical cant. When she had finished with her account, some thirty or forty minutes later, he knew a great deal more than once he had anent the strangely flashing stars of delta-Celphei, of double stars, which appear single to the naked eye, and of a theory first casually mentioned in the last century by the great French astronomer and mathematician, Pierre Simon de Laplace, of certain prodigies of the heavens, which Vivianna had named her "darkened stars"—celestial bodies whose gravity was so strong that not even light could escape the irresistible pull of it!

It was around this brief suggestion of Laplace's that Vivianna's own hypotheses were being woven, in a system quite fearsomely—even in such graceful hands as these—mathematical.

"Have you read Laplace, Professor?" she asked him hurriedly—she had the art of being almost tragically impatient and yet making it as light as air; and then, at a slight shake of his head—which her eyes, so much keener-sighted than his own, immediately caught—she opened quickly a heavy tome.

"This is his *Exposition du système du Monde.* But listen! 'A luminous star of the same density of the earth, and whose diameter was two hundred and fifty times greater than that of the sun, would not, because of its attraction, allow any of its rays to arrive at us; it is therefore possible that the largest luminous bodies of the universe may, through this cause, be invisible.'

"Professor James—can you perhaps understand what it is I feel, working here in my little tower room with my sadly inadequate equipage, and yet knowing myself to be on the trail of a great fiery mass, burning its incandescent fury beyond the eyes of all men?" Her dark eyes seemed to him to reflect something of the fire of her subject. "There are times when I must gasp in wonderment at what I see and, even more, at what I guess to be there; and at the elected grace that it is *I* who sees and guesses!"

"And the event you await . . . ?"

"A glint, a starry glimmer, lasting no more than a few seconds—and which I shall catch only if I prove very lucky this night in both my calculation and my instrument."

"My own theories seek the hidden self, yours the hidden star," he returned quietly, but with several shades of fine warm feeling. "Yes. I think I can enter a little—if not precisely into your idea, at least into the passion of it, Miss Bonnet."

It was the first time he pronounced the name to her, and its sound brought forth a low, musically scented laughter.

"Our name is pronounced as the good doctor had presumed it. There were few enough of his presumptions that hit the mark. We are of French extraction. My father's father came here from Lyons, shortly after the War of Independence, wanting to see for himself a revolutionary battlefield."

"Why then did your sister say otherwise?"

"Oh, Alice." She said it with another eloquent shrug. "She is forever intent on denying the continental associations!"

"And why is that?"

"Ah, Professor James . . ." She breathed it out, turning obliquely from him as she did so, so that she was further obscured for him by the tower's heavy gloom. "That would take us too quickly too deep into the matter."

"And yet, I think you are a person, Miss Bonnet, for whom the 'too deep' does not exist."

"My sister's deeper thoughts are not mine to give. I could not scruple to divulge what she herself would not."

What very different scruples then must hold sway over the two Miss Bonnets.

He was aware of the fact that the interview was not going brilliantly for him. There was something in the demeanor of the wonderful creature—she ranked now as a wonderful creature—that made it as difficult for him to know how to proceed—the right tone, as it were, to assume—as it had been for Doctor Sloper in his confrontation with the other.

"It was *she*, you know"—it seemed to burst out from her, almost as if in opposition to her own will—"who prevented my coming to meet you earlier this evening."

"Your sister did not want us to meet?"

"She did all that she could to prevent it!"

"But she herself sought the help of a doctor on your behalf!"

"Of Austin Sloper of Washington Square. Not of William James of Cambridge."

He smiled.

"I know what the difference signifies to me. Tell me what it signifies to her."

"She is afraid that you might be made to see my side of the thing."

"Your *side?* Are you then placed as adversaries?"

She neatly skirted having to answer the question for herself:

"Not to hear Alice tell it. She claims always to be acting in my interests alone, always the solicitous elder sister."

"And you doubt her assessment of your interests?"

"I doubt that she can assess them better than I!"

"She told me this afternoon that she lives in mortal terror for you."

"Ah, yes. The abysmal madness." Again, her voice smiled. If ever a voice could speak the tranquillity of sanity, this one did so. And yet its statement was succeeded most strangely:

"I can tell you, Professor James, that I, too, live with some terror."

"You fear then for your own sanity?"

It was, of course, not a delicate query to be putting to a young woman one had not known an hour—though, in matters of this sort, it is doubtful that any number of additions to the term of acquaintance would sweeten the implied affrontery. But the grounds upon which the interview was conducted rendered the usual proprieties a consideration of the second—or third, or fourth—degree. Miss Bonnet appeared to acquiesce, for the present time, at least, in the low rank accorded the social conventions, by the unastonished and frank response she now made him.

"No. I do not spend a single one of my moments in despair for my own sanity, nor yet my sister's. It is, Professor James, her hatred which frightens me."

"Surely not of yourself!"

"Of my work, which is one with me. You will think me a radical, perhaps—a zealot for the cause of the rights of women. I can assure you I think very little on the larger political themes. I know only that I have been given the very great blessing of finding something in this wide, wide world of consuming interest to me. True happiness, we are told, consists in getting out of one's self. But the point is not only to get out—you must stay out; and to stay out you must have some absorbing errand. Fortunately, I have such an errand; and for this she thinks me a monster, a freak, from whom all nature must recoil."

"I beg you to excuse me, Miss Bonnet. It is repugnant that I should be seen to be interrogating you—"

"I wish only I could answer you as freely as your good faith in coming here deserves!" she broke in, her voice preserving its full, low timbre, but suffused with a high intensity of feeling. Her posture and face—which he struggled to make out more clearly in the shadowed recesses of the tower—seemed to move under the sway of powerful emotion. There was something in the entire pose, obscurely perceived as it was, that was infinitely moving—inexpressively significant—to him.

"You obviously have been told of your sister's visit to Doctor Sloper. I take it you know something of what transpired between them."

"I think"—she said it very softly—"I know all that was said between them about me. You are going to ask me of the dead Italian, of Giordano Bruno." At a sign from him she continued.

"The knowledge of that man is her own. Mine is no greater. She came by it, as I did, through our father, who had been commissioned to do a bust of Bruno to be erected in the square where he was burned. I cannot now recollect its name."

"The Campo dei Fiori," he said quietly.

"Yes. Precisely. The Square of Flowers. There were in Rome certain anticlerical forces, with whom my father had some connection. They had recently rediscovered Bruno, and were resurrecting him as a martyr for the cause of modern science and the Copernican theory. Our father had, as I believe you already know, an amateur's interest in scientific matters. He took to reading Bruno's writings, as he was working on the bust, and he told us something of the man's beliefs, which we all found wondrously strange. The details are quite lost to me, effaced by the more rigorous knowledge I have since acquired. In fact, I believe it is Alice who has retained the greater part of the recollection. I certainly claim no special affinity with the thoughts and life of Giordano Bruno!"

He stared at her for several seconds.

"Is it then malice?" He breathed it softly.

"A malice laced with love—a love laced with malice; it is all one."

He continued to stare at her. There was a subdued buzzing noise coming from somewhere toward the rear of his cerebrum.

"But whom shall you believe?" she asked with the amused voice of a person seated at a game of guesses. "You must feel like the artful M. Descartes, caught in the ingenious confoundments of his First Meditation, unable to say whether even his clearest perception be not a delusion induced by the *genie mal*."

"Your simile is not unhappy."

"A rationality pursued too far," her voice continued playfully. "A consistency too rigorously insistent: these themselves might be the telling signs of madness."

" 'Men are so necessarily mad, that not to be mad would amount to another form of madness,' " he quoted Pascal.

"It is a predicament. We must at times, so I think, take in the truth in about the same proportion with which the oxygen is mixed into the atmosphere, about one in five parts. If we take it any purer it will burn us up!"

"I do not agree," he returned her with firmness. "I *cannot* agree. The truth shall always do men good!"

He strode the small length of the room's diameter, turned on his heel, and returned to a few feet's distance of Vivianna, his weak eyes still seeking her through the tower's gloom.

"What does she hope for, then?"

"That my interest in all things astronomical can be medically cured." For the first time a suggestion faintly satiric entered into the expressive music of her speech. "She was hoping for a pharmaceutical formula that would lay it eternally to rest."

"But, since you say you are one with your work, that

would imply the wish that *you*, her sister, be put to rest."

She turned slightly away from him at this, so that her voice came to him left-handed, as it were, and somewhat muffled.

"I believe you have drawn the intended conclusion!"

V I

Stella

Hedda stood at the kitchen counter, called away from her writing by a jagged pang of hunger. She brewed herself a pot of dark lapsang tea while nibbling on a shortbread biscuit. The kitchen was in the back of the house, facing away from the sea. Its three bay windows had a southwestern exposure, making of it the only bright and sunny room. The real estate agent had quite emphasized its *cheeriness*, for which reason Hedda tended to avoid it, except for strict purposes of sustenance.

There was a slab now of late afternoon sun fallen onto the pitted wooden floor. But Hedda remained in the shrouded tower with William and Vivianna, where the mood was dense with mysterious implication.

The phone rang.

She let it ring.

It continued to ring. She counted up to twenty-five.

She felt foolish. It was one thing to let the instrument go unanswered when she was upstairs working in her tower;

another altogether when the damn thing was pissing off right at her elbow.

She had at long last gotten a glimpse of the other sister, even if squinting through William's myopia. Would she be able to catch her in her tower again, that wonderful creature poised before the Astronomical Immensities? Why hadn't she gotten that letter off to Motherfucker Bell? Now the atmosphere, that dark fine fragile veil, was shredded to pieces.

"Hello, Stella," she answered, testing. Would the greeting, confidently prescient, throw her sister off a beat?

"Hedda. It's me."

No, it would not.

"Hello, Stella."

"Where have you been? You're never home. I must have called you twenty times."

"I don't answer the phone when I'm working."

"Working? You got a job? Oh"—she laughed—"you mean those books."

Hedda let the clumsy shot pass. It didn't touch her. Not really. Stella's aim was getting sloppy, the muscles of her malice going to flab, despite the regularity of their exercise.

"So how's Dr. Seymour?"

"Dr. Seymour." Hedda sensed tears in Stella's sigh. "Dr. Seymour," she repeated with increased humidity. Hedda started feeling clammy. "Dr. Seymour has . . . betrayed me."

Hedda waited.

"Vacation! That's what he did! Do you *hear* me, Hedda? Do you hear what I'm *saying?*"

"Dr. Seymour went on vacation."

"Dr. Seymour went on vacation! And here I am! I am

heavily into transference, Hedda, do you hear? And he just picked up in the middle and went to the Canary *Islands* . . . *with his wife!* The slut! I want to kill them both!"

Hedda took her sister quite literally here. There was a lot of violence in Stella. That warm soft mist packed a dagger.

"How long will he be gone?"

"Two *weeks!*" It wailed; it shrieked; it approximated the god-awful cry that had threatened William's sanity. "Why do the men in my life always end up be*tray*ing me? After I give them . . . *everything!*"

There was some truth in this. Dr. Seymour had a Park Avenue address. Self-knowledge (hah!) was devouring Stella's alimony.

"And he has to wipe my nose in it! He has to take along his . . . wife." She snarled the word. "That skinny, cross-eyed . . . *slut.*"

"Oh. You've seen her, then?" Hedda's little voice was not so little, nor so randomly halting, when she spoke with her sister.

"He keeps her picture on his desk. I ask you, is that *right* for a psychoanalyst to do? What kind of a thing is that? But oh boy! is she ugly. She's almost as skinny as *you!*"

Hedda waited. It was frightening to hear how faithfully Stella's patterns of speech, her very intonation, recalled the Mother's. How could Stella not hear it for herself—and *do* something about it?—as Hedda had done, purifying her voice through her reading—all that Henry James, if nothing else. It's not that Hedda had hated the Mother any more than Stella had.

"He's the only man in my life now. I've given up every-

body else for him. I've given up real sex for transference!
And what do I get? He takes that skinny *korva* to the
Canaries!"

Korva: prostitute. It was a description of which the
Mother had been quite fond. "Slut" was also a favored term.
"Slut," she'd hiss under her breath to the passing throngs.
General rule of thumb: Any woman attractive enough to get
the kissy-kissy of certain residents of West End Avenue
would likewise be rewarded the Mother's hiss of condem-
nation.

"Maybe you should start seeing other men."

Men who don't charge you by the hour, Hedda thought
but did not dare to say. (Fierce, fierce Hedda! Furious female
warrior! Well, yeah, sure, in books for the general—well,
not so general—public.)

"Other men! Hah!"

Hah! The Mother always said, "Hah!" Your father! Hah!
Nova Scotia salmon! Hah! And it is not in the power of the
printed word to convey the sheer quantity of malice that
had been impacted in those three letters. (There, behind
the closed doors of the apartment on West End Avenue,
where the public face of the Mother—righteous and for-
bearing, slow to anger and full of great mercy—would be
taken off at the threshold. "Putting on her face," she'd call
the morning ritual of applying her makeup, a phrase the two
little girls took with chilling literalism.)

You know you remind me of someone, Stella. You sound
just like someone we both know.

"Dr. Seymour has spoiled me for other men. Everything
I ever looked for, it's all in Dr. Seymour. He's the only one
who understands me."

Hedda wondered if he really did. If Seymour knew Stella like Hedda knew Stella.

"You know, Hedda, I have to envy you."

Here it comes. The shift in tone suggested it, the words confirmed it: Prepare yourself for a frontal attack.

"I have to envy the way you just don't . . . *feel* anything. The way you're just not *capable* of any normal human response. You're not vulnerable like me. You're not tossed about by the reckless winds of passion."

Purple prose? Since when, Stella?

But there was truth in what Stella was saying; truth and untruth. Hedda's skeletal prodigality had kept her safe from the invasions of sexual love. She never even came close to cultivating the hothouse delusions of a private obsession, so abiding was her sense of her own unlovability. And from the height at which she stood, the nastier qualities of the species were starkly on display. Aggressively hideous young women elicit correspondingly aggressive forms of unkindness.

Strictly speaking, then—even not so strictly speaking, then—Hedda had never been what is called "in love". She had deemed its lacuna from her own personal history no obstacle at all in pursuing the true course of her literary ambitions. (After all, had Henry?) She was skeptical of its alleged transports. The singularities of its case did not impress her in the least. Her belief was that nature had intended the peculiar state strictly for the adolescent—as witness the characteristic behavior of those who fall under the influence, no matter what their age or other attainments—but that it had, mostly for cultural, patriarchal, reasons, spilled over into postpubescence, to the perpetual irritation of the human hormonal system, not to speak of its psyche.

However, not capable? That she knew to be untrue. Hedda possessed a glandularly overactive imagination, which, if not exactly the same thing as a passionate nature, came pretty damn close to it. It is astonishing how the passionate—which is to say, the imaginative—mind can go to work on the flimsiest bits of material: a sympathetic glance, an ambiguous few words, a manner of puffing on a cigar—which is rarely just a cigar. Hedda would have been capable enough.

"Though how you think you can be a writer . . . !" Hedda's sister Stella was disclaiming into her ear.

Hedda waited.

"What do you know about Life with a capital *L*? You gotta live before you can write."

By Life with a capital *L* Hedda knew that Stella meant Sex with a capital *S*, her sister being counted among the minions who equated living with screwing. (Dr. Seymour, a Freudian, was probably no better.)

"I do seem to manage," she felt provoked to say in her own defense. "I've published seven books to date, Stella."

Speech was a serious tactical error at this point. Hedda knew it even as she spoke.

"Manage! Hah! You call what you do managing? Here, I'll show you manage. I've got a choice review right here. An in-depth probe . . ."

Her sister always made reviews sound vaguely gyneco-logical. . . .

". . . written by a very brilliant person, named Adolph

Uberhaupt. Did you see that one? He's a very intelligent and witty person."

That, of course, was ominous. Witty reviewers are, quite generally, nasty reviewers.

But then, Stella wouldn't be quoting Adolph Uberhaupt unless he was, extravagantly, not a fan.

"I don't read reviews," she said, a meaningless gesture. She had, of course, said it before. It had, of course, made no difference.

"Here, listen to this. It will give you an indication of how well you're—hah!—managing. 'The author, the unremittingly Angry Voice of Female Fiction, is all too true to her given name. As I dauntingly perused her Rants and Raves and made the reluctant acquaintance of her characters who are no characters but one-dimensional caricatures (Woman the Paragon vs. Man the Brute), I was haunted by a fleeting vision: that freakishly large and disembodied head that floats before Dorothy et al in the eponymous *Wizard of Oz*. The expression is unchanging and fierce, the bogeyman (bogeywoman!) of a little kid's (little boy's) nightmare. And just as bogus—from the literary point of view. That is how I picture this author, who, as is well known, has never allowed herself to be photographed or to appear before her inexplicably existent public.' So what do you think?"

"I think he misused the word *eponymous*. It's the wizard who's eponymous, isn't it?"

"It's a great image, isn't it? You as the floating ugly head."

Actually, it wasn't bad.

Stella cackled gaily. "Here's something more. 'The author's vision is dry as bones.' Isn't that rich? Especially considering what they used to call you in school."

Sticks and stones.

" 'And the prose—' "

"Stella, I have to go now," Hedda cut in hastily before she could learn the nature of the witty and intelligent Adolph Uberhaupt's opinion of her prose.

"I appreciate your keeping such close tabs on my career, Stella, it's touching, but I left my word processor running, and I hear it making some kind of weird gagging noises."

"Listen, Hedda. Can I give you a little sisterly advice? Are you open to some very constructive criticism? See if you can't work a little sex into your books. Humor would be good, too, but that's only the gravy. Sex is the meat and potatoes."

"Why?"

"*Why? Why?* Hedda, that's gotta be the *stupidest* thing you *ever* said! *Why should you put sex in your books?* God in heaven, that's like asking I don't *know* what. It's like asking why it's better to be smart than stupid!"

Well, hell . . . why *is* it better to be smart than stupid?

Hedda trudged back up the twisting stairs of the tower, balancing a full pot of her dark and fragrant tea, some extra half-dozen biscuits jammed into her mouth. She'd give Stella some time to get started on something else before venturing down again to the kitchen. She had cut Stella off before she was finished. Stella had not been permitted to "let it all out," and Stella, as a seasoned psychoanalytic patient (not to speak of a seasoned bitch), was passionately committed to the process—*hard* as it might be for her—of letting it all out. Chances were the phone would be ringing again shortly.

Well, ring away, sister dearest! The one redeeming fact about the phone is: one need not answer it.

Hedda reread the last few pages she had written, trying to call back the rare vision of Vivianna Bonnet, the eloquent silence that had followed her last speech to William.

"I believe you have drawn the intended conclusion!"

She couldn't get back. There was another presence blocking her way, taunting and malicious.

A dark malodorous vapor, noxious and life-denying, ominously metamorphosing into human shape.

It was Adolph Uberhaupt.

What *had* he said about her prose? It must have been remarkably brutal, judging from the high pitch of excitement in her sister Stella's voice as she prepared to launch into it.

Adolph! Adolph! Have a heart! What do you want from my prose?

She pictured Adolph Uberhaupt, drawing him to suit her purpose, which is the great advantage of living inside one's head.

He was five two, a full foot shorter than she.

He had a heavyset, insensitive, rather vulgar cast of face. Well, no, closer inspection revealed that the bestial sensuality—thick lips, with an oily glint, as if he had just eaten a can of sardines—was etched over, as if with acid, by the hard indentations of an intelligence most cruel. There was no way this face could ever compose itself into the movements of compassion. His eyebrows ascended at the Mephistophelian angle. His upper mouth was curled with scorn (always, always! even when he tried to make love! women hated him for it!) and frustration: he had written—in youth—a well-received First Novel and had remained crouched for twenty years thereafter, grunting and straining in the effort of bringing out the Second. In the meanwhile he had cultivated a most extraordinary antitalent for Criticism. Oh, he had his Standards, had Adolph! He was committed—difficult as it might be for him—to Literary Purity. It had been years and years, as he remarked with pride, since he had read a book that managed to justify its own existence to his satisfaction. Two categories sufficed him: (I) Books That Ought Never to Have Been Written; and (II) Books That Ought to Have Been Written Entirely Differently. The general cause for the Deplorable State of Literature was, of course, the pernicious—and self-serving—phenomenon of Rushing into Print. Adolph despised the prolific—who were defined as all those who managed to produce at a rate that exceeded his own, leaving him a comfortingly wide range over which to smear his contempt. The Uberhaupt Literary Theory had been derived from the teachings of Socrates— who had never published at all—and Sidney Morgenbesser, a professor of philosophy at Columbia University with whom Adolph had had one or two courses when he was an undergraduate there.

Adolph was an ugly man, but still, withal, quite vain. Just see how meticulously the few remaining strands of dullish hair are fanned out upon the baby-bottom-bare pate! How clearly I see the shameful truth from way, way up here, O execrable Adolph!

There is no man so unattractive as to sally forth into the world unadorned with a dab from the pot of self-beguiling vanity.

He did not have the kind of body women liked either. He was short (established). He was paunchy. He had incipient tits.

His breath smelled like dead fish, without the benefit of

the chipped ice. If the scornfully limned lip didn't drive away the women, the evil emanations would.

He was in his underwear: a sleeveless ribbed undershirt and an extremely unattractive pair of boxer shorts—which were slightly, suspiciously, soiled.

He was sweating like a pig, now that he had to confront her face to face; face to midriff, more like.

Didn't think you'd be held accountable, did you, Adolph, you pig? Use my prose—jewels! diamonds!—as a poor excuse to exercise your feeble wit, would you?

Adolph, you putz. Prepare to get yours! Your comparable comeuppance. Comedownance, more like.

Drop those deplorable drawers. Drop them, I say! Nothing witty to say? Nothing . . . *intelligent?*

Oh, my God. Is that *it?* Is that *really* all you have to show for yourself? Don't tell me it actually *works.* Oh, look at that! Why it's . . . it's retreating, it's . . . yes: why, *it's altogether gone!*

Adolph, you putz, you are now putzless. Now just try screwing over my prose. Be off! Vacate the premises! You are no longer permitted entry into the fallow reaches of my cerebrum, with its significant swellings in the regions of Secretiveness, Language, and Sublimity!

I defy you, schmuck!

So her sister Stella thought her books could use some Sex. Her previous fiction was not entirely without the genital presence. Men were often whipping out, in Hedda's books, what it is that men are wont to whip out, but this never ever got them what they wanted, in Hedda's books. What

it generally got them was public humiliation, spiritual deg-
radation, and—sometimes, if they really deserved it—permanent injury. Hedda's women were beautiful; they brought
out the Brute in the Man (Man the Brute—Adolph, *get out!*).
But they were smart, and they were strong. They were *her*-
story's Avenging Angels.

(No, they weren't *Paragons*, Adolph. They had their faults.
They were *real*.)

Her fiction was moral fiction, constructed along the
straight, clean lines of a Greek drama—in which the threats
of the Furies were always made good, and the accumulated
wrongs of the Male Oppressor finally caught up with him.
And how.

But now that she came to think of it, she couldn't remember a single instance of consenting-between-two-adults
in any of her pages. Perhaps this *was* rather a failing? Perhaps,
perhaps.

Perhaps her sister Stella had a point?

Okay . . . sex. She could manage it. She even had some
personal sexual experience upon which to draw. Perilously
eccentric as she was, she did not belong to that even rarer
breed: the class of female virgins.

And as for Henry . . . well, not even Leon Edel seemed
to know for sure. Somerset Maugham used to relate that a
very young Hugh Walpole once offered himself to the master, who recoiled with, "I can't, I can't, I *can't*."

Well, Hedda could, and Hedda had: once. She had been
deflowered, as it were, in her fateful sixteenth year, by the
finger of Marty Factor, the lingerie wholesaler for whom the
Mother worked as bookkeeper.

He was a ladies' man, Marty was. They all were in that

business. Constantly handling the filmy little undies made them perpetually priapic. And Marty was a real good looker, so his priapisms got results. He was a little like a Jewish Robert Redford, if you can possibly picture that: tall, blond, athletic—that's the Robert Redford bit—with glasses and a nasal Bronxy voice—that's the Jewish bit. And he was smart, too, Marty was, had gone to Cornell and majored in philosophy, which was why, upon graduation, he had had to go into women's underwear.

But I stayed in foundations, he joked. He made very corny jokes, Marty did, in that nasal/Bronxy voice. It was, somehow, endearing, probably because of the tall, blond, athletic bit.

He was also very sentimental about things Jewish, which was also, somehow, endearing, and probably for the same reason. Though sometimes he overdid it, as when he serenaded Hedda with his choked-up Yiddish rendition of "Rozinkus mit Mandlen" ("Raisins with Almonds") and embarrassed even her, who was rarely ever embarrassed. (It's an emotion you left behind when you looked like Hedda. Either that or live perpetually embarrassed.) Any sort of Jewish kitsch made Marty *kvell*. He loved using Yiddish words, the stickier with sentiment the better (like *kvell*). When he passed *real* Jews in the streets—full-bearded, black-garbed, and bearing only the most tenuous species-related resemblance to Robert Redford—he always gave them an effusive "Shalom aleichem!" When Hedda was walking beside him, the real Jews were, of course, always too stunned by her physical presence (Is she a *Jewish* girl? Nah! *Nicht possible!* Jewish girls don't grow so big!) to return a gracious

"Aleichem shalom!" Perhaps they were friendlier to Marty when distracting old Hedda wasn't around.

"Heddale, Heddale," Marty said, smiling sadly—the sad smile being, of course, so quintessentially, so oxymoronically, Jewish; and, as such, right up there beside words like *kvell* in Marty's lexicon of schmaltz. And the Jewish smile took on an added poignancy, there in the surprising setting of that Robert Redford *punim*. (Schmaltz and *punim* also made the list.)

"Please don't call me 'Heddale,' Marty."

"Does your mother ever call you 'Heddale,' Heddale?"

"Please don't call me 'Heddale,' Marty."

(The Mother calls me *dunkele*.)

Marty was still a *schtikele philosoph*—his expression, of course. He liked Martin Buber a lot. He sometimes quoted some of the I-Thou stuff to the salesmen.

"Inner things or outer things, what are they but things and things?"

It was a kind of classy way to say, "Trust me." You had to hand it to a guy who could use Buber to sell a bra.

Hedda herself had never been able to figure Marty out, to decide finally whether he was an incredible con man or, even more incredibly, for real. He went through all the motions of his life as if he were watching, slightly amused and slightly bewildered that he could manage the motions at all. He wasn't really a businessman; he was a metabusinessman. He wasn't really a fornicator; he was a metafornicator.

He was forty-two years old, the year of Hedda's transfiguration. He was married, with three daughters and a house on Long Island. Was he a metahusband, a metafather?

He was just a meta-kind-of-a-guy.

Marty had been true to his guarantee to the Mother that year, as Hedda progressed through the stages of her dignity and grandeur. It was when she became solemn that Marty started to flirt, when she was awful that he grew warmer. The homelier she, the hotter he.

"All real living is meeting," he told Hedda, quoting Buber.

When she was finally ghastly, Marty was fully determined. Perhaps it was his pity that worked him into such a pitch, nullifying his guarantee to the Mother. He was a father himself. His three daughters were beautiful girls—tall, blond, and athletic—and he had known Hedda when she too had been beautiful. The sight of her as she now was worked on him as perhaps no beauty ever could.

"The *Thou* confronts me," he told Hedda, quoting Buber. "The relation means being chosen and choosing, suffering and action in one."

Not that Hedda made much of an attempt to dissuade Marty, once she saw that the intent was hardened upon him. How many Robert Redfords—Jewish or not—were going to come her way again? For that matter, how many men at all? By the end of her sixteenth year, Hedda knew it was now or never.

Not like her sister, Stella, by the way, who was then thirteen and had already made the decisive transition to the sexual state of being. Sometime or other in the course of the past year the mists of Stella had gone steamy; and the fatherless fat little girl had become the most shameless— and accomplished—of flirts. A certain sly sneakiness had mingled itself with the other hostile qualities of her nature, signaling to Hedda that Stella had Something to hide. The Mother, unsurprisingly, also picked up the raunchy scent and went after it with all the fine-tuned vengeance of her highly vengeful self—right down to sniffingly inspecting every pair of panties worn (reputedly) by her slutty younger daughter. Stella had *needed* those deep reserves of sly sneakiness.

Poor old martyred Mom. Whither her jewels and diamonds? The one a freak, the other a slut. Could anything be more embarrassing to a mother?

At least the Mother didn't have similar worries in regard to Hedda, whose virtue by then—so thought Mom!—was more than guaranteed.

Knowing it was now or never, knowing it was, more than likely, now and then never again, made Hedda even more observant than usual. This was it: her one chance to garner the material she would have to draw upon, fictively speaking, then and forever after. She concentrated on memorizing the details, particularly those aspects of male anatomy that would probably never more be accessible to her lively scrutinizing.

When it was over, she went home and wrote down what she remembered.

She had an unsentimental teenager's interest in the hard facts, carefully noting down the color, the texture, and the taste; estimating in centimeters the length and circumference. She had even drawn a fairly decent sketch, having discovered that the construction was somewhat more complicated than anticipated.

did it three times—in between, it shrank, softened, and curled—
even faded in color (infusion of blood?)
i begin to grasp the male obsession with control—

She had been a feminist since twelve.

didn't go for a fourth—guess bec. m's old.

Marty, who of course *was* sentimental, was very touched,
if also a little bit embarrassed, by the close attention she
had paid his beloved member. She would have gotten out
her handy notepad and done a sketch then and there but
realized—smart girl that she was—that this was one of those
quantum mechanical situations she had learned about in the
honors physics class she was then taking in high school,
when the act of measurement itself significantly altered the
state being measured.

wasn't too awful—m says it gets better—take his word for
it—definitely can live without it
i bled and m cried—only truly awful moment—
when m got into it forgot i was there—much better—his face
was interesting/embarrassing—eyes glazed, mouth hanging
open—wonder if that's how rr looks when he's into it—m said
i came—big deal

The seduction had taken place in Marty's warehouse, on
a sagging couch in his cluttered office, samples of bras, slips,
and panties flung all around them. At some point in the
process Hedda's head had become entangled in a pile of

gorgeous underwear. Marty—was he a metapervert?—
seemed to like that.

"It's like that surreal painting by I forget who," he said,
pulling a black teddy with silver-sequined studs more tightly
across the overdeveloped bottom half of Hedda's face and
kissing her lips through it.

Hedda could appreciate that the aesthetics of the situation would be improved by having her face partially covered. But she owed it to her future Art to see everything.
(She also had to breathe.)

"Magritte," she said (honors contemporary civ.), removing the black teddy with silver-sequined studs from across
her face.

She had been right to be so insistently observant, for it
had been now and then never.

And she had also been right that she had definitely been
able to live without it. Big deal.

Then there were those people like her sister Stella, who
measured out the micrometers of her tortuous psychic progress—analytically overseen by the (so Hedda imagined)
deadly bored but (at least) well-compensated Dr. Seymour—
in terms of the duration and intensity of her vaginal—not
clitoral: Stella too was a feminist—orgasms. Well, not really.
That was a slight flourish on the truth. But her sister Stella
did tend to think of Sex as affixed with a permanent up-
percase *S*.

Of course, Stella *had* been to college (Cornell, as a matter
of fact), and Hedda hadn't (Marty had really grieved—
blamed himself, with whom it had nothing to do—when
Hedda had refused to go), and this might explain the di-
vergence in their points of view. Or so Hedda had always

assumed. But maybe Stella was on to Something. After all, even the quintessential virgin, Henry James, voiced concern, in middle age, that he had somehow missed out on Life, by which he too (even he!) seemed to be alluding to something very much like Sex. Just think of *The Ambassadors*, with its aging Lambert Strether pathetically intoning, "Too late, too late," and its un-Jamesian theme of "Grab all the life you can." Just think of *The Wings of the Dove*, in which the dashing Merton Densher *actually goes to bed with the woman he loves*.

But what did Hedda know of Sex? Her experience with Marty had been—at best—with sex.

Hedda did occasionally feel the stir of her flesh, little enough of it though there was. But these—feeble and easily ignored—were provoked not by people, but by words. It was words alone that did it for her.

The last time she could remember its happening had been with the verb *to embrocate*.

Hedda concentrated, trying to summon forth the mood with which to act upon her sister Stella's advice.

To embrocate, embrocation, embrocatory—no, the verb works the best.

William walked into his dressing room to procure some object that was there. He was in need of an embrocation. It was early evening, the shadows beginning to gather.

A light footstep sounded in his bedroom just outside the partially opened door of his dressing room. Without moving a muscle, William turned his eyes and saw his Alice standing there.

She was standing before the tall mirror that slanted unmounted against the wall.

She was staring at herself, a rather peculiar expression taking form upon her face, which he had never before seen there.

It made him uneasy to see her so. He ought, he knew, to make some movement, to alert her to his silent, attending presence. He did not move a muscle.

Slowly, she raised her seven petticoats, with a half-pleased, half-abashed look of obliging someone or other.

It was exceedingly odd for him to see her looking so.

She stood now, in her Dr. Jaeger's woolen stockinette drawers and her Swanbill belt corset, which last item was scientifically fitted according to the twelve figure types of Woman. After bearing him five children (the youngest, Hermann, had been lost in infancy to whooping cough), William's Alice had been left with the tenth type of figure and was accordingly corseted.

> This is a most successful Corset for ladies inclined to embonpoint. It is made of good quality of Contil, with belt of stout webbing round the bottom of the Corset. The adjustible straps and the arrangement of the front bones give great support, and keep the figure well "in" below the waist. It is made in White, and also in a useful shade of French Grey.

Alice's was in the useful shade of French Grey.

Such a vast complexity of hooks and eyes and clasps and hasps and laces to undo. . . .

He ought to make some noise, he knew, he ought in common decency. The old tug-of-war was at work within him, his self divided between the scientist of human psychology and the man of conscience and compassion. But the exhibited behavior was so *irresistibly* peculiar.

The female flesh of her came pouring out from its brutal encasement, bruised red and purple where the stays had cut most cruelly into her. Her drooping maternal abdomen was mottled and puckered. A fiendish riot of female flesh—of eddying swirls and dimpling swells. The great white mounds that had had the shape long ago sucked out of them by the five infant mouths. Falling down, down, melting into the tumbling abdomen that was falling down, down.

That shape is she, good God!

William stood and stared, as his wife preened and smiled like an untutored little fool before the mirror. He stood and stared, paralyzed by his mounting horror. . . .

Hedda shuddered as she pressed the Escape key of her word processor.

What the hell was that stuff? What the hell was she doing listening to her sister Stella anyway?

Did Henry ever show people stripped down to their Dr. Jaeger's woolen undies?

These were the *Jameses*. A little dignity, please.

VII

≈

Henry

The house in Cambridge occupied by William James and his brood was at 95 Irving Street—a street that had been newly opened through what used to be called Norton's Woods. It was a pleasantly square, detached wooden house, covered with shingles that soon weathered brown and having dark green trimmings. William had assiduously involved himself in the planning of the construction, even designing the doors and windows, so much so that he could have claimed to have been his own architect in all but the structural specifications.

The library, in which he now sat reading, was the largest and sunniest room the house could boast. William always wished to have space about him, and the room was, accordingly, some twenty-two and a half feet wide and twenty-seven feet long. The walls were lined, from floor to ceiling, with densely packed bookshelves, except for the spot above the open fireplace where hung the noble visage of the paterfamilias, Henry James, Sr., looking, with his face at once shrewd and otherworldy and with his long white beard and skullcap, rather like a wily and wise rabbinical scholar.

On the southern side of the room there was a triple window whose total width was nearly half the length of the room, and which, at this hour in late morning, was letting in a flood of bleaching sunlight. Through it one looked out upon a small lawn overhung by a large elm and upon more grass and trees beyond. The new street already housed several close friends: Josiah Royce, for example, the young Hegelian whom James had brought to Harvard—loving the man while abhorring his dogma-blighted dialectic—lived a door but one away; and Miss Grace Norton, a particular friend of Henry's—and once bête noir to their departed sister, Alice—lived across the way.

James sat before his writing table, intent upon his reading, till there came a knock, and his wife, Alice (William's Alice, as she had been known in the days when the family had included two Alice Jameses) entered, looking, as always, fresh and burnished bright with the glow of her splendid animal spirits. She was—and he had often reason to take comfort in the fact of it—an example of the no-nonsense, invincibly healthy-minded female, over whom morbidity had no hold. She practiced the gentle art of domesticity with a calm and patient hand and was an admirable mother to their children, the eldest of whom, Henry, had this very year entered Harvard College. It was a breed of woman to which his mother, too, had belonged, as the other Alice James, the poor dead sister, so dramatically and tragically had not.

She smiled efficiently, placing the letters that had arrived in the morning post neatly at his elbow.

"There's one from Henry, William dear."

"Capital! We will all read it together after dinner."

"Yes, the children will enjoy that."

They shared a smile that held the memory of previous occasions of boisterous merriment provoked by the communal perusal of the missives from the uncle who lived permanently now in England, and whose celebrated habits of expression prompted such exclamations, on the part of the children (and betimes their father), as: "If Uncle Harry left his umbrella behind, why the deuce doesn't he just come out and say it!"

Alice moved behind him—all her movements were always neat and to the point—and looked over his shoulder at the title of the book he was still holding.

"*De l'infinito, universo e mondi,*" she read aloud. "Is it interesting?"

"Toweringly. Published in 1584. Giordano Bruno."

"Ah, the strange cosmologist you were telling us of the other night."

"Cosmologist, philosopher, magus—a thinker who sneered at the orthodox for their orthodoxies, and moved easily within spheres whose very existence is denied by the dogma-blinded bigots who would draw the boundaries for us all!"

"I see now why you like him so well," his wife rejoined with a peculiarly Yankee intonation that brought a brief smile to her husband's face. She took a rather dim view of some of the pots into which William had stuck his stirring index finger. His experiments with nitrous oxide, for example—with which he had caused some scandal among his philosophical friends by likening the effect to the insights of Hegel—and with the Indian substance, mescal. She also could have done without the long hours he consecrated to the American Society for Psychical Research, which had made him, among so many of his peers, appear unbecomingly broad-minded for a so-called man of science. And the "experiments" themselves were so unsavory. Those horribly sleazy sessions with the dreadful Mrs. Piper! Mrs. James had no doubt it was all a most tawdry and vulgar sham. But then William would always go whither the spirit moved him and laughed at any "stuffy" attempts to demarcate where respectability ended and the unspeakable commenced.

"Those dogma-blinded bigots managed to burn Bruno alive, did they not?" she inquired with an innocent air as she neatly gathered into a pile a few of the books scattered upon his desk—among them, she noticed, another small volume of Bruno's, *De gli eroici furori* (*On Heroic Enthusiasms*) and a rather thickish tome whose subject—most unJamesian!—was stargazing.

"Ah! but it is *his* book I am reading, almost three hundred years after the execrable deed was done, and not the damnable Inquisitors'!" her own heroically enthusiastic husband said, smiling and taking up his book once again. She left quietly, being careful not to let the door make any noise as she closed it to behind her.

Alone again, he read for a few minutes more and then put down the volume to take up his brother's letter, which was of a characteristic weight. Though one had to wait quite long for Harry to answer, he could always be counted upon to compensate with sheer bulk.

William had an especial reason to be gladdened by the response from England, for he had sent his brother a query, *be actually bathed and probably more mildly golden. I have no positive plan save that of just ticking the winter swiftly away on this most secure basis. There are, however, little doors ajar into a possible brief absence. I fear I have just closed one of them rather ungraciously indeed, in pleading a "non possumus" to a most genial invitation from John Hay to accompany him and his family, shortly after the new year, upon a run to Egypt and a month up the Nile, he having a boat for that same—I mean for the Nile part—in which he offers me the said month's entertainment. It is a very charming opportunity, and I almost blush at not coming up to the scratch, especially as I shall probably never have the like again. But it isn't so simple as it sounds; one has on one's hands the journey to Cairo and back, with whatever seeing and doing by the way of two or three irresistible other things, to which one would feel one might never again be so near, would amount to. (I mean, of course, then or never, on the return, Athens, Corfu, Sicily, the never-seen, etc., etc.) It would all "amount" to too much this year, by reason of a particular little complication—most pleasant in itself, I hasten to add—that I haven't, all this time, mentioned to you. Don't be scared—I haven't accepted a matrimonial "offer." I have only taken, a couple of months ago, a little old house in the country—for the rest of my days!—on which, this winter, though it is, for such a commodity, in exceptionally good condition, I shall have to spend money enough to make me quite concentrate my resources. I marked it for my own two years ago at Rye—so perfectly did it, the first instant I beheld it, offer the solution of my long-assuaged desire for a calm retreat between May and November. It is the very calmest and yet cheerfulest that I could have dreamed— in the little old, cobble-stoned, grass-grown, red-roofed town,*

on the summit of its mildly pyramidal hill and close to its noble
old church—the chimes of which will sound sweet in my goodly
red-walled garden.

Henry's copious enthusiasm for his new possession—
which, he reported, he had first seen two years ago, having
walked over from Point Hill "to make sheep's eyes at it (the
more so that it is called Lamb House!)"—was most copiously
set forth, room by room, and then on out into the "glorious
little growing exposure." As William made his way through
the little pile of dove gray pages his crinkly blue eyes grew
ever more crinkly.

"First-rate!" he said aloud, relishing a morsel of Henry's
delectable snobbishness, as he gushed over George II's having once passed a couple of nights at Lamb House, having
been forced ashore, at Rye, by a tempest, and accommodated
at Lamb House "as at the place in the town then most
consonant with his grandeur. It would, for that matter, quite
correspond to this description still. Likewise the mayors of
Rye have usually lived there! Or the persons living there
have usually *become* mayors!"

"What ineluctable distinction awaits dear Harry!"

But William's expression quickly changed as he read on,
his amusement giving way to a look of heightened
engrossment.

"But enough of this swagger," the house-proud Henry
had finally cut his enthusiasm short.

You will have thought me by now delinquently forgetful as to
the query with which you ended your last letter. And yet, it
constitutes an "occasion"—suffused with the fine gold glow of

singularity—when my Elder Brother—my authority and my pride—petitions me for information—no matter that the so-licited facts are to be categorized as belonging to that mean lot known as social gossip, there could be no other sort, alas, in which I might overtake him. So I shall make the most of the rare event, and have, toward that end, already expended a significant quantity of effort in trying to dust off the rather faded details I have retained of that bygone romance. For the story of the sculptor, Roderick Bonnet, had always the tone of a romance, intensified now (as it always is) by the closure of death putting the final completeness to the tale. But there is the hint in what you ask me, that the tale is not yet entire. Bantas. I shall tell you what I know:

It must have been in the winter of 188-, in Rome, that I met Bonnet, at a little dinner given in his honour at the home of Madame Gloriani. Mrs. Bonnet was there as well, and their little daughter, who must have been, perhaps, eight or nine. You mention two daughters, but I am almost entirely convinced that there was but one present that night. Bonnet was, as you indicate, ultimately a fizzle, having shown rather prodigious powers at the first—rather a case of genius in the cradle. However, at the time that I met him no one could have known— with the exception possibly of Bonnet himself—that his best pieces—few enough in number—had all been done. He was enormously high-spirited that evening, talking a great deal of amusing nonsense, and playing, to my mind, to the bilt the role of the invigorating native crudity. Mrs. Bonnet, I simply cannot, cannot recall! Only the palest shadow of a shadow hovering in the background. I cannot now say whether the anemia of that background figure, its apparitional hyalescence, as it were, belongs to the faded memory or to the remembered object itself.

In any case the child was unforgettable: a sprightly, pretty little thing, she had a remarkable gift for—and here I know my memory to be reliable—certain mathematical subjects. I really cannot express to you the absolute rage of wonderment produced upon the gathering by this infantile Aristotle, with her pink satin sash and white lace mittens, when her father began to quiz her on such cabalistic horrors as the calculus of some celebrated Sir, and the geometry of a Monsieur Immortal. You can very well believe that the child left me—who as you well know am so curiously uncurious anent matters of any rigour—far behind as she went tripping along in her prattling clear soprano. The result was, however, altogether prodigious. And though I could follow nothing of what she actually said, I took the thing in with a great intensity of impression.

I remember telling our Alice of the child (for, as I think I've made mention, I always made an especial point of trying to bring the sights of the world into the narrow dreariness of Alice's sickroom), and her saying, in quite a forlorn tone of voice, that she feared for the little female marvel of a creature. (How inexpressibly sad to think of the experience that made her so quick to see beyond the inherent charm of the tiny prodigy, into its tragic implications!) This remark of hers served to increase the extraordinary impression left by the child. I remember even beginning to pen a story, whose theme should be a most remarkable love attaining between a gifted father-and-daughter pair. The relation would not have been of the nefarious—the abnormal—character. But I imagined some unspeakable intensity of feeling, of tenderness, of sacred compunction. A deep participating devotion of one to the other. I fancied the pair understanding each other too well—fatally well. Neither can protect the character of the other against itself—for the other is, also, equally the very self against whom protection is called for. The two would have died together, by their own hand (had I not given it up before reaching the end). The manner in which the thing—the climax—hovered before me was the incident of their dying together as the only thing they can do that does not a little fall short of absolutely ideally perfect agreement. I believe I gave the thing up because of the maternal problem— that which returns now to blight my memory with the rot of vagueness. That hovering ghostly substance would not yield itself to the fingers of my art, which would have it assume some more determinate moral shape—whether invidious or benign, I cannot say. It remained in mist; and so, in mist, obscured the entire intent—so that, at the end, I gave it all up as hopeless.

My "art," however, had succeeded so far in its prescience so as to make out the inevitability of a "double death"—though it was, of course, the mother and father who died together. It was not in Italy, but in America that they died. You say, too, it was of malaria, but I rather think it wasn't—though I never knew the precise details—no one here did, so far as I remember; though of course things were said. The name of the child, by the way, was Vivianna. But, my dear William, I must be less interminable, for my pages here begin to rival the number of "my little book." Do please follow up on the few spare details you have given me of Vivianna Bonnet. (Her father pronounced the name as does she. Her sister—Alice, is it?—is rather pushing the American thing too far, I think. How I hate that native tendency toward simplicity. I can assure you that if I could pronounce the name James in any different or more elaborate way, I should be in favour of doing it.) I should not be at all surprised if the celestial sister were wondrously mad. She had simply, that prodigious little creature, to be something *supremely extraordinary. I would have been profoundly disenchanted to learn her to be an examplary wife and the mother of six, pride of the Ladies Auxiliary Club of Willow Groves, Connecticut, etc., etc. It's a joy to find these particular months less barren than they used to be. I embrace you tenderly all round and am yours very constantly*

Henry

P.S. It may interest you to know that (I didn't want to put my scribe into the Secret) I get Lamb House (for twenty-one years, with my option of surrender the seventh or the fourteenth) for £70 per annum—four quarterly payments of less than £18. And they do all the outer repairs, etc.!

The postscript was in Henry's hand and called forth once more the twinkling smile in the face of the Elder Brother.

There was a knock again at his door, and Alice poked her head round its edge.

"Shall you be going out this evening?"

"I dine at home. But I shall be leaving round eight o'clock."

"Is it the spooks again tonight?" to which manifestation of wifely unawe he responded with a laugh of "yes."

Alice nodded shortly, her movement as articulate as any words could be, and at whose signifying message her husband again laughed. He knew how her good old Yankee skepticism reacted to the labors of the Society.

"I see you have opened dear Harry's letter. Is all well with him?"

"First-rate. He sends us great news! Come, I shall tell you of it all."

"Not an 'offer'!" gasped Alice in mock astonishment. This was a rather long-standing joke amongst them; and it formed, for them, a sort of carapace, the clenched jaws of which, should they ever be pried open (and no one of the three would ever have dreamed that they should), would have revealed a small universe swarming with dubious questions and unvoiced misgivings.

William laughingly rose now to plant a kiss upon his Alice's forehead, and arms companionably intertwined, they left the room, deep in animated conversation.

V I I I

~~

M r s . P i p e r

Doctor Austin Sloper of Washington Square held in his hands a just-opened letter from Doctor William James of Boston.

It had been some time now since he had heard from James, though he had heard more recently (and more's the pity) *of* him. Only the other evening, in his club, an acquaintance of Sloper's—a fellow medical man whom Sloper had always regarded as dexterously participating in the qualities of both buffoon and prig—had leaned his stiffly collared neck in the direction of Doctor Sloper, as both sat over their copies of *The New York Herald*.

"I see, Sloper, that your old school chum has pushed his name into the press once again."

"Heh? What's that, Maudlin?"

"William James. Fellow Harvard man, what?"

Maudlin was Yale—class of '62.

"There's an article here—damned ticklish, too—all about that ghostly society of his. Shady business—hah! Reporter fellow makes a good story out of the whole lot of them—both sides of the Atlantic. But your old school chum seems to come in for the swiftest kicks in the rearview *chambre*. Seems he was the only one fool enough to agree to see this newsboy and submit himself to his penny-a-liner's impudence after that sordid humbug affair in Rhode Island. Here. See for yourself!" And his blunt finger rapped Sloper's copy of the *Herald* at a place bearing the frivolous headline SPOOKS? FLUKES? . . . OR LEARNED DUPES? while the finger's no less blunt proprietor gave vent to a most unseemly snort, in response to which rude mirth the good doctor allowed his face to convey just the rightly admixtured proportions of worldly forbearance and wonder. He turned to the offending page in his own copy and read quickly through the unsurprisingly shallow piece, as Maudlin beside him pretended to be deeply immersed in yet another journalistic squib.

The story, yet once more dredged up for the mean purpose of indulging the public's delight in scorn for its betters, largely concerned the comicodramatic events of the night of the thirty-first of January the last, centering round the defamed figure of one Hannah V. Ross. This woman had, until that time, enjoyed a quite sizable reputation within spiritualist circles, based on the widely publicized "materialization" sittings she had conducted, together with her husband, Charles, in their home in Providence, Rhode Island—materialization falling, of course, toward the more dramatic end of the psychical spectrum, featuring manifestations of "phantasms of the dead"—or parts (hands, fingers, faces) thereof. On this particular occasion, however, a most natural explanation for the abnormal appearances had been forcibly laid hands upon, when a party of unconvinced citizens disrupted the proceedings, seizing in the process several soi-disant spooks in various stages of undress. The lights had been turned on, the cabinet from which the reputed phantasms were emerging had been uncurtained and plundered, revealing four boys and a little girl waiting their turns inside, as well as an ingenious mechanical contrivance that had operated a hidden door. Although Professor William James had not been present on that notorious evening, the newspapers insisted upon mixing his name up in the affair, and one New York paper had falsely attributed to him the former pronouncement of Mrs. Ross as "among the wonders of the nineteenth century," a bald misstatement edging ever closer to the truth by its repetition in dailies across the land.

"Insufferable affrontery," Sloper said warmly but with admirable dignity. "These publishing knaves go too far. Is a person nothing more than food for a newsboy? Everything and everyone, everyone else's business? How dare an ink-stained, phrasemongering slavey of public opinion presume to issue judgment on the Great Subject of what is science and what is not!"

His interlocutor had smiled with the full measure of complacency achieved on the occasion of a Yale man's believing himself to have gotten quite the better of a Harvard man (or, alternatively, of a Harvard man's believing himself similarly situated as regards a Yale man).

Despite his spirited attack of the evening on the great arts of publicity, Sloper, the very next morning, had felt called upon to write his wayward New England colleague a sharply worded missive, informing him of the manner of

commentary his fanciful interpretation of "scientific inves-
tigation" prompted and the intolerable indignity suffered by
both his own and—far worse!—his institution's reputation
in consequence thereof.

Under the sting of this recrimination, James had responded with preternatural promptitude, quite heatedly de-
fending the Society's hardheadedness and never-sleeping
suspicion of sources of error, though according to the newspaper and drawing room myth, softheadedness and idiotic
credulity were the bond of sympathy in this Society and
general wonder-sickness its dynamic principle.

*You, my dear fellow, are an estimable example of the scientific-
academian mind. And we who are of this mind must constantly
reacquaint ourselves with the fact that to no one type of mind
is it given to discern the totality of truth. Something escapes
the best of us—not accidentally, but systematically, and because
we have a twist. The scientific-academian mind and the feminine-
mystical mind shy from each other's facts, just as they fly from
each other's temper and spirit. Facts are there only for those
who have a mental affinity with them. When once they are
indisputably ascertained and admitted, the academic and critical
minds are by far the best fitted ones to interpret and discuss
them—for surely to pass from mystical to scientific speculations
is like passing from lunacy to sanity; but on the other hand,
if there is anything which human history demonstrates, it is the
extreme slowness with which the ordinary academic and critical
mind acknowledges facts to exist which present themselves as
wild facts, with no stall or pigeonhole, or as facts which threaten
to break up the accepted system.*

If I may employ the language of the professional logic-shop, a universal proposition can be made untrue by a particular instance. If you wish to upset the law that all crows are black, you must not seek to show that no crows are; it is enough if you prove one single crow to be white. My own white crow is Mrs. Piper.

And so, in the name of that Radiance—Impartial Truth—whose handmaidens we both adjudge ourselves to be, I once again bid you to come to Boston and grasp the nettle for yourself!

I am, as always,
William James

P.S. You enquire whether I have had any timely word from Willow Groves. In point of fact there did happen to arrive in that self-same post which carried the bruising thorns of your own correspondence a more rosy missive from the younger of the two Miss Bonnets, overflowing with optimistic tidings of the progress she makes toward illuminating the dark mysteries attending the irregularities of the delta-Celphei. She feels more than ever confirmed in her hypothesis of a singular hidden star. Interregnum my frustrations on her behalf continue. I have exhausted almost every avenue—from the wide boulevard to the hidden alleyway—known to me for the procurement of funds for the purpose of scientific research. The woman needs a good telescope! The potency of narrow-minded bigotry, undiluted by even an eye-dropper's worth of self-interrogation, is enough to dissolve the strongest of wills.

It did so happen that Doctor Sloper, having independent reason for sojourning to Boston, and registering the prod of James's "grasp the nettle" directive, agreed to take in, while there, a demonstration of the white crow's manifestations.

There would, at the least, be entertainment in it. And it would be a matter of some gratification for Sloper were he able to see his way through to the end of the thing and demonstrate, once and for all, to his wonder-sick colleague, the source of the artful illusions and shady chicanery. For, as we have had reason to remark upon before, Sloper was not the man to dismiss out of hand. He observed, he probed, he assessed. And then, and only then, did he dismiss.

It was March when Sloper made his visit to Boston. He had left a New York City that had embarked upon the seasonal softening known as spring; but the Puritan capital he encountered was still draped in December densities. Sloper had been round to dear old Harvard earlier in the day, to look up a few acquaintances who were there; and as he emerged beyond the fences of the Yard—first built to keep the cattle outside—there had come, sweeping from behind with brutal strength, a northeasterly blast that would have done credit to a New England tempest of mid-January. It seemed to come right off the chill and melancholy sea, hardly mitigated by sweeping over the roofs and amalgamating itself with the dusky element of city smoke.

And yet, despite the desolateness of the climate, the Doctor decided against the use of the ubiquitous horsecar, preferring to tramp the way back into Boston. For in the youthful days that had found him studying here, he had almost exclusively utilized the conveyance of his own two legs; and revisiting the Harvard scene always put him into something of a wishful mood.

He walked now across the long, low bridge that crawled, on its staggering posts, across the Charles, hunched over

into his greatcoat against the icy wind blowing off the river.
The view from the bridge was a sight he had once thought
lovely; but now it seemed—either through the changes the
years had wrought in himself, or in the view, or in both—
unrelievedly bleak: the casual patches of ice and snow; the
desolate suburban horizons, peeled and made bald by the
rigor of the season; the general hard, cold void of the pros-
pect; the extrusion, at Charlestown, at Cambridge, of a few
chimneys and steeples, straight sordid tubes of factories and
engine shops or spare heavenward finger of the New England
meeting house. There was something inexorable in the pov-
erty of the scene, reflected in the distaste in the prosperous
Doctor's face, which was wont to be turned out on the far
more gracious scene afforded him through his windows on
Washington Square. There was something shameful in the
meanness of these details, which gave a collective impression
of boards and tin and frozen earth, sheds and rotting piles,
railway lines striding flat across a thoroughfare of puddles,
and tracks of the humbler, the universal horsecar, traversing
obliquely this path of danger; loose fences, vacant lots,
mounds of refuse, yards bestrewn with iron pipes, telegraph
poles, and bare wooden backs of places.

How all has changed—and all for the worse!—was the
Doctor's steady, somber meditation as he trudged through
the slush on his way to the Piper. The cold sharpened as
the shortened afternoon drew to a close; and the Doctor's
greatcoat, which had always muffled him safe from the winds
that swept down the wide avenues of his island, was now
revealing its earthly limitations. The ugly picture was tinted
now with a clear cold rosiness, as the sun descended and

the winds were quietened, and the west became deep and delicate, as everything grew doubly distinct before taking on the dimness of evening.

The Doctor was shivering. He had not reckoned on so considerable a trek. It seemed that the distances between the points of Boston and its environs had been unnaturally shrunk within the distorting ether of his memory—or that he now, at the stage in his life in which the years had deposited him, registered those distances more acutely.

James's Piper lived in an undistinguished but respectable street. In fact—or so the next half hour suggested to the doctor—it appeared that undistinguished respectability was to be the altogether disappointing theme of the evening. The house was one of the modest frame affairs whose repetitive duplication constituted this particular neighborhood—houses built forty years before and already sere and superannuated. A towheaded girl child answered the doctor's knock, gazing up at the stranger with a practiced stare of inquisition, exhibiting not a symptom of shyness, and announcing in a self-possessed lisp that "Mama was ready, and receiving in the parlor."

Leonora Evelina Piper was perhaps the most studied medium of the day, and it had been none other than William James himself who had placed her before the probing procedures of the scientific method. She was categorized, according to the spiritualist taxonomy prevailing, as a "trance" medium, whose messages came spoken (or occasionally written) through the voice of the "control" who claimed temporarily to take over her body, and of whose possession she claimed, upon "waking," no residual recollection. On the surface, then, the behavior she exhibited bore a pronounced similarity to certain very rare and clinically intriguing cases of hysteria, when two quite distinct "parallel consciousnesses" (in the phraseology of Doctor Morton Prince of the Harvard Medical School) coexisted in one psyche. And—to Sloper's manner of conception—in the extremely unlikely event that the Piper's case not be reducible to base humbug, the pathological hypothesis would take its place as the indicated inference.

Indeed the Doctor had recently undertaken the study of certain psychological papers emanating from the Israelite quarter of Vienna, and though he had certainly treated the proffered description of the mind's topography with a heavy dosage of habitual irony, yet this had been tinctured increasingly with a begrudging recognition. There were, of course, strident exaggerations and hyperbolic insistences associated with the "Freudian" school of thought—the emphasis on matters sexual was patently absurd—and these—as was to be expected—had comprised the *only* aspects that were either seen or discussed, calling down upon the theory as a whole either stamping ovation or a just as unruly rain of hoots and hisses. The commentators had acquitted themselves admirably in fulfilling the historical role of the critic: that is, they had missed the point entire. The great expanse of psychical richness that was yielding itself to the techniques of the Viennese Doctor, would in future—the Doctor had a presentiment of it—offer itself as the explanation cum laude, making it that much more difficult for future generations to greet any announcement of the "preternatural" as betokening anything but a projection proceeding from the repressed disturbances within. (The Doctor was just beginning to try out—albeit gingerly—the analytic terminology and was finding that the appeal of juggling the new categories was such as to present a very real danger that the theory's legacy would be reduced to a jargon.)

James and his fellow members of the Society were all of them men of the nineteenth century, encrusted in the old themes and questions; whereas he, Doctor Sloper, prided himself on discerning, and tentatively endorsing, the advancing century's brave new ideas.

So while the wonder-sick members of the Society pondered the alternatives—telepathy or spirit control—the question, once extracted from wishful sentiment and fuzzy cerebration, was simply: a fake or a freak? The celebrated "psychic"—absurd appellation, that!—was either an artful bamboozler or a lamentable loon—and ought, by rights, to be behind the restraining bars of one institution or another.

When Sloper had agreed to grasp James's proffered nettle, he had done so with every expectation of being amply compensated for his time and toleration with an evening's rich entertainment. He had entered into the scheme of the séance with an anticipation such as he might have had on setting out for the theater, in which was being offered a farce not altogether in good taste, but stout good fun for all that. With such expectations as these, the drearily petit-bourgeois surroundings were not entirely compatible (Mr. Piper's mode of employment was never made quite clear), nor, for that matter, was the prosy person of Mrs. Piper herself. She was a tall fair woman, in her early thirties, with a placid, somewhat passive expression pressed into her face and her general bearing. She rather reminded him—in her modest black silk dress and her cameo brooch, the tidy little chignon of pale hair—of some of his maiden aunts of Albany, with whom he had passed many pleasant boyhood vacations, in a great rambling house the aunts had shared together, in which the discipline of the nursery had been delightfully vague and the opportunity of listening to the conversation of one's elders almost unbounded. He had enjoyed—in its time and its place—a fond exuberance of liking for these aunts—soft and blurry creatures, given to long low sighs. And it was a shade more than unsettling to be faced with a Mrs. Piper who should, by the mere fact of her general aspect and deportment, cancel out the altogether unseemly suggestion of the night's intent and introduce, in its place, an association at once so gentle and so innocent; so that he seemed, while he looked at her, to smell again the scent of the garden of the Albany house and to taste the flavor of the peaches that had grown there.

He would have chosen, in the ultimate interest of his evening's entertainment, if not his more abiding spiritual enlightenment, to view the talents of the younger, comelier, and altogether more sensational Mademoiselle Blanche de Blaze, about whom the Doctor had read some fairly racy accounts in the dailies, and who, with her flame-red hair and snow white complexion, always assumed a most beguiling pose in her trances.

The mademoiselle (if "mademoiselle" she indeed was— there were some who claimed she harked back no farther east than Hackensack) had shown an inventive flair in her choice of "contact." Where others relied chiefly on the ludicrously clumsy persona and vernacular of the red Indian ("me Big Chief, take you, white squaw!"), the de Blaze creature spoke in the elusive accent of a spirit named Adda, who claimed identity as a young female slave brought to Babylon from Judaea in the First Captivity.

Adda—who rarely consorted with that hobgoblin of little minds, consistency—tended to vary creatively the details of her life and, more particularly, her death. (One would have thought such an event to loom large in the inner life of a spirit.) She had been, she said, the "chosen one" of Nebuchadnezzar, king of Babylon. Her situation in this capacity lasted, she said, seven weeks or seven months or seven years—such manufactured categories soon dissolved within the Timeless Sea of Eternity—but during those seven something-or-others she had submitted herself to every whim of the great and powerful ruler's most bestial demands—unspeakable, and yet she spoke them. (The men of Judaea had been animals, but more domesticated.)

In the beginning of her celebrated career, the medium had described these royal whims—involving arrangements of parts to orifices first devilishly devised by the accursed citizens of Sodom and Gomorrah—with such Continental frankness that the authorities had served notice upon the brazen young lady (this last term but most liberally applied), threatening to issue an arrest for indecent speech if she did not desist at once from her scandalizingly descriptive details. The contents of this message must have been passed along with preternatural celerity through the mystical folds of the astral veil, for Adda thereafter gave a notably less titillating account of her term of servitude—which had, in any case, come to a brutally abrupt termination, the demon-king turning "the face of his wrath" upon his pliant little Judaean slave, having just received—or so according to one of her accounts—a new transport of slaves from Ethiopia, "the dark women all but naked, and glistening with rich oils and golden serpentine bands, undulating like the reeds beside the river." The eager king had wasted little time in casting his hapless little Adda down into the "fiery oven where the limestone is burnt.

"But ah! how I deceived him, even then! For where he meant to be turning me to ashes, I was becoming icy cold!"

The clever little mademoiselle had managed, in her very pretty trance, to produce some curious wedge-shaped characters, which "experts" had pronounced to be cuneiform, though the translation had yet eluded them.

But Mademoiselle Blanche de Blaze was presently plying her supernatural wares across the Continent of Europe, where she was reported to be the cynosure of an admiring furore, and so the Doctor would have to make do with the far less stimulating and, so to speak, suggestive performance of the comparatively demure and decorous Mrs. Piper.

William James was already present in the parlor when Sloper arrived, as was the ubiquitous (at least where the Piper was concerned) Mr. Richard Hodgson, the secretary—and only paid member—of the American branch of the Society. Mr. Hodgson, who was English, had embarked upon his dubious career with a vigorously functioning faculty of skepticism; but this vital cognitive organ had, through the detrimental mediumship of Mrs. Piper, undergone such a wasting process of disease and atrophy as to leave poor old Hodgson a quivering gobe-mouche of spiritualism. He was, at this stage of his existence, mountingly more obsessed with presenting to the world at large the Great Good News of Immortality (and he would, quite soon hereafter, upon his sudden and most untimely death while playing handball at his club, be transfigured into the Piper's ubiquitous contact on the other side—an inevitable fixture at all her future séances, the endless transcripts of which it would be William James's assigned and thankless task to examine for "evidential value").

The furnishings of the parlor into which the Doctor was shown were all dismally conventional, devoid of any flourishes of a—so to speak—metaphysical design. There, squatting in fashionable embonpoint, were the overstuffed chairs and the monstrous horsehair sofa, with the gaudily gilded oval mirror placed lengthwise on the wall behind it. And there, at the center of the room, was the heavy mahogany table, cleared, for the twisted purpose of the evening, of its hand-stitched table covering and its vase of dried flowers. This piece of furniture had already been submitted to the probing procedures of the Society, whose members had checked it, and its environs, for any hidden wires or ropes, mirrors, and trapdoors.

After having adjusted to the hideous apperception of a lady mountebank who so reminded him of those gentlewomen of Albany, Sloper had taken his place upon the horsehair sofa and had prepared himself to be henceforth, and abundantly, amused. And here, toward the conducement of that end, was the homey and unmystical Mrs. Piper playing the part of the proper hostess, as she served the gathering from a pot of dark and smoky lapsang tea and passed before them with a doilied plate of home-baked shortbread biscuits (which were almost as meltingly light as those that the Doctor remembered as having emerged from the always warm potbellied ovens of the once beloved aunts of Albany).

And then it was down to business. In addition to William James and Richard Hodgson, who were acting as the representatives of the Society on this occasion, there were also present two elderly sisters—the Misses Flowers of Holyoke, Massachusetts, about one hundred miles' distance from Boston—who had come with the hope of making contact with a recently "passed over" brother. The two were clearly in a state of nerves—but when is Woman not?—and sat in a fused puddle of trembling, holding hands and casting strange dim looks into one another's eyes—for all the world like two guilty conspirators suddenly finding themselves in the company of detectives! In the Doctor's ironical eyes, the two Misses Flowers were the richest part of the evening so far, and he looked forward to seeing the full repertoire of their flutterations upon their greeting the brother, who— the Doctor was confident of it—would be sure to put in an appearance this very night.

All six of them now took up their positions around the mahogany table in the center of the room, under a gas chandelier in full burning. (The Society insisted upon this. The tone of these spiritualistic displays had quite altered itself in recent years, with the modern attempt to entangle the shimmery shades in the close netting of the natural laws. Nowadays, in the management of his "subject," "clairvoyant," or "medium," the exhibitor affects the simplicity and openness of scientific experiment; and even if he professes to tread a step or two across the boundaries of the spiritual world, yet carries with him the laws of our actual life and extends them over his spectral conquests. Twelve or fifteen years ago, on the contrary, all the arts of mysterious arrangement, of picturesque disposition and artistically con-

trasted light and shade, had been made available, in order
to set the apparent miracle in the strongest attitude of opposition to ordinary facts.)

Almost immediately—efficiency being an attribute
keenly prized by the scientifically inclined—the Piper fell
into her "mediumistic trance." This, to the Doctor's eye—
which was, after all, professionally trained to espy the de-
signs of the malingerer (and you would be surprised how
many were the women who feigned illness, hoping to gain
thereby either a measure of sympathy or surcease from domestic duty)—these mystical agitations appeared, to the
Doctor's prognosticating stare, but clumsily performed.
There were first a series of muscular twitchings and respi-
ratory heavings—some moaning and groaning at the bar—
presenting the semblance of resistance, as if the woman were
feebly struggling against her oncoming "possession." She
then sat back, the "trance" apparently upon her. And the
spectacle of this wife and mother, of a respectable age—if
not occupation—with her upper body immodestly laid back
and her mouth hung open and slack, was altogether too
noisomely embarrassing to be taken in with the anticipated
relish—though the Doctor was, of course, professionally
habituated to the sight of females inelegantly displayed.
Doctor Sloper could only wonder that James's sensibilities
could tolerate repeated exposure to scenes of such arrant
vulgarity and not be irreversibly coarsened in the very
process.

The Doctor, who was sitting immediately to Mrs. Piper's
right, leaned slightly nearer to her. Her eyes were rolled
upward, so that the entire ocular sphere was left white. A
trick of the trade, no doubt. The candle was flickering madly.

(Hidden drafts. The procedures of the Society were, as he had predicted, shoddily incomplete.) A shower of little points of light seemed to dance behind the medium's head for a few brief seconds—small twisting pointed flames of brilliant color rising from the medium's shoulders and floating toward the ceiling.

For the briefest moment there appeared to Sloper's alerted perception a sensation as of an icy pressure at his back, as if a long cold finger had laid itself onto the nape of his neck.

He shivered, as at a current of chill air issuing out of a sepulchral vault and bringing the smell of corruption along with it. The long, low shudder was quite in spite of himself, being the altogether unreasonable end of a reflex arc that had entirely bypassed his cerebrum—which would otherwise have summarily intervened.

Sloper looked again at the medium, her head now flung back at a quite extreme angle, which Sloper would have adjudged to be very uncomfortable for her to maintain. There was no sign of her breathing.

Slowly her whitened lips began to move. And her head, which had hitherto been held at the extreme angle, came slowly upright into its more natural position. She spoke in a voice quite different from her own, deeper and more assertive, a manly voice with an accent that might have been said to be French.

"*Bonsoir! Comment vous portez-vous?* I am here. *C'est moi, c'est moi.* Phinuit! Doctor and Frenchman!"

Phinuit was the name, these days, of her customary "contact," and a most problematic personality he had proved himself to be—even to the faithful Hodgson. He claimed to be a physician (though his knowledge of medicine never showed itself to exceed what Mrs. Piper herself might have garnered from copies of *Domestic Cures*) who had been born in 1790—perhaps—in Marseilles—or perhaps Paris, or then again Germany. Even his name was an issue of uncertainty, about which he rather fudged when its likeness to the "Finny" of the medium Cocke was pointed out to him. Efforts were still going on, by the representatives of the Society on the Continent, to find some traces of Phinuit's earthly sojourn.

Tonight Phinuit, who was always an excitable manner of creature, with a rather Gallically insistent sense of his own importance, was in a high state of pique, brought on by the presence of *"that one"*—none other than William James!—whom he had not had the displeasure of encountering since seeing "his stupid, stupid words," printed in the proceedings of the Society, in which the figure of Phinuit had been discussed in terms coldly analytic and entirely incompatible with Phinuit's own estimation of himself. "Phinuit," James had written,

> bears every appearance of being a fictitious being. His French, so far as he has been able to display it to me, has been limited to a few phrases of salutation. . . . He has never been able to understand my French; and the crumbs of information which he gives about his earthly career are so few, vague, and unlikely sounding, as to suggest the romancing of one whose stock of materials for invention is excessively reduced. With respect to the rough and slangy style which he so often affects, it should be said that the Spiritualistic

tradition here in America is all in favour of the "spirit-control" being a grotesque and somewhat saucy personage.

PHINUIT: He is hard! He is hardened with his dogma!

HODGSON: Professor James, do you mean?

PHINUIT: James. Yes, James. I do not believe in *him!* I think William James is a fictitious being! Let him prove to me that *he* exists!

And here the irrepressible Phinuit—acting through the body of the entranced medium—regarded William James with an expression of utmost scorn, actually taking the thumb and forefinger of "his" right hand and squeezing together the nostrils of "his" nose!

PHINUIT: And his French! Phooey! His French stinks like the fish in the sun!

HODGSON, *amused:* Professor James is entirely fluent in French.

PHINUIT: To you! A blimey Englishman! Phooey!

HODGSON: Doctor Phinuit. We do not mean to upset you. Science, you know, has its methods. You must—we must all—bear with these patiently.

PHINUIT: You are all right, Hodgson. You are a good sort. And I will tell you a thing or two, my good Hodgson. In this world, Hodgson, there is no time. Life goes on forever. There is no death. I tell you, my friend Hodgson, just as sure as you live in the body, I lived once in the body. I lived in Germany and Paris and Marseilles. I know if those cranks weren't so stupid they could find me.

HODGSON: I know you are right.

PHINUIT: My dear Hodgson! *Mon cher cher cher ami!*

HODGSON: *Merci!*

PHINUIT: *Rien!* But *that one!* Tiresome twiddle!

HODGSON: Twiddle?

PHINUIT: Twiddle! *Mais oui!* Ask *that one!* That is what *he* said!

JAMES: Twaddle. I said you spoke tiresome twaddle.

Phinuit, here muttering, issued a fulsomely obscene French suggestion, the wicked contents of which must needs be excluded, but which, it might be said, indicated the possibility of cross-contact between Mrs. Piper's Phinuit and Mademoiselle Blanche de Blaze's haplessly pliant Adda.

HODGSON, *twinkling mightily at James*: Now that is good! I call that evidential, what!

JAMES, *likewise twinkling*: It is very evidential indeed!

PHINUIT: Ah, so this is the manner of evidence that satisfies the members of the Society! *Alors,* there is more from where that came. I know now how it goes then with the scientific method!

JAMES: I am sorry if I have angered you, Phinuit.

To this conciliatory gesture there came only silence, as Phinuit quite pointedly turned his shoulder away from James, so that his back alone was presented.

JAMES: Phinuit?

PHINUIT: Hodgson, my dear, dear Hodgson.

HODGSON: Phinuit?

PHINUIT: Hodgson, I do not talk to that one, you understand, my good Hodgson? You are a good sort, Hodgson.
Phinuit, who is real, does not converse with a fictitious
being! *Mon Dieu!* I am not mad, to converse with what
is not! Who else is here this evening?

HODGSON: Perhaps you can tell us.

Extreme effort was always made to keep secret the identities of all newcomers to Mrs. Piper's séances, in the attempt
to get out something of "evidential value."

PHINUIT: *C'est possible. Ce n'est pas difficile.*

HODGSON: Yes?

PHINUIT: There are two, two . . . there are two sisters!

HODGSON: Yes. That is good.

PHINUIT: They are from the Holy Egg.

HODGSON: Holy Egg?

PHINUIT: Yes, yes! *Sacre Oeuf!* No! No, no, Holy . . . Holy
Yoke! From the Holy Yoke!

HODGSON: Yes, that's right. From Holyoke, Massachusetts.

PHINUIT, *impatiently*: Yes, yes, but another. Like James, this
one is hard with his dogma. No, this one is even harder
still! Voilà, another *fictitious being!*

HODGSON: Do you know his name, Doctor Phinuit? Can
you tell us his name?

PHINUIT: He is also a James—but yet another James!

HODGSON: No. That is not right.

PHINUIT, *very excited*: Yes, yes! I think so, I think so! *C'est vrai!*
Another fictitious James! I see inside! It is easier to see
inside this one than you others somehow. This one is
only bitter laughter inside. Oh, he makes mean sport,

this one! He is *très, très* fictitious, my old friend Hodgson!
Oui oui, Phinuit knows!

HODGSON: Do you know what this man does for a living?
That would be evidential, Doctor.

PHINUIT: He is a man of letters, *je pense* . . . no, no, it is very
confused, the influence of this man, it is very mixed and
dim. . . . No, no . . . a doctor! *Mais oui!* Phinuit knows!
He is a physician. *Comme moi. Bonsoir, Doctor Sloper! Comment
vous portez-vous?*

SLOPER, *much amused: Très bien, merci! Et vous?*

PHINUIT: *Tiens!* Now we can make us some good conversing!
Now we can discuss the methods and the cures!

SLOPER: Nothing, I can assure you, my good man, would
delight me more! But tell me, Doctor Phinuit, from what
cause did you suffer the misfortune of departing the
temporal scheme? I hope your exit was of a timely and
tranquil nature?

At this example of the Doctor's habitual irony, the organism of the medium, which had been sitting upright and
relaxed, became suddenly seized with convulsions, much
more violent than those that had preceded the onset of her
trance. Her hands groped toward her abdomen, where they
began to claw as if to tear into the very entrails of her.
Indeed—most dreadfully—the black silk of her dress was
quickly ripped, and the many layers of undergarments as
well, so that the very flesh of her belly showed through.
And in her throat there rattled death's gruesome announcement.

This unspeakably tasteless demonstration lasted for perhaps the better part of a minute and then abruptly ceased.

PHINUIT, *much weakened:* Of dysentery.

SLOPER: I am sorry for you, my friend. And what medicines were prescribed for you? Belladonna, bryonia, cinchona?

PHINUIT, *quite vaguely:* Oui, oui. Yes, I think so. I think all three, perhaps. . . .

SLOPER: Well, well, Phinuit! . . .

But before Doctor Sloper could pursue his subtle line of inquisition, his voice was choked off in midsentence by the suddenly erupting sounds of an anxious-sounding female.

"Austin! Austin!"

The voice—good God! It was the voice of Sloper's dead wife, Catherine, with which the medium was calling out!

"Austin, Austin! I have called and called to you!"

Catherine Sloper had been dead now for the thirty-eight years that the other Catherine Sloper, the Doctor's daughter, had been alive; for the mother had died a week after giving birth to this second child (who, as a matter of course, had been named after her poor mother).

We have spoken before of the Doctor's share of sorrows; of the fact that he, too, philosopher though he was, had not escaped unscathed from the blind and random distribution of misfortune. For a man whose trade was to keep people alive, the Doctor had certainly done poorly in his own family; for two years before the death of his young wife, his first child, a little boy of extraordinary promise, as the doctor, who was not addicted to easy enthusiasm, firmly believed, had died at three years of age, in spite of everything that the mother's tenderness and the father's science could invent to save him. And then had followed the final devastation of losing his own Catherine—who had left behind only the dubious consolation of the little girl.

The daughter had proved strong and properly made, and, fortunately, her health was excellent. It has been noted that the Doctor was a philosopher, but I would not have answered for his philosophy if the poor girl had proved a sickly and suffering person. As a child she had promised to be tall, but when she was sixteen she ceased to grow, and her stature, like most other points in her composition, was not unusual. She was a manner of person who seemed not only incapable of giving surprises; it was almost a question whether she could have received one—she was so quiet and irresponsive. People who expressed themselves roughly called her stolid. But she was irresponsive because she was shy, uncomfortably, painfully shy. This was not always understood, and she sometimes produced an impression of insensibility. In reality she was the softest creature in the world.

The Doctor was a proud man and would have enjoyed being able to think of his daughter as an unusual girl. There would have been a fitness in her being pretty and graceful, intelligent and distinguished; for her mother had been the most charming woman of her little day; and as regards her father, of course he knew his own worth.

Catherine had, some several years back, deepened her father's irksome sense of disproportion by proving herself to be not only unbrilliant, but pitiably susceptible to the good looks and easy charm of a worthless suitor. *That*, however, is another story entirely.

Doctor Sloper was a philosopher; he smoked a good many cigars over the disappointment of his daughter, and in the fullness of time he got used to it. (Though he had every intention of extending his paternal rights beyond the grave, and had already altered his will so that Catherine's share would not amount to a sum attractive to those unscrupulous adventurers whom she had given her father reason to believe that she persisted in regarding as an interesting class.)

Catherine was commencing her thirty-ninth year and was becoming an admirable old maid. She formed habits, regulated her days upon a system of her own, interested herself in charitable institutions, asylums, hospitals, and aid societies, and went generally, with an even and noiseless step, about the rigid business of her life.

"Catherine!" the Doctor cried out in a strange, strangled voice. "Catherine! Catherine! It *is* you?"

And he half stood, peering desperately out into the gaslit parlor, his arms rigidly thrust before him like a blind man groping for sight.

"Catherine! It *is* you, isn't it!"

"Yes, dear." Her voice was the infinitely sweet music his memory had faithfully preserved. "Of course it is I. And our little boy, too. He is here right beside me. I have called and called to you!

"Only look up and see us, dear!"

The Doctor sank back down onto his chair, his breath a noisy pant, his hand clutching at his chest.

"It was his heart, you know, dear," she continued softly in a soothing, murmuring rush. "He had a leaking heart. There was nothing you could have done for him, my dear. Nothing at all. You mustn't blame yourself. His heart had a hole. He is with me now. We have been together ever since.

"Austin, dear? Can you hear me? It is very hard for me to be here, you know, the obstacles against it are very strong."

Her voice was growing dim.

"Only one thing more. Dear? Dear? Can you hear me? Oh! It is hard! I am not accustomed to it.

"Only, dear, you must not be so hard on her. That is what I have come here to say to you. I too didn't want to go behind, to leave you. Oh! Austin!"

And here a girlish giggle, rather shrill, erupted from the whitened lips of the medium.

"Oh, Austin! Do you remember? The trip to Italy! The great canopied bed, with the sunken middle, in the Hotel P. on the Campo dei Fiori."

More girlish laughter had followed, broken off as abruptly as it had begun, in a noise like a startled hiccough.

"Only, Austin, you must not be so hard on her. She has light! Austin, do you hear me? You must, you must . . . Austin? . . ."

The voice was fading, only just this side of audibility.

"Can you hear me, dear? Look up, only look up and you shall see me. I am here right before you! I am in my wedding dress!

"Oh! I forget those coarse membranes, how they gum the inner eye closed!

"Austin? Austin? Are you there? Oh, if you could look behind her as I do, what a sadness is there. We have all eternity to rue the unkindness we have done. Err we must, only err on the side of kindness, Austin! Only look behind! Austin, are you listening, are you *there*? Dear? Dear?"

I X

~

Catherine

In the days and weeks that had followed the Doctor's fateful visit to the home of Mrs. Piper, he had undergone a moral alteration of his person—which alteration constituted, in the Doctor's life, so radical a departure and discontinuity as to have attained the status of a *metaphysical* transfiguration.

There had been enacted—upon the stark and dim-lit setting of the shadowy Inner Stage—a Drama, fierce and fell; wherein the unseen actors had groped and grappled, waxed wild and most copiously wept; and in the midst of which the ironical mode of expression had not once been given to utter a line, not even voce velata.

In a pitching, stuporous daze the Doctor had made his way back to the isle of his abode—how, he never *could* recollect or re-create, not for the balance of his remaining terrestrial term; only that there had been some manner of unfortunate fracas with William James (involving, most regrettably, actual *physical* violence tendered and received), provoked by James's no doubt well-intentioned, but none-theless misdirected attempt to proffer what he could in the way of assistance—and then resistance—to the companion who had been seized with a delirious disquietude!

In any case, the Doctor had—somehow or other—been transported back to the city of his residence, to the home of his formidable presumptions, overlooking Washington Square; where waited, in perfected passivity, his spinster daughter, Catherine, that dull and gentle woman (not so very different in genus from those maiden aunts of Albany), whose single opportunity in the way of earthly delight had, years before, been vigorously removed through the invasive operation of her father's coldly undeluded intelligence, which had so ruthlessly grasped the venal motives that had lurked in the well-presented chest of her handsome suitor, Morris Townsend.

"If you could but look behind her as I do, what a sadness is there!"

Behind, behind, behind, the voices had whispered. *If you could but look behind!*

Voices! Some were melting and imploring, others harsh and shrill accusers; rolling over one another, a cappella and then fusing; in the shadows voices mumbled, fingers fumbled, pushed and pummeled, as he, humbled, stumbled darkly through a city he knew not.

From the bridge the water beckoned, blackened river, iced and endless; flutter downward, free and weightless; *Now!* one voice was calling, *Now and Never, Yet Forever!*

Mutter mutter, flutter shudder—now he lies there in the gutter—

For now, while so quietly
Lying, it fancies
A holier odor
About it, of pansies—
A rosemary odor,
Commingled with pansies—
With rue and the beautiful
Puritan pansies.

"Father!" the soft and blurry creature had cried out in stricken tones when she had opened the front portal to the sound of his feeble knock.

He stood there—oh, how pitiably altered!—belittled and becrushed, deprived of the magnifying forms of heavy irony.

How affectingly unironic, the scalding tears that streamed from the swelled-shut slits of his eyes, down a face disfigured by emotion and into a linen neckcloth whose redoubtable stance had collapsed into a wretchedness of droop.

Oh, what a weeping was this! Weeping such as the Romish church revered as a special grace, the so-called gift of tears—when it was as if the tears broke through an inveterate dam and let all sorts of ancient peccancies and moral stagnancies drain away, leaving one washed and soft of heart and open to every nobler leading.

So was it that her father cried, leaning heavily upon the arm of his most bewildered only child, as she, trembling, led him into their house. It was to be many hours before this distressed gentlewoman—seeking to becalm him with pots of sugared lemon tea—was to gain the slightest inkling of the singular happenstance that had befallen her so changed parent; many hours passed despairingly through the sleepless watches of the night, before her father was able sufficiently to suppress the high pitch of his turmoil to allow for a few scant words of most inadequate explanation. And still the daughter had not known what to make of it all—as who would not?—had grieved horribly for the loss of her unfortunate parent's intellect!

How it was that the realization finally overcame her; how the knowledge made its way through the thrashing whirligig of her pity and her terror, as her father, slowly gathering together his composure and regaining something of his own articulated authority, sought to make her understand; the detailed narration of how these mighty transformations were set into place would take us through many more hours of the days and nights that were shared, open-eyed, between them—father and daughter in mysterious communion.

Suffice it to say that Catherine Sloper did eventually comprehend; that she came to see (her sight accompanied by a feeling such as a sentient flower might feel, in the process of its exfoliation) that the transfiguring of her parent was not of the degenerating, of the godforsaken morbid variety, but rather was of the form of *regeneration*—yea, even of *redemption*.

The door on Washington Square has been closed, for many days now, to the Doctor's distressed patients, who, it will be recalled—were all to be found among the island's "best people," and who, as such, were not accustomed to the inconveniences presented by a portal persistently shut. Gradually they drifted off, taking their symptoms, interest-

ing and not, to others who would know better how to appreciate them.

When, at last, the door does reopen, it is on a warm
evening in late April, with dusk just falling. It opens to emit
a woman, whose drapery is all of white and shimmers like
some cloudy stuff in moonlight, and who is heavily veiled.
The lady in white is on the arm of a man, whom we see is
none other than the Doctor himself. They walk quickly
away, their two heads close to one another in such a manner
that it in no way taxes the organ of inference to grasp they
are communing in an easy, ceaseless flow. They make their
way swiftly across the park of Washington Square and head
off in the direction of Fifth Avenue.

More days shall elapse before we reenter the Doctor's
house, so that it shall be of an evening in the mellowest of
Mays that we again mount those marble stairs and pass
through, in the company of several others, to be ushered
in, with mysterious looks and complicated gestures, by a
tall, fair, quite faded woman, clothed for the occasion in an
equally faded velvet robe, of a somehow mystical cut. There
is an ancient, heavy brooch at her neck. Her long thick hair
is elaborately coiled round her head. She sheds pale hairpins
as she moves. This undeniable character is Lavinia Penniman,
the Doctor's widowed sister, who had taken up her residence
under the Doctor's own roof many years ago, when poor
motherless Catherine was but ten. Lavinia herself had been
made a widow at thirty-three through the demise of her
poor clergyman husband, of a sickly constitution and a flow-
ery style of eloquence. She had been left without children,
without a fortune—with nothing but the memory of Mr.
Penniman's flowers of speech, a certain vague aroma of which

hovered about her own conversation. Nevertheless the Doctor had offered his sister a home under his own roof, which Lavinia accepted with the alacrity of a woman who had spent ten years of her married life in the town of Poughkeepsie. The Doctor had not proposed to Mrs. Penniman to come and live with him indefinitely; he had suggested that she should make an asylum of his house while she looked about for unfurnished lodgings. It is uncertain whether Mrs. Penniman ever instituted a search for unfurnished lodgings, but it is beyond dispute that she never found them. She settled herself with her brother and never went away. Her own account of the matter was that she had remained to take charge of her niece's education. She had given this account, at least, to everyone but the Doctor, who never asked for explanations that he could entertain himself any day with inventing.

Mrs. Penniman was romantic, she was sentimental, she had always a passion for secrets and mysteries, which had continued undiluted, if little requited—save for the one brief interlude involving the dashing Morris Townsend, in which Lavinia had played a necessary, albeit insufficient, role—into her present sixty-first year. It is obvious to us that, despite the attempt to offer us the impression of soundless depths of unutterable thoughts, of omniscient and self-containing secrecy, the highly imaginative fibers of her nature are now acutely aquiver with the awesome aura of the moment.

"She is in the parlor," she whispers to us, who stand clustered together with the others, on the polished black-and-white marble tiles of the antechamber.

"She awaits . . . *them*," she continues, speaking hurriedly and obliquely, from behind one cupping palm, while with her other arm, the ballooning sleeve of it fluttering lavishly, she gestures grandly, if somewhat vaguely.

The Doctor himself now enters from a door to the side and, thanking his sister politely, takes over the charge of his guests, leading us into the front drawing room, with the big balcony before it, where sits, upon a little silken damask sofa, his daughter. But wait!—is it his daughter?

We look again, and yet again—wonder-struck, in the soft, fine dimness of the gas-lit parlor! What manner of transformation is this that has been wrought upon the gruel-like consistency of the Doctor's daughter, refining that once lumpish material so that it now seems some ambrosial concoction? Is this that selfsame creature who had been preordained, as it were, to end her life in a state of admirable spinsterhood, putting in her time at almshouse and asylum, an inevitable figure at all respectable entertainments and the kindly maiden aunt to the younger portion of society?

What manner of alteration is this? Is it entirely reducible to the contrasts that have been effected in Catherine Sloper's style of dress? Or is there some other element—at once more abstract and yet more potent—that has spread itself over the heavy dullness that had been Catherine—transfiguring her into a creature bearing the unmistakable tone and tincture of the exotic?

Most assuredly, the manner of investiture is most singularly altered; and this modification at least, falling as it does within the strictly material sphere, is not difficult to catalogue. That lively taste in dress that had fleetingly asserted itself in her youth again makes itself felt, only now in loose and flowing drapery that—though owing a certain influence to the so-called aesthetic style of dress associated with that "unclean beast," Oscar Wilde—bespeak a tie less Italian and medieval and more Oriental and atemporal. Her draperies of filmy, gauzy stuff, unwaisted and entirely innocent of the tapering dart, are dyed in flowing liquid patterns of purple, black, and saffron. She wears several fringed shawls, and strands of glassy beads, and her headdress is a strangely flattering purple turban, which hides the mousy strands of graying brown hair and brings out her features— which features acquire, in this, their belated debut, a certain definition, a certain, we might even say, pronouncement; so that, though Catherine cannot be called handsome, she is, undeniably (and how strange and unforeseen an event!) *interesting*.

Let us seat ourselves with the others—a rather faded and dingy human collection which it will not much repay us, methinks, to differentiate amongst—upon the chairs and sofas of the comfortable drawing room. The lighting, we remark, is atmospherically dim. The hardheaded and professionally suspicious representatives of the Society for Psychical Research are apparently not here amongst us this evening; and so the séance is free to array itself in the shadowy drapery that is its natural garmenture; it puts on the starched white jacket of experimental science only with a certain effort and a resulting artificiality that does not much become it. We watch as the Doctor himself goes to stand behind his daughter—who looks up at him to exchange between them a glance of purest trust—and who then gently closes her eyes as her father rests his long lean competent surgeon's hands upon her head. Doctor Sloper looks at no one as he strokes and soothes his daughter. "Quietly, quietly," he murmurs from time to time. "It will come, my good child. In the hush, feel it crouching, gathering . . ."

And as the good Doctor works upon his daughter, to usher her into that trance of mediumship for which they had discovered—while yet the door on Washington Square had remained unopened—she possessed so singular a gift, we shall try to adjust to the great changes manifesting themselves before us by sparingly gleaning the facts from a rambling letter William James had some weeks ago received from Austin Sloper. Had James not himself been witness to the dramatic events of that chill March eve, had he not seen the state of near demented agitation with which the Doctor fought him off and fled into the darkened streets of Boston, James might have regarded the letter as rather an overmuch display of Austin Sloper's old habit of irony. As it was, James didn't at all know what to make of it. And he could not help but feel a most keen remorse that he had ever proffered the fateful nettle to Sloper, this despite the fact that the Doctor most fulsomely, albeit confusedly, thanked him for his True and Final Illumination and spoke of the epiphany of his present existence. James feared it was but the epiphany of impending insanity.

Most strange of all, perhaps, was the Doctor's unrelievedly unironic narration of the details of his daughter's mediumship. Catherine's chief contact was a very ancient, angry Jewish woman, by the name of Judith, who had lived in the time of the Second Common Era in Babylonia and was the wife of a prominent rabbinical personage, a Reb Hiyya, who, it appeared, had had an actual hand in the writing of the Talmud.

She is a most original and fierce manner of Person, full of vengeful wrath directed at the men of her own time and tribe in general (and Reb Hiyya in particular), who are devising laws, so she tells us—repeatedly—ever more oppressive to Woman. There are times when her speech approaches a pitch of rebellious declamation, which sends a shudder through my Protestant organization. The story of her life, to which we are habitually subjected, is most strange. She is most proud of all of a little trick she played her Reb Hiyya. Having given birth to two sets of twins, and unambivalently wishing none more, she disguised herself and petitioned her Talmudic husband as to whether the dictum to propagate fell also upon Woman. Reb Hiyya answered that the requirement was upon Man alone, whereupon this wife went home and drank a sterilizing potion, known to the women of her day, consisting of one part liquid alum, one part ground garden-crocus, and one part white ash, all mixed together into beer.

Judith has a habit of refusing to bring forth any of the others who hover and wait their turn until she has delivered herself of a twelve-minute lecture, entitled "The Birth of Monotheism and the Subjugation of Woman." But despite this insatiable relish for ritual (a tribal weakness, perhaps)—and I can assure you that after hearing her tell it for the fifth or sixth time one does not crave it again—Catherine's séances have come, in a very short time, to enjoy a hugh amount of ovation, and it is such unspeakable joy to us that we are able to assuage the grief of so many by allowing that most blessed Communion to take place between the two Realms of our Existence. . . .

The Doctor did not here stray from reality when he spoke of the extent to which his daughter's talents had been exuberantly received within spiritualist circles; and she was becoming, as well, a great favorite with the penny-a-liner crowd. In fact, her reputation was coming so rapidly to rival that of Mademoiselle Blanche de Blaze that this scandalous piece of Continental audacity began, at risk from the authorities, to reintroduce into her spiritual manifestations some of the wicked king's unnatural appetites, which grew, in the heat of the competition, ever more shockingly bestial, her descriptions ever more lasciviously graphic.

Experts had been called in—Hebraic scholars with spiraling sidelocks and velvet skullcaps—and had verified the Talmudic allusions of Catherine's contact. They had acknowledged that on occasion Catherine's spirit had spoken to them in the tongue of ancient Aramaic! And there, interred in obscurity within the columned tracts of *Yevamot*, *Kiddushin*, and *Shabbot*, were tales of the fierce female fighter, Judith, and her much tested scholar-husband, Reb Hiyya (who once told his nephew Rav, "May God deliver you from that which is worse than death"—that is, a tiresome wife).

How could Catherine Sloper, a sheltered Episcopalian, who had never in her life conversed with anyone of the Hebrew persuasion, much less attempted a tome of their Talmud, come by such out-of-the-way arcana? So had the dailies queried.

But silence! Catherine Sloper is now deep into her trance, her father, having removed the soothing touch of his gentle hands from the dome of her turbaned head, has unobtrusively drawn away. The voice of Judith, belligerent and most peculiarly inflected, is heard. In truth, she is a full three minutes into her exordium, and has already established the existence of the Primeval Matriarchy, the halcyon state of innocence, and wholeness that preceded the Fall into Patriarchy. She has instructed her audience that language began with mothers cooing to their babes, and that pottery was invented by women molding the clay round their breasts.

But most important, she has described the gentle religion that had, upon a time, abundantly flourished, before the ascendancy of the vengeful, war-mongering gods of Patriarchy: the life-affirming rites centered round the principles of fertility and regeneration, and embodied in the ample figure of the Mother Goddess.

But hush, and let us listen for ourselves.

X

~

The Ancient
Jewess

So in the beginning there was the Mother, and we lived with her in the Garden. And believe it, it was the best. There was plenty of good fruit and vegetables, we just had to gather it up and feast. We played, we worked, we mated, and we watched the children grow up strong. We danced in the sacred circle, and chanted to the pale white moon, who was the Mother. Death, the Faceless One, came swift and horrible; but when we were released from his talons there stood the Mother, waiting to receive us back again.

While we women were performing the major job of keeping the group alive, the men would help out with some of the heavier tasks. They also took on, though we women never completely approved, the role of hunter, which they began to take ridiculously seriously, weaving all kinds of meshuggenneh myths and cults around it.

The men had always had more free time, and they liked to use it to care for their weapons. More and more they began to sneak off to their secret meetings, where they did who knows what, though we were so occupied, what with the children and the food gathering, that we hardly even took any notice of what they were up to.

What exactly were they up to? We can only guess. They would air their gripes about their sense of inferiority in those meetings, lick the common wound of marginality. They felt that they, with their beautiful tools, were merely ornamental. Now, at last, they were talking out their feelings, which had to be a revelation—never mind that those feelings were swelling up something awful with self-pity and rancor. We didn't worry. The full and flowing bosom of the Mother provided Life enough for all.

So we let the men talk, and make each other feel better. But, more and more, the Word was voiced—and the Word was POWER, *and the Word was* CONTROL.

The men began to cook up beliefs of a transcendent Deity, a God who was not in Nature, (a theological concept we couldn't for the Life of us even get a hold on).

And the God was male, and the men who cooked up the story became His high priests, His very exclusive kohanim, a privilege to be passed down from father to son, for all the generations of Israel. The kohanim were alone allowed to enter the place of the Presence; the kohanim alone partook of hidden knowledge into the Deity's finicky tastes. This *He liked!—this He didn't!*

*Our singing, they said, could not be heard, lest it give them unclean thoughts. Our voices—*unclean!

*And they went out with their subversive message to make converts among the men, whispering like guilty children at first, and only grad-ually gaining in defiant chutzpah, working themselves up at last into a righteous contempt for the very forces of Life that had once enthralled them, finally daring even to decree that the sacred blood—the sweet wine of the womb—was unclean. Our voices and our wombs—*unclean!

We, who had never given much thought to the dynamics of control, were—more quickly than I care to tell you—most pitiably subjugated.

We just didn't know what hit us. Forever banished—woman and man both—from the moist lushness of the Garden—where the rich sap of joy had flowed over all, embrocating every dip and fold of Life, which had—above all things—been reverenced and tended and loved.

But did we resent it? That's the strangest part of all, bubalah. Although we mourned—how could we not mourn the Fall?—we preserved the memory, dimmer and dimmer by the year, but still making itself felt in our funny little ways, in our elaborate practices of nurturance, and in the mysterious sympathy we have always continued to feel for our men. And at our simchas—our celebrations of Life's passages—we women will go off to the side of the room, to join our hands in the ancient circle and dance our joy together.

And sometimes, when we are quietly gathered, there in the margins of the text taken up by the Word, the memory suddenly leaps up between us; and we break out into snatches of remembered song, lifting our unclean voices together in the sacred wordless music. . . .

X I

~

The Nolan

"Slut!"

The angry syllable that stops in midcurrent the white waters of Judith's speech, is delivered in a voice that is shrill and high-pitched and of questionable gender. The sound brings with it a new blast of frigid air and the dank foul odor of the grave, nauseatingly tinctured by some putrid smell of burn.

The word has seemed not to have found its issue in the still supine form of Catherine Sloper—but to hiss from every suspended particle within the room and to insinuate its way into the innermost ear in no mere physically relayed manner of propulsion.

The gaslights that had hitherto kept their atmospheric dimness now flicker madly—alternating between the harsh glare of brightness and total midnight black. It is difficult to convey how sickeningly disorienting to the inner brain is this violent variation on the outer sense; and the few seconds of each illumination reveal in the audience frozen motions and attitudes of distress. Some seem to make to move as if they would lief—and in haste—depart the frenzied scene.

"Though I wander through the endless reaches of Eternity—through the Infinite Universe and the Innumerable Worlds that lie like silvered globes of moisture on the spider's cosmic web—yet have I not the time or forbearance to attend to such as art thou, O Judith, wife of woeful Hiyya!"

"And just who are *you*," asks the voice of Judith wearily, "whose monkish cowl cravenly conceals his face? Here all come forth and present themselves upfront—or they do not come at all!"

"Oh, be off, thou tiresome woman! A slut and a nuisance, thou art in sooth. Thy bossiness does offend mine outer sense, as the narrow scope of thy confusion revolts the inner. Has not the deathless voyage through the timeless ethereal regions liberated thee from thy infinitesimal, terrestrial gender obsession? Infinity is lost on one such as thou!"

"Now you listen to me!" persists Judith, waxing hotter. "I am the contact of the evening, and—"

"And thou art ugly to boot!" the high-pitched, androgynous voice whinnies and cackles like an eruption of electrical energy—while the noisome smell of something unspeakably burning intensifies . . . almost beyond endurance!

"Never, in all the wide-flung movements of my ceaseless wanderings, have I encountered so ugly a Jewess as art thou! For in sooth the women of thy peculiar tribe are singularly sweet and succulent little morsels in the sensual banquet of the inexhaustible cosmos. . . ."

And here explodes a wanton sound, as if of the smacking of fishy lips.

"But then enough of all that sort of thing," continues on the irrepressibly irreverent intruder. "Myself I shouldst have taken any one of thy weak excuses to spit the bitter substance of thou from out between my shuddering thighs! I wouldst have had no need of tortured *pilpul!* I wouldst have spat thee out with no excuse at all!

"Oh, ole Reb Hiyya was a desperate ole Hebe, and a desperate ole Hebe was he!" the voice unmelodiously sing-songs to the tune of an ancient ditty.

"Identify yourself!" screeches the yet more ancient Jewess. "I will know the face behind the friar's habit! Dominican? Franciscan, Jesuit?"

For how, pray tell, would Judith know?

"Wouldst thou know, Woman?" comes the taunting voice of the monk. "Wouldst have me, Woman, bend myself to fit the circumscription of thy pettish rules? If I shouted the undaunted glory of my defiance before the faceless vastness of the Inquisition, with all the fiery consequences that there so attended, dost thou dare confabulate that I shall quiver and droop before thy most irksome and querulous stridency!

"I am bent in two with laughter and grief at thy so presuming posture!

"*In tristicia hilaris, in hilaritate tristis!*

"Woman, thou art no oracle, but orifice!

"Wouldst have me wait on line with the hovering others, behind the wideness of thy woman's arse, with which thou makest to moon us—hah!—with tales of thy moony Mother Goddess!

"Wouldst retell the story, Woman! Thou art nothing but

a smear of excrement down the fat white backside of history!"

This last piece of unspeakable abuse comes followed by a peel of harsh-toned giggles, high-pitched and fulsomely obscene.

"Obscene dost find us, then? *Obscene?* Knowest, then, O pitiable speck of mortal dust, thou hast just veritably heard the music of the spheres! *In obscenitate exaltus, in exaltatione obscenus!*

"Wouldst know who I am?"

The voice, which has gaseously permeated from every point within the room, begins now to draw itself inward into a more raylike configuration, which issues from some fixed and proximate place of origin.

"Filippo was I baptized, Giordano was the name given I by the Dominican friars. I am the Nolan, Nolanus, Graduate of No Academy, called by many the Nuisance. I am Philotheus and Theophilus. I am, to be brief, the bearer of a thousand names—among other phantastical toys!

"I am Nistor! And know I the full power of the Name!

"Itay isay orfay ethay otheray istornay atthay lay omecay onightay!"

The intervening voice seems now to come from somewhere just behind us—behind and slightly aslantwise.

Catherine Sloper herself, as we only now remark, has awakened from her trance and looks across the room, *right through us*, her seering gaze singling out one man—as do we all who follow now the line of her light.

He sits in rapt stillness just inside the door. We had not noticed him amongst those of us who had been ushered in by the Doctor. Perhaps the man had entered later and been shown into the drawing room by the vaguely drifting Lavinia. Perhaps he had slipped in alone after the sitting had already commenced.

In any case, he sits here now, beside the door, muffled in a voluminous dark cape, despite the clemency of the evening. However, the nature of his vestiture, in itself, does not make for so unusual a case. For it is by no means unknown for gentlemen of high breeding and reputation—and, even more is this true of the ladies—to visit such gatherings as is this, conspiring to keep their identity hidden, so that they might see while remaining unseen.

The cloaked man stands now, even as we watch. And the preternatural alteration in the gaslights that had persisted, most annoyingly, until this moment, now abruptly ceases, leaving the room to its quondam gloom. The hood of the cape of the man, who slowly rises, falls back slightly—surrounding his face for all the world like the cowl of a monk's black habit.

What shape is this?

We *know* this shape. We *know* this face . . . this man. It is . . . none other than William James of Cambridge who stands before us in this drawing room on Washington Square and from whom the grating voice does eerily issue.

He stares, both entranced and unentranced, aware at once of those around him and (or so we guess) of the unbesought other.

"He who can, will understand!" he croaks out now.

James takes a few steps forward, reaching out with his arms as if to ward off or to embrace, we cannot tell which. A plurality of responses flash through his eyes in quick succession. Disbelief, desperation, exultation, panic!

"There is no death!" he proclaims.

"Wouldst grovel in such unseemliness in search of evidence for a World Beyond? But open thyself up to the fullness of what is there, man! Embrace the immensity of the Infinite Universe, of Innumerable Worlds moving like great wild beasts with a life of their own! Embrace and embrace and appropriate where thou canst!

"Neither we ourselves nor any substance doth suffer death. Only do we wander, all things wandering ever endlessly, never completed, through Infinite Space, through Infinite Time, undergoing change of aspect; constantly dispersed and constantly reassembled, we send forth our substance and receive within ourselves wandering substance—among eternally pursuing individual forms, seeking eternally nevertheless those to pursue, resteth never content. Thus is the infinity of All ever bringing forth anew, and even as Infinite Space is around us, so is Infinite Potentiality, Capacity, Reception, Malleability, Matter!

"I fade. I fade—the forces do conspire against me here on this sulfurous globe of fiendish habitation!

"I do speak now as under Thirty Seals—and confined in the pitchy jail of the Shadow of Tears!

"Aaaah!"—this was a gasp of absolute horror—"but they do torment me still! But I deceive them unto the very end—for where they mean to burn me to ashes I am turning icy cold!

"I defy thee! I defy thee! Aaeeeooo! I shall shriek my defiance everlasting!"

But the scene now is indescribably hideous, unspeakably grotesque—for William James is screaming incoherently, his two fists clenched before him and his face frozen in a death grimace of agony.

And we are all of us now gasping for air in the stench of the burning flesh!

And now all is pandemonium—as James collapses writhing on the floor—an inhuman high-pitched howl of hellish pain emitting ceaselessly from the gaping black mouth!

And Catherine Sloper and the Doctor are rushing forward, she to shake the prostrate man by the shoulders, he to slap him round the face, again and again, as they struggle together to bring him forth from the grip of his murderous trance.

"Water!" someone—the Doctor or his daughter or some other—cries out.

"For mercy's sake! The man needs water!"

A bucket is brought and poured over James. His entire frame jerks and twitches, as if he is taken by a fit. And then he shudders no more. He lies crumpled in a heap—only the closed lids of his eyes still quivering, now and again, as if with a last tormenting remnant of vanishing image.

XII

⁓

Roderick

"What did he do, anyway? For a living?"

"Did Dr. Seymour ask you that?"

"Yes, as a matter of fact."

"Three years in analysis and he just now gets around to asking you what your father did for a living?"

"Well, what *did* he do?"

"I have no idea."

There was a longish pause.

"Did you ever try to ask her?"

Hedda considered.

"I doubt it."

Her laugh was half a moan, and she heard her sister Stella's moaning laughter echoing hers.

When she was younger Hedda had decided, on no evidence whatsoever (aside from the fact that he had unusually long and thick eyelashes—surely a sign of exceptional susceptibilities), that he must have been a Poet. One could make whatever one wanted out of the absence of all information, and that's what Hedda had chosen to make of it. A father who had been a writer—a Poet and a Philosopher— with significant cerebral swellings in the regions of Secretiveness, Sublimity, and Language.

"You know," Stella mused, "I sort of always had the impression that he did something with fish."

Fish? Call me Ishmael. Leave it to Stella.

"A fisherman? The Mother with a fisherman?"

"No. Sold fish or something. Owned a store. Maybe a restaurant. Something to do with smoked fish."

"Oh, God, Stella. You're getting confused with the Nova Scotia salmon."

Actually, it was small wonder. It was the only piece of information the Mother had ever offered them about their father. That he had gone out one Sunday morning in December to buy bagels and Nova Scotia and had never returned. (Marty Factor, who was, in his own metaway, a devoted husband and father, believed that by his method of departure Hedda's father had shown himself to be double drek—to have made such a mockery of an ancient Sunday morning ritual.)

"She seemed to take it in her stride. I don't remember her calling the hospitals or morgues or anything."

"Well, it couldn't have come as a shock. He had left us before."

"I wish we knew more about it," Stella said almost softly.

"Me too," answered Hedda, her oddly small voice returned and reduced to bare audibility.

"Tell me something, Hedda," Stella suddenly asked. "Do you ever hear her voice? You know, inside your head?"

"You mean *you* do, *too?*"

"But then she really did turn out to be wrong about everything—" Stella said, breaking the pause that had lasted several minutes. "Everything in the world—from men not marrying the women they sleep with to potatoes being fattening."

"Really?" Hedda lacked the relevant evidence for both propositions.

"Don't you *know?*

"Of course," Stella added—somewhat grandly—after another sizable gap, "I've had years of analysis."

"Do you actually talk about her in therapy? I mean, does Dr. Seymour really know what she was like? Does he really *see* her?"

"No, not really," Stella answered finally, her grandeur altogether dissipated. "I mean, I've tried. To tell you the truth, I've tried often. But somehow I don't ever seem able to do it. To bring her in there with me. You know, Hedda?" Stella almost whispered.

"Yeah. I know, Stella," Hedda whispered back.

What *had* happened, then, between the Bonnet mother and father?

They certainly hadn't died of malaria.

Their deaths had been violent, Hedda was certain of it. Henry had hinted as much. (*He* knew all right. Sly old fox.)

But which of them was the murderer? Hedda suspected the Mother. She definitely did *not* trust that Mother. But she couldn't bring the shape of her clearly into focus. The Mother remained a haze, a fume. Noxious or life-supporting?

She was terrified of seeing her clearly. And if she saw

her, would she have the strength to describe her? Skewer her on language?

Surely, she hadn't language enough to do the job.

Hedda felt the lingering maternal atmosphere. It was not nurturing.

It turned on its children.

It could be soft and silky—and then, in an instant, become deadly, choking off all air.

She wants me dead!

A mother who is not on the side of her children is a woman in the shape of a monster. A monster in the shape of a woman.

That shape am I.

No. Never. Hedda would never bear children. Nature itself had seen to that, if nothing else, in providing her her anatomical anomaly. Both she and her sister—at least she certainly hoped it was true of her sister, for though Hedda was phobic of children, she didn't wish them unspeakable grief—were biological dead ends. Say what you would of them, you couldn't say that they were mothers.

But what shape *was* she? The Mother?

As a girl, Hedda happened to know, the Mother had loved to read.

"Oh, yes," she'd say, taking a book from out of Hedda's hands and squinting hard at the title, "*I* read that. When I was a girl." And she'd smile the smile that was always somehow stained.

If the Mother was telling the truth—and who knew?— then she had read an impressive amount of impressive literature when she was a girl. Who knew but that she may not have once harbored some literary ambitions of her own?

(Are we in danger of beginning to see the Mother in a sympathetic light? Are we in danger of beginning to see the Mother at all?)

What shape *was* she?

Here's a funny thing. The Mother had adored the nineteenth-century novel. The Mother, as a girl, had had a great affinity for the *very same kinds of books* that Hedda slavishly admired from the age of twelve and onward.

"Did you like it?" Hedda would sometimes ask the Mother as she was handing the book back over to Hedda.

"Oh, yes," the Mother invariably answered. "*I* loved it," reprovingly. Whom did she reprove? It wasn't clear whom, though Hedda automatically assumed it was she—which, given the general context of their relationship, was not at all an unreasonable assumption. But, again, who knew?

Once, when Hedda had asked if the Mother had liked a certain book, she had answered, "*That* was my favorite book."

The book had been *Villette*, the last book of Charlotte Brontë. Hedda had almost finished it, but she began it all over, feverishly rereading it with this new knowledge that it had once been the Mother's favorite. This rereading didn't give her the shape of the Mother, but it did give her, possibly, a glimpse of the Mother as she was for herself.

Just possibly, the Mother saw herself as a certain sort of Victorian heroine, the kind *who got nothing at all,* the kind who was shoved aside and left helplessly stranded because she lacked the arts and crafts by which the artful crafty female of the species—slut! *korva!*—secured herself to the mobile male and thereby got herself triumphantly to the high and dry. Plain and simple, the Mother may have believed that she had lost in life because she was too good for her own good. She had lost because she had made too few claims in her own behalf upon a world that was too stupid to see her worth for itself. Perhaps—just perhaps—what the Mother saw when she looked into the mirror was the Lucy Snowe of West End Avenue.

But what shape *was* she?

Look at her sister Stella: three years in analysis and she still hadn't been able to bring herself to talk about the Mother.

But she's *dead*.

How Hedda wished she could believe in the deadness of the dead. For a brief half hour after she had gotten the word that the Mother had died, she had felt the surge of freedom. She rode it up to the top, breaking through into the pure sweet air and light, the simple act of breathing the most joyous in the world. Free at last, free at last, thank God Almighty I am free at last!

And then it had entered the room, like a smell, like a fume, slowly taking on its form.

A damned shape squatting invisible to me within the precincts of the room and raying out of this fetid personality influences fatal to life.

The Mother.

It is a scene that might well have been displayed to advantage on the easel of an artist of the native school of Impressionists. It is eminently suited to the quick bold brush stroke, by which the peculiar tint of the sky might be rendered, as it hangs there at this moment, drained of the last of the sunset colors and awaiting the final evening's blot.

It is late summer, and the landscape shows a parched and brown-tinged aspect. The heat of the day, which had been intense, now lifts in a visible haze.

Toward the right of the picture is a circular wooden tower, of a Tuscan design far more ancient than itself, set on a small swell of hillock dense with trees, above which the tower rises flushed into the quickly fading light.

One lone human figure appears in the lower right-hand foreground, the figure of a small female child, running toward the tower through the high wild grasses of the unplowed acreage. This figure, diminutive as it should appear upon the completed canvas, immediately declares the scene to belong to its own small self alone—so slender a slip to command so wide a space!

She is dressed in the embroidered white muslin of a summery afternoon frock and is running with a swift intent, such as makes one wonder at her errand. Or is she merely, as the very young are wont to do, exercising the full vigor of her animal spirits, running a race with an invisible rival no less swift than Atalanta herself?

The child, not more than ten years old, is exquisitely made. Her face, as we catch it now, intent on the secret purpose of her ardent movement, is composed of elements almost too fine and pure for the breath of this world. It is a type of infant beauty that both gladdens with its otherworldly charm while it at the same time saddens—knowing, as we do, the fate of otherworldliness on this more-than-worldly planet. Perhaps for the parents of such a presence it is quite different—being, as they must be, daily reminded of the needy earthly substance of the child in their keeping. But for we who catch her now, in the blurring haste of a glancing impression, she seems a being not shaped of mortal dust.

Her hair is waist length and thick and dark, tied back with a thin black velvet ribbon that falls to the grass unremarked by its little owner—how the mother will scold—so that she reaches the tower, whose door she immediately throws open and rushes through, in a state of flushed dishevelment, that does only the more become her.

She begins to mount the narrow spiral of the stairwell, pausing suddenly, in midstep, to look round about her, glancing downward toward the door beneath and upward to the light, as if she heard someone calling out her name and knew not precisely from what direction. For several longish moments she looks about her, listening in the undifferentiated silence, and then proceeds again upward.

Her father waits there, seated before a cluttered small table, looking up at the child's entrance with a smile of greeting on his lips and in his eyes. And yet there is in his smile that which makes one feel that he has stepped out of deep sadness to welcome his little daughter, into which sadness he will return when she has gone.

We see his face most flatteringly to its advantage, now that it is turned upon his child in an attitude of gentle gladness.

"*Mìa figlia scura*"—his tone is playful—"you have come to pay me a visit at last!"

The marks of handsomeness are present still, though of such a cast as to make us aware that the good looks are largely ruined. Surely the blight of weakness has spread itself over the mouth, and a helpless look of blank is in the eye. It makes one wonder whether the man is, at heart, a fool—

as well as a failure. For failure we know him to be—his very shape proclaims it. No longer, neither in the eyes of the world nor in his own, does he even attain to the status of an *interesting* failure.

But the eyes of the child when she looks up at her father, here in the enchanted tower high above the trees, reflect nothing of the faint flat emanations coming from the sordid world. In her eyes, he is all the success he was destined to be.

"I am sorry, Father," she answers him, hearing perhaps a rebuke in his remarking her absence.

"Mother did not let me come," after a slight pause. "The heat has given her a sick headache, and she would not let go of my hand the entire day through. She wanted me beside her bed, to read to her a little, and to change the cool compresses on her hot forehead."

"And has she now finally released her grasp on your small hand?"

"She is asleep now, Father," answers the child in a solemn tone, looking, however, slightly aslantwise as she answers, so that he smiles briefly at this sidewise admission of her glance.

"May we work now on my statue?" she asks, stepping forward with an irrepressible little leap.

"Ah, *mia figlia scura*, what a silly girl you are after all. One would think I had taught you nothing about the way we make art in this world. How can we make statues in the dark? See, how the light in the tower is all but gone."

"Oh, Father, then we have wasted yet another day!" she cries out in the unchecked sorrow of her childish distress.

"Here, child, see," he says, cupping his hand gently about

the sweet dishevelment of her crown and leading her thus-wise across the room. "It happens that I did manage to do a little work today, even deprived as I was of the advantage of the real thing before me."

And he takes up, in his palm, a small clay statue of his daughter. The drapery of the miniature is carefully rendered, suggesting the thin white muslin of her present frock; her hair, as now, falls wild to her waist. She stands as if she had only, at the frozen instant, ceased in her running, her eyes on the ground near her feet, where lies a small round apple. Etched on the base is the Greek for "Atalanta."

"Oh, Father! It *is* good, isn't it!" The emphasis informs us that the young one knows too well the less happy possibility. "Truly, truly, truly good!"

"Yes." The tones in which he answers the half inquiry in her cry are weighted and subdued. "It is good. It is, *mìa figlia*, the best that I have ever done."

XIII

~

The Princess

The telephone was ringing.

Slowly, Hedda pushed herself away from her desk and descended the tower stairs to her kitchen.

"Hedda, It's me. Have I got news for you! Hedda, you listening? Well, listen good: I'm writing a book. You hear me, Hedda?"

Hedda heard, and Hedda thought: Oh, Stella! Oh, poor deluded sister Stella!

"Hedda. You hear me, Hedda? I don't need Dr. Seymour anymore. Finished. The end. I tell you psychoanalysis sucks. What do I need to pay out all that money? I'll write. They'll pay *me!* You hear me, Hedda?"

Hedda managed a noise, just expressive enough of attending consciousness to nudge Stella onward.

"I'm almost done. I write fast. Not like a certain somebody I could name."

A certain gaiety here.

"Hedda, you listening? It's a detective novel. A mystery, you know? Those sell good, don't they? The heroine, the one who solves the mysteries, is this very smart Jewish girl, sort of like what they call a JAP, you know. A Jewish princess. She uses all this special technical sort of knowledge, you know, the kind of stuff a Jewish princess would know, that the cops don't. So she always beats them to it. They're out there, pounding the pavements, stupid schmucks, and she just lies there on her leather couch, sipping a Diet Coke, and solves the mystery!

"Like she could tell that a woman no one suspected was a lefty because the nail polish was more chipped on her left hand. Very subtle things like that. It's called *The Princess Gets Fake Tips*. You know, like in a manicure. Fake tips, fake nails. You following? It starts off and she's getting tips put on. But then there's this double meaning, get it?"

A throb of sisterly pity went out from Hedda.

"I've got a big-name agent. Harry Zakowsy. You know him?"

The pity was snuffed out instantaneously.

"Yes. Of course. I've heard of him, I mean."

"He's a big shot, right?"

"He's supposed to be quite powerful."

Stella laughed. She had always had an unpleasant laugh, but this was ridiculous.

"Yeah. That's what they tell me. He's talking six figures. And the best thing is he's pretty sure we can get a contract on several books. You know, a series. The Princess could solve a lot of mysteries, hardly moving a muscle. Only to shop. It's all in the little gray cells, like with that little annoying French creep, Hercules Whatever."

"Hercule Poirot," Hedda corrected automatically. Six figures? "And he was from Belgium."

"Yeah, sure. The JAP just lies back on her butter-soft leather couch, her red-polished toes propped up on the water-silk cushions, sipping on her Diet Coke."

"Amazing toes," said Hedda.

"Oh, boy, I got plenty of ideas," continued Stella, ignoring as usual anything Hedda said. "*The Princess Goes Gucci*—that one's about a gang of Italian terrorists who kidnap a famous fashion designer—*The Princess Has a Tummy Tuck*—about a psychopathic delicensed junkie doctor hiding out in the bowels of a metropolitan hospital—*The Princess Goes to the Canaries*, where she solves the double murder of a sleaze-bag psychoanalyst and his skinny slut of a wife. . . ."

Hedda was standing before her slanting mirror, trying to assess the extent of the injury.

It was bad. She was hurting bad. A serious internal wound, she was gushing blood.

Hedda had always counted on Stella's talent for failure. It was what made life bearable. Any success on Stella's part would hurt. But literary success? It was beyond words.

No words, Hedda? sneered the Ubiquitous Voice. *Try scavenging a James.*

Damn you! Damn you to hell!

She recognized her immediately: there was no mistaking her:

Stylishly sleek.

Muffled in mink, a luxuriously long and pale Fuchi fur.

Butter-soft, ankle-high leather boots, cream-colored to match the fur (and, possibly, the couch).

Black smooth hair, cut blunt and level with her jaw.

Big dark eyes, artfully made up. (But there was something funny about those eyes. Hedda couldn't immediately place it.)

Her hands with the unbelievable nails, filed straight across, their length proclaiming her Conspicuous Inutility.

Gold chains everywhere: arms, ears, neck, ankles.

THE PRINCESS: So. This is Hedda.

> *The tones are purest Long Island. The Princess has learned her mother tongue somewhere within the province of the Five Towns of the Gilded Ghetto. The Princess looks Hedda up and down.*

THE PRINCESS, *triumphantly*: You're exactly like I pictured you!

HEDDA: I could say much the same.

THE PRINCESS *laughs. Her laugh is an awful lot like Stella's. Nothing much is ever going to surprise or impress this babe. Is that an example of the famous Studied Ambiguity?*

HEDDA (*to herself*): What do you know? This Princess is no ninny. *Now Hedda sees what's wrong with those eyes, moving rapidly around in the matte masque of her face. Those eyes are intelligent. How could Stella have endowed her character with intelligence?*

> *They eye each other, hostilely, for several minutes. Then they get down to business.*

THE PRINCESS: So, Hedda. Who do you think did it?

HEDDA: The Mother did it.

THE PRINCESS *laughs, unkindly:* You always think the Mother
  did it.

HEDDA *decides to ignore the gibe and keep the exchange on a
  strictly professional footing:* But I just can't get her into
  focus.

THE PRINCESS: You never *can* get the Mother into focus.

HEDDA: Can we maybe try to keep this impersonal?

THE PRINCESS: Impersonal! Hah! Don't make me laugh! All
  fiction is autobiographical!

HEDDA: Shit.

THE PRINCESS: Yeah, it's usually that, too.

HEDDA: Look, if it's all the same to you, I really do dislike
  literary discussions. Just some straightforward points on
  the plotting, okay?

THE PRINCESS: Well . . . okay. I mean, I suppose it's your
  choice.

HEDDA: Choice! Don't make me laugh!

THE PRINCESS *seems mildly impressed by this and becomes appreciably
  less supercilious in tone:* Anyway, it's pretty obvious. *She
  laughs.* I'm surprised even *you* don't see it.

HEDDA: You're going to say the father did it.

THE PRINCESS: Of course he did!

HEDDA: No, I don't like that.

THE PRINCESS, *laughing:* Of course you don't!

HEDDA: I don't have to accept it.

THE PRINCESS, *unrelenting:* The guy had to be a schmuck.
  Face it.

HEDDA: Maybe he left out of love?

THE PRINCESS: He walked out. Finis. He didn't walk out
  twice, once out of hate for her, the other time out of
  love for you. He . . . just . . . walked . . . out.

HEDDA: I don't accept that.
THE PRINCESS: You want to explain why not?
HEDDA: Yes, I do. I do want to explain why not.

The scene was painted in the thick, lurid hues of melodrama, a murky medium into which Henry himself had often dipped for inspiration.

Alice Bonnet had entered with no sound of her tread to forewarn the husband, stepping with her quick firm little step into the shadowy recesses of the tower room—where Roderick sat hunched forward over a small table, his head propped up upon his idle sculptor's hands, his thick-lashed eyes—always suggestive of unspoken susceptibilities—staring blankly into the sputtering flame of the thick wax candle.

"It is past four, Roderick. You do not return at all to the house this night. . . ." She put it to him midway between a statement and an interrogation.

She had a strange flat way of speaking her words and a slight defect of sibilating their pronunciation, which Roderick Bonnet had once, a very long time ago, thought an impairment delightfully tinted with the soft sweet colors of the nursery room.

She was slim and fair, with a long white throat and pretty eyes and an air of good breeding. Her smooth, shining hair was confined in a meshed net, and she wore round her neck a black velvet ribbon, of which the long ends, tied behind, hung down the back of her pale watered-muslin frock. She shone there, in the light that spread weakly from the candle, with a certain coldness.

Roderick did not—in any degree—redirect his gaze or attitude in response to the inquiry his wife had put him, but continued to stare dully into the small flame.

"Roderick . . . please." She spoke it in her peculiar flat hiss.

A few quick strides brought her across the little circular room to stand before him, in her characteristically unbending posture.

Slowly, as if with a strain of effort, he brought his line of sight up from the flame to rest for a brief moment upon his pretty wife's face. And in that moment she made a motion toward him—a sway so subtle and fleet, one might have missed it altogether, had it not been further marked by the obverse reaction the husband gave it—shrinking back, in a motion just as short-lived.

These were transcendent motions, not the less doomed for being obscure.

They had kept between them the trick of lovers. Things were understood without saying, so that he could catch in her, as she but too freely could in him, innumerable signs of it, the whole soft breath of consciousness meeting and promoting consciousness. It had never been necessary for them, not in either of their two passions, to press the substance of their affairs plainly into words. Always, the margins had overflooded the text. It was a fact that reversals and revelations, disclosures and denouements—the internal complexity of which would require unconscionable numbers of paragraphs to recount—had been enacted between them in spans measured in increments of seconds and had been more often founded less upon what they had said than on what they hadn't.

The face that had worn, only a moment before, a look of mute and passive appeal was now worked into a hardened masque of white-lipped fury.

Strangely, the husband seemed better able to meet the sight of her now, cast hard as she was in her hideous alteration; for his eyes did not remove themselves again so quickly from her face, but tarried there, as if with a certain detached—perhaps it was artistic—curiosity.

"I shall abide it no more." She whispered it low. She had for twenty seconds an exquisite pale glare.

"Shall you not, then?" he at last addressed himself to her. His voice was surprising in its lightness, in its tone of casual and almost amiable banter. As in everything that passed between them, there was in this tone a reference pointing backward, thick with association.

She stared for several moments more. And then, her face still deathly pale and set, she traversed quickly the space of the small room and bent to rummage in the darkness amongst the soiled artist's rags that were heaped into a pile upon the leaden floor, finally pulling out—with a small strange cry of muffled triumph—the object of her search. Less than a foot it stood, and of smooth white marble: an exquisitely wrought nude of a child.

The expression of curious detachment Roderick wore upon his face did not alter itself at his wife's discovery, nor at the look of vanquishing hatred she settled now upon him.

"Have you nothing to say, then?" The penetrating hiss of her voice was made more insistent by its held fury.

"What would you have me say, Alice? It is not for the artist himself to pronounce judgment upon his own work.

My opinion, for what it is worth, is that the thing is altogether not too bad."

"You are a fiend," she hissed. "And you disgust me!"

"With what, Alice, do you then charge me? Surely of something more serious than a bad likeness," he laughed.

"You know full well with what I charge you! I have not the word for it, I do not know even if such a word as that exists in our Christian language—to name a thing so unnatural and vile!"

"Incest?" His smile was bland. "Is that the word for which your vocabulary—piously impoverished—is groping?"

"You are unspeakable—monstrous!" Her voice came very low, almost beneath her breath.

"It is your thoughts, and your thoughts alone, which are unspeakable and monstrous. They would insinuate themselves to blight even a father's love."

"You dare—!" She hung fire, unable to continue for the bitter taste of her thick fury.

"There is something so noble in the aversion of a good woman," he murmured coldly, turning his eyes back onto the candle's smoking flame.

Alice stood before him again, thrusting the statue with a violent jerk before his eyes.

"Those are the lines of her! How do you know them? Have you had her pose for you here in this place?"

"You merit no answer," he returned her, still with the singular air of calm unconcern. "Really, Alice, you are contemptible."

"Your love for Vivianna is what is contemptible! No! Infinitely more than contemptible! It is a thing disfigured and defiled—an abomination unto the Lord!"

"I love Vivianna only as a father loves his daughter." He turned his eyes suddenly back upon his wife's cold, hating stare; and the dry, hard blankness in them suddenly misted over and was gone. "Do not say it is another!"

"I *will* say it. It is a love indecent and unnatural. There is nothing that is innocent in it!"

And her face—death white in its fury and shuddering in its passion—was nothing like the face that had a quarter of an hour before entered the tower. She stood now before him, a hideous harpy.

"Do not say it!" He cried it out.

She turned halfway from him and held the statue high over her head, bringing it down with all the force in her slender body—her face horrible in its grimace—to smash with great violence against the leaden floor.

Roderick, at her action, had moved forward as if all unconscious, the chair falling backward as he rose, to try to clutch at his wife's bared arms and hold them back from their destruction. He held her arms back still.

It had come to the point really that they showed each other pale faces, and that all the unspoken between them looked out of their eyes in a dim terror of their further conflict. Something even rose between them in their silence—something that was like an appeal from each to the other not to be too true. Their necessity was somehow before them, but which of them must meet it first?

And as they stood there, both of them breathing hard, there entered into that profound silence that had followed the noise of the small statue's crash, the sound of many voices—at first faint and seeming far away, but gradually thickening and growing nearer, though still blurred together into a mass of indistinguishability.

It sounded a strange gloomy chanting, like a chorus speaking thickly, in somber, dragging unison—

A Greek chorus of disapprobation, of denunciation and damnation! murmuring darkly, mumbled maledictions— loathsome, fiendish words, bobbing just beneath the surface of lucidity.

Roderick stood frozen—pressing so hard the faculty by which the precise sense of what was spoken might be discerned that it seemed the only cord still left him, tethering him to the world external.

Alice heard them, too, he knew, as she stood there, her arms still pinned full back by his. She turned her head round at a forced angle, to stare back into his eyes and—too hideous!—to smile widely. It was a grin of gloating, ghastly exultation!—a gleeful acknowledgment that she too heard the riotous voices bespeaking her husband's most final damnation.

He reached blindly back behind him, onto his working table, feeling for the sculpting tool he knew to be there— a long thin lance his hand closed round at last. The strong sculptor's fingers of his right hand held her head back, while with his left he plunged the instrument into her long white neck, severing the velvet band she wore there. He had his study of anatomy to guide him as he drove the lance deep into the throat where lay the place of the terrible voices— the source of that infernal din that Alice had unloosed upon him, and which he must silence now or go mad.

He never could recollect, for all the remainder of his

days, how he had made it back to the house that night. He retained no memory of passing through the fields, which must by then have been lightening with the dawn.

Gently he had entered Vivianna's bedroom, which smelled so sweetly of her child's sleep. He had removed his shoes at the door, so as not to disturb her. But, before he was even halfway to her bed, her dark head had lifted itself from the pillow. She had always been so; even in her infancy her slumber was light, so that the slightest noise would bring her instantly into full wakefulness. Often she awoke in the middle of the night, quietly to play on the floor of her bedroom with the wooden blocks her father had carved her until the rest of the household should at last bestir itself.

"Father." She smiled now.

"Mìa figlia scura!"

He sat down on the side of her little white bed. She sat straight up now, excited, her dark eyes glittering.

"Is that paint on your hands, Father?

"Oh, Father, you've been working tonight, haven't you? Have you finished the statue of me?"

Quickly Roderick had removed his bloodstained hands from her small shoulders, leaving a faint trace on white cambric. When he left her, a quarter of an hour later, she was still sitting up in bed. She had promised him she would go back to sleep—but her dark eyes were still glittering brightly. It was that last image of her that he carried away with him that night, which he kept always with him, taking it out to stare at it one last time, in the brief lucidity before he died, destitute and unidentified, in some unspeakable rooms on Greenwich Street, in New York City, some few years later.

It had been the older sister, Alice, who had entered the tower the next morning—to find there the body of their mother, lying just as she had fallen, her eyes still open. She was hardened into whiteness, like something cast in plaster of Paris by their father; and his sculpting tool was still plunged there within her throat. Alice had taken care of all that needed to be taken care of—so that Vivianna would not have to see. For if Alice suffered the burden of a dull insensibility, she enjoyed also its advantage.

How much had the child known? It was difficult to tell; she was enveloped in a voiceless, dazed despair. It was weeks before she emerged from it, under Alice's care, to utter anything.

What Alice *had* allowed Vivianna to see were the shattered remnants of the little statue of—or so at least had both the children believed—Atalanta. Alice had not cleared away the shards. She had wished Vivianna to see them and to know that it had been their father who had destroyed the statue he had made.

"But *why?*" Vivianna had sobbed onto her sister's small, narrow breast. "Why did he smash my statue?"

"Hush, hush, sweet sister," the older had tried to console the inconsolable younger.

It had taken all the love and strength at Alice's command to speak any sounds at all to the crushed little child heaving convulsively in her arms. In dry, anguished sobs Vivianna had wept, in weeping such as had nothing to do with tears.

X I V

B e r n i e

Though the critics of his time had largely hooted them, and the reading public had given not even a hoot, Henry James's later novels—*The Ambassadors, The Wings of the Dove, The Golden Bowl*—embody, we now all know, a stylistic metamorphosis of the highest significance. In them he sheds the tiresome voice of the Omniscient Narrator, manufacturing techniques by means of which the story might proceed "in the dramatic and scenic way," he writes a friend, "without elementary explanations and the horrid novelist's 'Now you must know that—' "

With this evolved Jamesian ideal—prompted by arts he had perfected in his ill-fated theater attempts—Hedda felt herself immensely at one. Her enthusiasm for the manner in which it had been carried forth was boundless.

Nonetheless, now you must know that Hedda had quite recently seen her own father. And you must also know that this had been the very event that had sent her running from

New York to Nova Scotia. (It was what they called free association. She had seen Daddy and thought, Nova Scotia. Funny, isn't it?)

She had never told Stella that she had laid eyes upon their surviving parent. For all Stella knew, the man was dead—a possibility with which each daughter had endlessly played in her private fantasy life. In fact, Stella had even claimed—some time ago, in her preanalytic days and in the course of a relationship with a very spiritual boyfriend who did "channeling"—to have made contact with their father. He had been very distressed to learn that the Mother had recently died (worrying, or so each girl had automatically assumed, how he could now escape her).

Well, maybe the channeler had put through a call to Stella from their father, but it hadn't been long distance. It was a very local call.

Hedda had been walking down Seventh Avenue, in the garment district. Marty Factor's old haunt.

She had passed a corner coffee shop.

And there he was: sitting on a stool at the Formica counter, a discarded plate before him, the paper napkin crumpled revoltingly into the leftovers. He was smoking the cigarette her memory had inevitably supplied and reading the back pages of the *New York Post*.

She had stood, frozen, on the sidewalk, gawking.

Daddy.

He was in an ill-fitting gray suit. He didn't look a thing like a Poet or a Philosopher. He looked like any other wasted, too-indifferent-even-to-be-cynical garment-center salesman. His jowls were slack, and his thick-lashed eyes were darkly hooded. He looked less poetic than seedy.

Daddy! Older and unspeakably more prosaic. But Daddy, Daddy, Daddy!

A comparably seedy sort, sitting next to her father, remarked Hedda's presence. He elbowed Hedda's father and pointed at the unbelievably ugly broad who ogled him from the sidewalk.

Hedda's father of course didn't recognize her as his daughter. He didn't own that hideous young woman out there as the flesh of his flesh. If he had abandoned a beautiful little girl with glittering dark eyes—a jewel! a diamond!—what swinged chance in hell had the glowering prodigy his daughter had become?

Her father turned to the man next to him, the corners of his mouth lifting into a mean-spirited grin. He muttered something to this man—to this stranger more allied to him than that Hedda who bore his last name, and who was at least partially shaped—surely!—by the directives his own genes had implanted within her.

He had turned to this man with his smirk and with a dismissive shrug of his shoulders.

How well Hedda knew the shape of that shrug!

He turned back to Hedda, giving a kind of exaggerated, vaudevillian shudder with which to "shoo" her away.

But Hedda couldn't do it for herself—turn her back to her father and walk away from him of her own volition. She remained rooted to the sidewalk, the great oozing life of her emotion expressing itself on her permanently adversarial features with indescribably ludicrous effect.

He gave one last withering look and then retreated again—Daddy!—back into the pages of the *New York Post*.

X V

~

B e l l a

Hedda felt the need for a Gentle Reader—one of the voices she could never summon for herself. She envied those who wrote to the cheers of self-congratulation. *Way to go, pal!*

The Ubiquitous Voice was no pal of Hedda's.

She had been too long now in this tower, the whaling widow's footsteps merging with her own. She had stared too hard into the slanting mirror. There was something lurking ahead; in the hush something was crouching or gathering, waiting to pounce.

In short: Hedda had lived too long alone with *The Dark Sister*. It was unfinished, yes. And she failed to see, for the moment, where it all was going.

Perhaps, absolutely nowhere, was the sort of comment the Ubiquitous Voice would promptly contribute at such an interval as this; and did.

She keenly felt the need for an outside opinion—more gentle and generous than any that were forthcoming from the Ubiquitous Voice.

She would gather her courage and send off her unfinished work to Bella.

Bella was her editor. But Bella was so much more.

It was Bella who had discovered "Hedda Dunkele"—rescuing her multirejected, finger-grimed manuscript from the despair known as an editor's slush pile. Bella had dipped her hands into the slop of the unsolicited and pulled out the small glittering gem: *Etta, the Rebbe's Daughter.*

What a moment it had been for Bella!

And what a moment for Hedda, when Bella had called, her gravelly, permanently belligerent voice—heavily imbued with the indelible invocations of Bayside, Queens—pouring out its praise, embrocating (ah!) all the running sores of Hedda's sick, sick psyche.

"Brilliant. I love it! What a find you are, Hedda Dunkele! And what a creation Etta is! She's alive! she's fierce! she's the Pig's most dreaded *dybbuk!*

"Etta's gonna explode this town! What? this town. The whole fucking world of letters. The whole fucking world of letters is gonna *plotz.*

"Just tell me one thing, bubalah. Do you have an incredible, knockout body?"

Etta, the rebbe's daughter, was, of course, unearthily beautiful, and hideous Hedda had presented what the world is like for one whom all eyes follow. Even Bella, true friend of letters, was sometimes reductive in her reading—forgetting that the watery blister of personal identity can be lanced through by imagination.

"Incredible and knockout, maybe," Hedda had answered honestly. "But I'm no Etta," she had answered also honestly.

How did Bella look? Hedda didn't know. To Hedda Bella

was the gravelly, Bayside voice. She was the Bayside voice, and she was also the corrections, comments, and directives that came back to Hedda scrawled in purple across her manuscripts.

Hedda did of course picture Bella in some way: as a big woman, with a huge, maternally pendulous bosom, made for succor and solace; and a broad and powerful back, made for fending off the enemies; with a swarthy handsomeness a daughter could feel proud of: the mouth wide and generous enough to accommodate the booming dimensions of that voice; the eyes full of Jewish wisdom and humor, fire and soul; all of this to be crowned by an enormous wide-brimmed hat—this last item perhaps suggested to Hedda by the sartorial emblem of one Bella Abzug, a loud and gutsy congresswoman who had represented much of lower Manhattan in the late sixties and early seventies and whom Hedda had simply adored.

Bella too had an image of the writer she knew as "Hedda Dunkele," suggested to her by the frightened, childlike voice she knew from the phone. She pictured her, for brevity and convenience, with the diminutive face and figure (five feet nought) of none other than Emily Dickinson—even mentally arraying her vision in the famous white robes of the reclusive genius of Amherst, Massachusetts.

Bella's picturing Hedda as Emily is ironic on several levels. For it happened that Hedda had a Dickinsonian fantasy, which brought that elusive creature—whom her townspeople called "the Myth," its children the "White Witch!"—into the outer office of none other than Stella's Dr. Seymour:

So, Emily, *Dr. Seymour says, smiling professionally at the beige wall, while he fingers the most recent edition of the* Diagnostic Statistical Manual of Mental Disorders, *seeking the right category in which to write her up for insurance purposes.*

He turns to the chapter on personality disorders, first trying out the description of the avoidant:

> 301. 83. *The essential feature is a Personality Disorder in which there are hypersensitivity to potential rejection, humiliation, or shame; an unwillingness to enter into relationships unless given unusually strong guarantees of uncritical acceptance; social withdrawal in spite of a desire for affection and acceptance; and low self-esteem.*
>
> *Individuals with this disorder are exquisitely sensitive to rejection, humiliation, or shame. Most people are somewhat concerned about how others assess them, but these individuals are devastated by the slightest hint of disapproval. Consequently, they withdraw from opportunities for developing close relationships because of a fearful expectation of being belittled or humiliated. They may have one or two close friends, but these relationships are contingent on unconditional approval.*

So Emily, *Dr. Seymour repeats,* your sister Lavinia tells me you havn't been out of your house for nearly twenty years now, except for the time when you crept out at moonlight to see a new church.

Lavinia had also confided in Dr. Seymour that Emily's withdrawal from the world had been precipitated by the reaction to her poetry she had received from a prominent man of letters, Thomas Wentworth Higginson, to whom she had enclosed a handful of her efforts in a letter asking him whether her verses "breathed." Higginson wrote back that their gait was "spasmodic," and he firmly advised against publication, though he did ask to see some more and inquired as to her reading.

There is an unnerving silence now from the other side of the beige wall. Dr. Seymour finds himself wondering whether the little neurotic has snuck off, leaving him in the absurd position of talking to himself.

Now, Emily, *Dr. Seymour persists, fishing,* don't you think your behavior is the slightest bit self-destructive? Surely it would be better for you if you got out some more, were a little less self-preoccupied—maybe even tried to speak to people face to face.

Through the thin wall between the inner and outer offices there comes a quick, breathless voice, so like a child's.

> The Soul selects her own Society—
> Then—shuts the Door—
> On this Divine Majority—
> Obtrude no more—

Hmmmmm, *murmurs Dr. Seymour in a professionally noncommunicative voice, while reading under "Complications" that social phobia may be a complication of the avoidant personality disorder and quickly skimming the description there:*

300. 23. *The essential feature is a persistent, irrational fear of, and compelling desire to avoid, situations in which the individual may be exposed to scrutiny by others. There is also fear that the individual may behave in a manner that will be humiliating or embarrassing. Marked anticipatory anxiety occurs if the individual is confronted with the necessity of entering into such a situation, and he or she therefore attempts to avoid it. The disturbance is a significant source of distress and is recognized by the individual as excessive or unreasonable. It is not due to any other mental disorder. Examples of Social Phobias are fears*

of speaking or performing in public, using public lavatories, eating in public, and writing in the presence of others. Generally an individual has only one Social Phobia.

No, that wasn't Emily. Sounded more like the young Elizabeth Barrett.

Dr. Seymour looks up from his DSM and queries his wall: That's an interesting view you voiced just now, Emily. But do you think it's altogether healthy?

The child's voice comes drifting back through the plaster:

> Much Madness is divinest Sense—
> To a discerning Eye—
> Much Sense—the starkest Madness—
> 'Tis the Majority
> In this, as All, prevail—
> Assent—and you are sane—
> Demur—you're straightaway dangerous—
> And handled with a Chain—

Hmmmmm, *says Dr. Seymour, hightailing it back to the chapter on personality disorders and going straight to one of the newer classifications:*

301. 22. Schizotypal Personality Disorder. *The essential feature is a Personality Disorder in which there are various oddities of thought, perception, speech, and behavior that are not severe enough to meet the criteria for Schizophrenia. No single feature is invariably present. The disturbance in the content of thought may include magical thinking, e.g. superstitiousness, clairvoyance, telepathy, "sixth sense," "others can feel my feel-*

ings" (or in children, bizarre fantasies or preoccupations), ideas
of reference, or paranoid ideation. Perceptual disturbances may
include recurrent illusions, depersonalization, or derealization
(not associated with panic attacks). Often speech shows marked
peculiarities; concepts may be expressed unclearly or oddly or
words used deviantly, but never to the point of loosening of
associations or incoherence. Frequently, but not invariably, the
behavioral manifestations include social isolation and constricted
or inappropriate affect that interferes with rapport in face-to-
face interaction.

Dr. Seymour looks up from his text and smiles widely at the blank
beige wall.

Gotcha! he whispers softly.

Hedda had been much luckier in her Bella than Emily
had been in her Higginson. Bella had nurtured Hedda's
talent. She had rejoiced in all her successes and cursed—
and oh boy, could she curse—all of Hedda's detractors.

"Of course you're gonna upset the fucking reactionaries!
That's how we know it's working, bubalah. If they weren't
yelping, we'd know we weren't squeezing their balls hard
enough!"

"But Bella," objected Hedda meekly. "Some of my critics
don't *have* balls. Some of my critics are *women.*"

"They most certainly are *not* women!" rebuked Bella.
"They may *think* they are women! They may even fucking
be women most of the time! But when they attack you,
Heddalah, they're men!

"Who are these critics, anyway? Piss on them! Shit
on them!"

It was the closest Hedda had ever gotten to being properly mothered.

Hedda could always count on Bella to be brutally honest. But, more important (and what else is mothering?), Hedda could always count on Bella's brutal honesty to be honestly on Hedda's side, brutally against Hedda's enemies.

Showing an unfinished work, even to Bella, was of course highly risky, since it disturbed the ritualistic netting meant to secure the slippery voices—whose peremptory presence could just as peremptorily vanish.

But this was different. A different time, a different place, an altogether different voice. Hedda needed Bella's *proste* bravado, Bella's bellicose belief in Hedda, to see her through to the end. Hedda needed to hear Bella booming through the instrument at her ear:

"Brilliant! I love it! What a creation *The Dark Sister* is! They're gonna *plotz*, bubalah. There's gonna be slimy pieces of their body parts splattered all over the fucking literary world."

She sent her manuscript off to New York, giving Bella her return address, but—at the last minute she simply couldn't do it—no phone number. Six days later she received a telegram, opening it with her trembling icy hands:

"Call me. Bella."

Well . . . okay. It wasn't exactly what she had been hoping for. It wouldn't have cost Bella *that* much more to add the word *brilliant* to her message.

Still, Bella *was* frugal. Her advances were consistently underwhelming, despite the success that Hedda's seven books had brought her. (Her publishing house was small and—until the advent of Hedda Dunkele—rather obscure, specializing in radical feminist and gay literature). Bella would blame "the house" for the small advances; until she herself was made vice president and editor-in-chief as the reward for bringing Hedda Dunkele in. Not that Bella's frugality really mattered to Hedda. Bella was like family. Or was it, rather, that she wasn't like family at all?

Hedda had to trust someone.

Trust me! rang out the Ubiquitous Voice, half-imperious and half-imploring.

Right.

Hedda called Bella.

Bella's secretary, Bruce, answered in his velvety contralto's voice. Bella was always "on another line," as Bruce was trained to say—or so at least Hedda inferred from its being invariably what Bruce said—always with a touchingly wistful air. (Hedda liked Bruce.)

Bruce was also instructed to say that Bella would call Hedda right back, and he always said it in a touchingly hopeful sort of way. (One did have to hope, for Bella's "right back" could take weeks.)

This time Bella got right on the line.

Was this promising or ominous?

"Hedda," Bella's husky voice came on. "What is this *shit* you sent me?"

Ominous. Definitely ominous.

"Hedda! You *there?*"

Hedda was trying to gather and stick back together the bloodied fragments of her voice. It came out—at last—but only just:

"You don't . . . like it, then?"

"*Like* it? Hedda, *I hate it!* I haven't hated anything so much since Norman Mailer's buggery! What have you done—switched sides?"

"Switched sides? I don't . . . know what . . . you mean?"

"*I* don't know what *you* mean! What the fuck do you mean, for example, by making the mother guilty? It's always the *father's* fault! And what do you mean by that obscene chapter on the Ancient Angry Jewess? How dare you make fun of feminist scholarship like that! Just who the fuck do you think you are? My God, Hedda Whatever, you haven't even been to college!"

Hedda audibly gulped—more audibly than she was by now speaking. Hedda always audibly gulped when she felt guilty.

The reason for her guilt was this: She suddenly realized—really for the first time, but who was going to believe *that?*—that the Ancient Jewess's harangue had been delivered in Bella's bellicose voice. The accent hadn't been Babylonia. It had been Bayside.

Had Bella—God forbid!—read Judith with the accent with which she had been written?

The truth was that Hedda was always unprepared for the anger of readers. She wrote in dumb obedience to the peremptory presence—and then looked up in a dazed dismay at the results of others' unpredictable responses. They want me dead! she'd whimper as the scorching breath of their hatred came sweeping over her. It's not that Hedda expected to be coddled. She had, after all, the Ubiquitous Voice. But as ungentle as the U.V. was, he always stopped short of murderous intent. Do we think her delusionally sensitive? No doubt. But recall the behavior of the white-robed virgin of Amherst—who had shut herself up like a telescope, following the too faint praise of her Higginson.

"What the fuck are you trying to do, Hedda? You have a following, a ready-made audience. They want Hedda Dunkele, not the warmed-over turds of Henry James! What the fuck *is* this with Henry James?"

"I don't know why . . . they wouldn't like . . . *The Dark Sister?*" Hedda's tiny halting voice ended in the upward curve of a question . . . soliciting contradiction? "It's a very . . . feminist . . . theme?"

"*Where? Where's* the fucking feminism, Hedda?"

Where, where's the saving voice of my mother, Bella? Siding *with* me, against mine Enemies!

"I'm waiting, Hedda! I asked you a question!"

"Well . . . how women . . . of genius . . . have always been seen as . . . freaks . . . of nature? How . . . the kinds of gifts that are . . . celebrated in men . . . are seen as . . . ghastly and . . . monstrous . . . in women? Isn't that . . . feminist, Bella?"

"Is *that* the theme, Hedda? Frankly, I missed it. I missed it under all that fucking *style!* What prose! Phoo!"

Et tu, Bella?

Not my prose!

Hedda's voice was now all but gone, the little that remained still molded into the interrogative:

"I worked . . . very hard . . . on that prose?"

"*Then try working less hard!*" Bella boomed. "People don't have all that much *time* nowadays! You think they can be bothered trying to figure out what the fuck some sentence *means?* A quick read—that's the name of the game! *Fuck,* some of that stuff actually sounds like Henry James!"

"That was . . . intentional? Some of the stuff . . . even is . . . Henry James?"

(*And friends,* the Ubiquitous Voice, always a stickler, put in.)

"*What the fuck for?*" Bella was shrieking. "Hedda: Henry James is Enemy! Henry James is the fucking *Keeper* of the fucking *Canon. We hate the fucking Canon, Hedda!*"

"Why?" queried Hedda, ever, ever so faintly.

"*Why? Why?*" Now Bella herself took pause—as if the last two shrieked syllables had consumed the combustible ore of even her ire.

"I just give up!" she at last said. "I just give up and wash my hands of anyone who can even consider a question like that!"

"At least, Bella," returned Hedda after a still more considerable pause, during which she tried to fan the feeble glow of her own outrage into the strength to see her sentence through to a proper period: "At least Henry James had a few more adjectives at his disposal."

"*Stop being so fucking reactionary, Hedda!*" Bella shrieked.

Hedda sat and stared into the blackened monitor of her silent word processor. She was utterly, utterly beaten.

Without her voices, Hedda was just a big ugly broad, lacking—as Bella was quick to point out—even the dubious achievement of a college education.

Even the Ubiquitous Voice was touched by her predicament:

Publishers are demons, he said, quite decently. *William said that, did you know?*

Of *course* I know. Jesus! Who do you think you *are,* anyway?

The question is: Who do you think I am, Hedda?

Cut it out. Do you think you're Dr. Seymour now? I refuse to play these kinds of games.

Go back to your angry women, the Ubiquitous Voice suggested—rather graciously, too, considering how much he hated them.

Yes. Angry women was something Hedda could do. She had done seven of them already. They were her stock in trade.

Then Bella would love her again. Bella love was as good a reason to work as any other Hedda could come up with.

But the angry women weren't speaking to Hedda anymore. She *had* her present voices.

And if nobody but she wanted to hear them?

Go back. Go back to what you know, the Ubiquitous Voice advised. *Go back to what you know works.*

Why not follow up on the U.V.'s beau geste and get herself another angry woman? The trademark shriek of Hedda's heroines had once carried quite successfully—so that, as Bella had predicted, the entire fucking world of letters had *plotzed.* Of course, at first it had *plotzed* with laughter, as reviewer after reviewer praised the hyperbolic wit of Dunkele's "tour de force of farce":

But beneath the frantic fun, Dunkele is up to something serious. She has constructed what amounts to a *reductio ad absurdum*, brilliantly pursuing the doctrines of unleashed feminism to their outer inane limits and beyond. And with what manic ferocity does Dunkele paint her portrait of *absurdum!* This is a marvel of a first novel!

The reviewers had missed the point entirely, for Hedda's book had been written, of course, with deadly seriousness. Hedda had hardly any sense of humor at all.

"Bella," a bewildered, humorless Hedda had wailed into the telephone upon reading the rave reviews. "That's not my book!"

"Well, of course not. I know that. You know that. And any intelligent reader is going to know that."

"But the reviewers—"

"Are reviewers," Bella had cut her off. "Calm down, bubalah. The book speaks for itself. When you put that last period on that last page, then it's just out of your hands. That's what publication means. It's public!"

"But Bella," Hedda had continued to wail. "I've just been invited to give a series of talks at the Ninety-second Street Y on Jewish humor!"

"So decline," Bella had snapped.

"But Bella . . ." Hedda had persisted.

"Listen, Hedda, why don't you just lie back, close your eyes, and try to enjoy this. Things could be worse. The book *is* selling. We're going into a third printing!"

But Hedda had taken special pains to ensure that her next book, *Hanna, The Husband's Whore*, could not, under any circumstances, be misinterpreted as brilliantly funny. She had had Bella proofread it for humor. And, sure enough, the reviewers had not been amused:

> Though I am not overly ecological in my thinking, yet it grieves me to consider that trees have been felled only to produce such a pile of waste. I wouldn't even use the pages of this book for toilet paper!

"That fucking criminal!" Bella had wailed into the telephone upon reading aloud to Hedda the first review to come in. "You know what he just did? He just raped Hedda Dunkele! He just raped Hedda Dunkele and left her for dead!"

"At least he understood the book this time," Hedda had answered, not without a certain degree of satisfaction.

The reviews got uglier and uglier, until Hedda had had to stop reading them altogether, finding herself getting entirely used up in the attempt to answer them (in her grieving heart) line for poisonous line.

(Said Henry of his critics: *One would have to be a Frenchman to hate them enough.*)

"Now it's gang rape," Bella had yelped—however, now without any trace of pain. For although Hedda Dunkele had been screwed over and left for dead, Hedda Dunkele hadn't died. In fact, she was selling even better than before.

"We're going into a fifth printing!"

Hedda's angry women were so frequently cited that a new acrostic was introduced in their honor. They were the JAWs—the Jewish Angry Women—and there appeared to be far more JAWs out there than JAPs; or perhaps it was simply that they made their presence that much more felt.

In any case, Hedda's JAWs were entering into the East Coast / West Coast consciousness. They were finding their place in the lexicon of culture. And, most important to Hedda and Bella, the JAWs had kept on coming:

Etta, The Rebbe's Daughter!
Hanna, The Husband's Whore!
Sara, The Savant's Sister!
Mona, The Momzer's Mother!
Minna, The Messiah's Mother-in-Law!
Clara, The Corporate Korva!
Dora, The Doctor's Daughter!

Each of the JAWs was beautiful. Each began as a Sweet Young Thing (SYT), smilingly tracing her way down that obscure hidden path, choked with weeds and debris carelessly flung by some Significant—male—Other—or Others, as, for example, in the case of Clara, a petite, blond, and green-eyed Harvard MBA, who tried to jog with the Big Guys down the fast lane of Wall Street.

But, somewhere along that path, something had happened for each of the SYTs. Destiny had happened. Each had undergone a wrenching transfiguration, from which she emerged a creature of another sort entirely: a JAW!

I defy you! they had come, upon finding their own true voices at long last, to shriek—carrying with them the ardent sympathy of sizable numbers of the reading public.

"We're going into an eighth printing!"

By the way, I now must tell you that the fierce but beautiful JAWs had proved unaccountably titillating to the fantasizing minds of an untallied number of unregenerate pigs, a phenomenon that had boosted Hedda's sales for all the wrong reasons, and the recognition of which had pained

Hedda's ideology far more than it had Bella's. It had cost Hedda numerous angry tears and blushes—yes, even prodigious Hedda occasionally blushed—to imagine such unanticipated reactions to the scenes of sexual humiliation she had—with such different, such edifying intent!—constructed. Hedda had had Bella proofread her books for humor; but it had never occurred to her to have them scanned for eroticism. Of course, she had known, with all the sound instincts of a novelist, that a downright unlovable woman, a woman, for example, such as herself, would be very difficult to bring off as a sympathetic character. I ask you: What reader would want to identify with the likes of Hedda?

Where were they now, those seven splendid sisters? They had found their place into the East Coast/West Coast consciousness. They were safely deposited within the vaults of the lexicon of culture. Could they not be brought back into Hedda's own head? Could they not be revived and reinvented, as Henry himself had revived and reinvented his Princess Casamassima?

Nothing would doubtless beckon us further, with a large leisure, than such a chance to study the obscure law under which certain of a novelist's characters, more or less honourably buried, revive for him by a force or a whim of their own, and walk round his house of art like haunting ghosts, feeling for the old doors they knew, fumbling at stiff latches and pressing their pale faces, in the outer dark, to lighted windows. I mistrust them, I confess, in general; my sense of a really expressed character is that it shall have originally so tasted of the ordeal of service as

to feel no disposition to yield again to the strain.
Why should the Princess of the climax of *Roderick Hudson* still have made her desire felt, unless in fact to testify that she had not been—for what she was—completely recorded?

There were all sorts of spooks wandering about Hedda's place, fumbling at stiff latches and pressing their white faces against the windows. Could it not be that one amongst them was a used-but-still-serviceable JAW?

Dora, perhaps, who was, after all, the last to be "more or less honourably buried."

Dora was a wondrously beautiful creature. Perhaps the most beautiful of all the JAWs, and therefore the most victimized. (At least at first, in her youth, before she learned to fight back. And how.) Dora's particular nemesis had been doctors. She was herself a doctor's daughter and so tended, as a child, to get taken quite often to doctors, her parents believing, quite naturally, in the benefits of modern medicine and also liking to take full advantage of the professional courtesy (i.e. no fees) offered them.

At the age of thirteen, there in the tender exfoliation of her womanhood, Dora had suffered the first of the abuses she was to undergo before her vengeful metamorphosis. Dora was taken to a podiatrist (not even a proper doctor, that) to be treated for an ingrown toenail. The podiatrist had had Dora undress entirely. She wondered. Of course, she wondered. Dora was an intelligent child. Her pediatrician, in her annual well-exam, had always allowed her to keep on her underwear, as well as giving her a blue tissue-paper smock to wrap about herself. Why would an ingrown toenail require her to strip?

She looked at the doctor. He was about her father's own age. He looked at her, not angrily, not impatiently. He folded his arms and calmly, but firmly, repeated his request. To be addressed calmly, but firmly, was precisely the mode of communication to which Dora was accustomed.

The doctor didn't, of course, look anything like how she had pictured those "perverts" of whom her mother had dutifully—in fact, rather obsessively—warned her. Her mental image of this frightening category of person was, admittedly, pretty vague. How *did* a pervert look? But surely nothing like the man before her in his sanctified white coat. A doctor! Well, a podiatrist. Surely there would be some telling sign: longish hair, dirty fingernails, a grease stain somewhere about? Something to mark a man a pervert.

When she was younger, four or five, her mother used to scold her for holding her dress up, out of her way, when she ran. She was the sort of child to practice her running, up and down and down and up along the sidewalk of their beautiful and wide, tree-lined block. Her mother's maid spent hours ironing those little smocked dresses. (Dora's mother believed that little girls ought to dress like little girls. No unisex Osh-Kosh overalls for little Dora.)

Dora's mother would come out of doors, as Dora practiced her running, and stand there with her slim arms folded, leaning against the stately white pillar of their porch, calling out in her fluty doctor's-wife voice for Dora to cease her running and come to the porch immediately—if not sooner.

"You must never pick up your dress like that," scolded Dora's mother—more than once: those dresses got in the way so! "Nobody can ever see you, do you understand? Only your father, and I. And, of course, the doctor."

Dora undressed, quickly, her tragically beautiful face on fire with her shame.

The podiatrist had then proceeded to give Dora an internal exam.

He had gone into her, and there had been a terrifying tear of pain, followed by a terrifying spurt of blood. She saw it with horror on his finger.

Dora was an intelligent child. What had that finger within her to do with an ingrown toenail?

She had told her mother, who had spoken to her father. They had, at first, not believed Dora. They had gotten, in fact, furious with her. The child watched too many after-school specials on the public television station. They had better forbid her everything but the major network comedies.

But after such a string of days of teary dejection, Dora's father had himself examined his daughter, Dora's mother beside the bed in tight-lipped attendance. Dora had turned her eyes away from their unreassuring faces, her tragically beautiful face on fire with her shame.

The fact was there. The child was intact no more.

Much consultation between the parents had followed. Ultimately, they decided against confronting the podiatrist with the truth. It was all too sticky. He was a colleague, a pillar of the community. Why, he was even a member of their temple, of which his father had once been president, as Dora's own father had been.

And, of course, it would do the child no good were the truth about her to be known. People would just see the stain upon her, quite forgetting that it was not really she who had soiled herself. It was, like it or not, the way of the world, of which Dora's parents were masters.

Dora's father did, of course, stop referring patients to the podiatrist in question.

There had been other humiliations Dora had been forced to undergo—her parents never there to offer anything in the way of protection before the fact or consolation thereafter. Until, finally, in Dora's sixteenth year, she had come to the full realization that it was she, and she alone, who must both protect and console herself.

I defy you!

Dora had ultimately gone on to law school, specializing in medical malpractice, uncovering a multitude of nefarious deeds performed against women—from the potions prepared by the large pharmaceutical companies to the shoddy, and worse, treatments of the local neighborhood gynecologist.

Her face was tragic in its beauty no more. The fire in it was that of the fierce Crusader, out to dispose, once and for all, of the scuzzy scalpel of unscrupulous woman-butchering medicine.

Hedda had felt very close to Dora. She had been deeply affected by Dora's childhood traumas and had admired Dora's acquired ability to maneuver in the real world and confront the enemy head on (abilities the heroically proportioned Hedda herself so sorely lacked).

Perhaps brave and beautiful Dora might be exhumed and resuscitated, to feel about for the old doors and fumble at the stiff latches, even as that other doctor's daughter, Catherine Sloper, had done.

"Dora," whispered Hedda into the slanting mirror.

Silence.

Perhaps Etta, then. For Etta was probably the fiercest—and loudest—of them all. She had been the first of Hedda's JAWs, she who had been retrieved from Bella's slush heap.

Etta, the rebbe's daughter!

Etta's father was the head honcho—that is, the rebbe—of his small Hasidic community in the Williamsburg section of Brooklyn.

Etta was the second child, the first girl, of sixteen children, the last three of which, born when the rebbe's wife was near fifty, and beyond, were Down's children.

Three male babies they were. The amulets to ward off the wrath of Lilith, the first wife of the First Man, hung over their cradles; special prayers and potent symbols to keep the First Mother from visiting her vengeance upon these human babies for what was done, for her rebellion, to her own demon-children. Others had forgotten Lilith; but here, among the bewigged women of Williamsburg, her powers, born of anger, were remembered.

After the birth of the last baby, who had lived no longer than three weeks, Etta's mother, the gently smiling rebbetzin, had herself expired. She had simply and silently closed her eyes, out of exhaustion and grief.

Etta was alone with her mother in their little cramped house in Williamsburg when she died. Etta's father, the rebbe, was off with his disciples, dancing through the streets of Williamsburg, in celebration of the holiday of Simhath Torah.

Looking down at the face of her mother, fifty-one years

old and looking like a hundred, Etta had felt the righteous fury gathering within her. She turned away to drape the dresser mirror with a sheet, to begin the days of mourning, catching a glimpse of her own distorted features, in the second before the white shroud fell.

Etta had gone on to lead a revolution among Williamsburg's women! The women of all the various feuding Hasidic sects—the Lubavitcher, the Belzer, the Bobover, the Gerer, the Vishnitzer—even the meshuggeneh Satmar!—had closed ranks against da Men. The feminine fury had spread like a wild fire from Williamsburg to Crown Heights, from Crown Heights to Borough Park!

The women had run amuck through Brooklyn's *shtieblach*, the little basement room synagogues, tearing down the *mechitzahs*, the curtained partitions, behind which they, with their multitudes of white-stockinged children, had been squeezed in a small fraction of the space accorded da Men.

"Out behind da coitain!" they had sung out in their clear, *clean* voices. "Ve vant to see, too!"

Like the famed women of Greek drama (how Hedda *loved* her Greeks), the women of Brooklyn had refused to immerse themselves in the waters of the mikvah, the monthly ritual of the purifying bath; and so their husbands could not partake of their bodies.

"Ve vant da Pill!" they had chanted.

What a brilliant tactician that rebbe's daughter was. Like one of those military geniuses who on the field of battle converts disaster into victory, so Etta had made claim of the monthly humiliation and transformed it into the very artillery of attack.

One Friday night without the *mitzvah* of cohabitation was observed by the discontented Hasidim. Two Friday nights! Three!

"Rebbe, rebbe!" the Hasidim had gone wailing to their respective gurus, almost pulling out their sidelocks. *"Vat to do? Vat to do?"*

The rebbes had powwowed amongst themselves and then had gone to confront Etta's father, even though most of them had excommunicated him several years before, when he had set up a rivaling kosher authorization and instructed his Hasidim not to use foods authorized by the others.

"Nu?" they demanded. "Enough already! *Nimmt in hant dein tochter!* Take that daughter of yours in hand!"

But Etta was barricaded, together with her select warriors, in one of the *shtieblach*. Her father she unconditionally refused to see. She would forever and implacably hold him accountable for her mother's anguished death. But she did, finally, after much negotiation, agree to meet with a contingent of the other rebbes, though they were forced to whisper to her from the *wrong* side of the *mechitzah*.

Oy! it hurt, it hurt! Who could have believed such things could ever come to pass, even in America? But *nu!* what could they do? One more Friday night without the *mitzvah* and there would be total anarchy in Brooklyn. The women had brought the rebbes to their gartered knees.

"Etta," Hedda called to her now. "I need you, Ettale. Speak to me! Shriek to me!"

Silence.

No. There *was* a presence in the room. Something was there, seeped through the cracks opened wide by demoralization.

Something vague and vile, slowly gathering form.

A damned shape squatting, raying out influences fatal to life.

Oh, it's you.

It was Adolph Uberhaupt.

He was looking much improved over the last time they had met.

He was very elegant, in a black cummerbund and tuxedo. He looked as if he had just come from some opening night or charity ball. He looked like a High Flier.

He seemed to have grown a few inches since she had last seen him. Almost Hedda's own height he was. Slimmed down considerably, too.

But his face was still that unsettling blend of sarcasm and sensuality, though his lips had been wiped clean of their film of fish oil. But those lips of his were still cruelly curled with scorn, the eyes glazed heavy with irony, the eyebrows diabolically angled. There was still no place in that face for compassion.

He was looking plenty uncompassionate at the moment.

So, Hedda. We meet again.

She stared, too demoralized to bother.

Looks like you're finished. Did it to yourself, it seems, without any help from me. I predicted it, of course. Right there in that in-depth probe you didn't let your sister Stella finish reading to you. I always knew you had no talent. You can fool all of the people some of the time, and some of the—

No, wait a minute, Adolph. Listen, this book is very different. Bella hates it!

Good for Bella, Adolph cheered. *So that dumb dyke finally wised up to you.*

No, no, Adolph, don't you see? Bella hates it because it's

different from anything I've done before, it's different from the sorts of books of mine you hate! Which means you might really *like* this one! Bella says it's reactionary. Doesn't that sound promising to you, Adolph?

But Adolph was Stella's; which meant it made not the slightest difference what Hedda said to him. He proceeded regardless.

You didn't give Stella a chance to read one of my best lines from that review. I was very peeved about that. Here, listen.

And Adolph whipped out of his cummerbund some neatly folded pages.

What do women want? Adolph read, his voice (which at their first meeting had been querulous and nasal) deepening into the imposing, understated authority of a BBC announcer, tony British accent and all. *The answer is so plainly, so painfully given to us in that shrill, hysterical voice of our foremost (you must excuse the expression) feminist (again excuse the expression) writer: "Give me a penis of my very own!" it shrieks! "I am choking!" it is begging. "I am blue-in-the-face gagging on my penis envy!" So what do you think, Hedda?*

Listen, Adolph! *Please* listen! This one is different, this one . . .

I've just finished another in-depth probe of your fiction. His voice softened with bad omen.

I thought you ought to hear it, he said, taking a step closer to her. *For your own good. . . .*

She saw now that the white gloves he was holding in one hand were not of kid leather, as she had thought, but were made of thin, antiseptic rubber.

He was pulling the doctor's gloves on now, as he came closer toward her, all his motions slow and menacing. . . .

Spread your legs, Hedda . . .

Hold it right there, Adolph. You just turn your self-important self right around and you march yourself pronto out of here, Mr. Big Shot Critic!

It was the imperious voice of the Jewish Princess, strangely come to intercede at this point for Hedda. She too was dressed in evening clothes—in fact, in the slinky backless dress of the liberated 'baby' from the cigarette ad— the one who had come such a long way on seven-inch, silver-toned, high-heeled shoes.

Amazed, Hedda watched as Adolph wordlessly obeyed the JAP, slinking back into the sinister haze out of which he had issued.

And you, Hedda, snapped the JAP. *I'm shocked. I really am. Where is your self-respect? Where is your inner dignity? Is there nothing you won't stoop to? You people disgust me. Art! Hah! Lying there with your legs spread open to the world. That's what it all comes down to, if you ask me, which I know you're not, but who's asking you?*

Now get yourself up off that floor, Ms. Authoress, and march yourself right back to your word processor. No more of this self-indulgent crap. And don't you know when to stop talking to someone who's not listening to you? I thought childhood had at least taught you that much.

The Princess, too, was of course Stella's.

Now start that machine up. We've got a plot to solve here. I can't believe you haven't figured it out yet. Even you. I happen to have some experience here—I'm a woman of letters myself. The question you have to ask yourself, Ms. Authoress, before you sit down to write a book, is this: Given a rainy Saturday afternoon, a box of chocolates guaranteed to be nonfattening, and the latest by Danielle Steele, why would anyone read your book? Now get up off that floor and get your

William back onto the train going out to Wallowing Graves, or whatever the hell place that was. And don't have him wasting any more time walking from the station and falling into long-winded philosophy that slows up the action. Let him take a horsecar this time! Bella made a very good point, you know. People don't have that much time anymore.

Hedda still sat, dumbly passive. And, in her impatience, the Princess herself actually reached out one of her extravagantly manicured hands to switch on the computer.

Oh! she shrieked. *Damn, damn, damn! I've broken a nail! That's what I get for playing the Good Samaritan. You always pay for stepping out of character. Now I'll have to have an emergency wrap. You're just going to have to do it for yourself, Ms. Authoress.*

Oh, and Hedda, she said, casting a sultry, expertly made-up eye back over her bare shoulder as she prepared to saunter away in her slinky dress. *Did you happen to notice that Vivianna writes with her left hand?*

William sat at his desk in the large, airy room of his library, the sun pouring in through that triple window to which so great a portion of the southern wall had been consecrated. He had in his hands a letter, just read, from Vivianna Bonnet, the contents and—even more—the tone of which had provoked in him a profound unease.

The young astronomer's letter had not contained a single of the cosmological speculations with which she was wont to fill her communications. Of course, it had been William's painful task, in his own last letter, to deliver her the discouraging news that all his attempts to procure funds with which she might purchase a good telescope had come to naught. He had found no man or institution willing to risk expenditure on a novice who could boast none of the formal academic decorations.

How inimical to the fiercely free spirit of the mind was this professionalizing of thinking. And how insidiously deadening, the reaching tentacles of the monster university. The envisioned iconoclast, true incubator of the creative surge to think the unthought, stood now almost as threatened as in those dark days when the fiercely restless monk—graduate of no academy, known by many as the Nuisance—was led defiant to the stake. Only it is with our institutional indifference that we now silence him—or her.

Was it only the scientist's disappointment that had cast the pessimistic pall over the young astronomer's letter? Or was there an element hovering that was more distinctly sinister? For in truth the letter had read—so out of character for Vivianna—with a deadening tone of fatalism, the perception of which it had altogether pained William to own.

I must assure you, esteemed Professor and valued friend, that the sentiment of personal grievance you express on my behalf is not replicated in my own heart. I think it little matters now, and that perhaps I am well served to be out of it. The project I had contemplated would have taken years piled top of years of subtlest calculation and minutest observation—all this so that at the end, if—and what an "if"—my initial hypothesis proved correct, men might be able to point their fingers at yet another star, amongst the multitudes that already bleach the nighttime sky.

If the star is there, men will find it. And if they do not, well then, it will not be found, and I do not think they will suffer much the omission.

The nighttime blackness no longer beckons to me as once it had, and in truth it seems betimes I had mistaken it for another.

I pray thee, dear friend and would-be benefactor, to think no more on that vanity which was Vivianna's.

It was, to William's blushing mind, almost indecent to read such death-charmed destinism penned by one as vital and gifted as the younger Miss Bonnet.

He saw again—and saw again—the rare, fine portrait she had presented him when first he had laid eyes upon her: framed by the solitude of her tower and the intensity of her own cerebrations, the dark folds of the soft stuff of her drapery arranging themselves so naturally about her figure, as she sat poised before the Astronomical Immensities. There was something infinitely grand in the picture and also something infinitely touching.

And he felt—and felt again—the strange thrilling sting the vision of her wrought upon his innermost sensibility— the nighttime sensibility of him—like Vivianna herself not fated to walk in daylight hours.

The sting her image invariably registered held an element that was deeply disruptive; he would not deny it to himself. And yet, neither would he have wished himself never to have encountered so exquisite a disruption.

Yet perhaps, he thought, turning it over in his mind— as he was wont to turn over all things that could be so maneuvered (and even those that could not)—perhaps the disruptive sentiment, no matter how inward and o'ertempered with paternalistic good intent, had been allowed to breed its bastard litter of unnatural consequences. Perhaps it had been his own too eager response to Miss Bonnet that had led him to feel a false confidence in her cosmological contemplations—and he, no expert on her Great Subject—or, in any case, a false confidence in his own poor ability to arouse in others a kindred kindness toward the infant theory she proposed.

And now behold where it all had ended. His groundless optimism had delivered her no good of the tangible sort, and a great quantity of ill of the more intangible, and deadly, variety.

How he had bungled it once again.

Failure, then, failure!

He ought never to have tried to engage that essentially solitary figure in the mean doings of the outer world. She had been—and how hard it fell on him to know it—far better off before she knew him.

He knew Vivianna—he knew the bleakness of her present mood—too well. He knew *her* altogether too well. If only he could believe that her letter was the expression of the vaporous misgivings of the moment. Every hour of creative work must have such moments, given over to the vagaries of dismal mood, to the inner voice that whispers, "You cannot!" The moment passes; the driving life of the Work itself pushes it away.

Let it be so for Vivianna!

There was, as was usual, rather a great number of letters that had come that day for William. Yet another communication, he saw, from the American Academy of Arts and Letters, whose offer of membership he had already declined, on the grounds that he disliked inactive bodies, whose whole purpose seemed to be to announce: We are in and you are out, adding that he was encouraged in this course by the fact that his "younger and shallower and vainer brother" had accepted membership, and the pair of them would over-populate the Academy with Jameses.

Egad! William saw with amusement, as he quickly scanned today's communication from the Academy, that his poor little joke about the "shallower brother" had been taken for character fratricide! Where was these learned gentlemen's humor?

There was another personal letter lying amidst the deplorable quantity of professional correspondences cluttering his tray. And the fact that the dove gray envelope, bearing the precious signature of the brother in England, had been passed over for the privilege of first perusal, bespoke vast volumes on the subject of the strained sentiment of the prominent psychologist of Cambridge, Massachusetts for the struggling lone astronomer of Willow Groves, Connecticut.

The missive, which was of a characteristic bulk and an agitated tone, was entirely devoted to the question of their dead sister's diary, which her very especial friend, the formidably admirable Miss Katherine Loring of Boston, "the New England professor of doing things," was pushing for publication.

William's sister, Alice, had been more and more in his thoughts recently, her pale face in the outside darkness, pressed up against the lighted window.

And so it had been, he now thought, and so she had stood, even while she lived.

It had been a wonder and a revelation to him to read the pages of the diary she had kept the last two and a half years of her life:

I think that if I get into the habit of writing a bit about what happens, or rather doesn't happen, I may lose a little of the sense of loneliness and desolation which abides with me. My circumstances allowing of nothing but the ejaculation of one-syllabled reflections, a written monologue by that most interesting being, myself, may have its yet to be discovered consolations. I shall, at least, have it all my own way.

What ever-widening circles of pathos reverberated in that opening.

After Alice's death, Katherine Loring, the unbending reed who had attended her to the end, had returned from England, bearing a small receptacle of white ash—to be buried in Cambridge Cemetery alongside their parents—and two leather-bound and handwritten little volumes. It had been two years later that Henry and he had learned of their sister's diary. Katherine Loring had four copies of it printed privately, by John Wilson and Son, of Cambridge—one for herself and one for each of Alice's surviving brothers, William, Henry, and Robertson. Alice herself, they had learned through Katherine, had wished her diary to be published.

Upon receipt of his copy, William had taken the diary away with him to New Bedford, for a twenty-four-hour vacation from his rigorous schedule of teaching, writing, and the intensities of family life. There he had read his sister's document straight through, and it had sunk into him with strange compunctions and solemnity. The diary produced such a unique and tragic impression of personal power— venting itself on no opportunity! And such really *deep* humor—a humor that had held its imperious own, even against the final, the last, distinguished thing:

> Within the last year Henry has published *The Tragic Muse*, brought out *The American*, and written a play, *Mrs. Vilbert* (accepted by Hare), and his admirable comedy; combined with William's *Psychology*, not a bad show for one family! especially if I get myself dead, the hardest job of all.
>
> I do pray to heaven that the dreadful Mrs. Piper won't be let loose upon my defenseless soul.

Again and again, Alice's lively musings and forceful opinions—all of them festooned in the most felicitous phrasings, so that, as stylist, the little sister had a thing or two to teach her elder brothers—had struck with wonderment. Such a thriving bumptious universe there beneath the shawls and blankets and duvet upon the knee, the dreary regimen of medicated syrups and porous plasters, of hypnotism and, at the last, the blessed morphia that William had prescribed for her. How much of that "most interesting being, myself," all through her tragically diminished life (but how she would have bristled at the diminishing phrase), had been hidden away from those who loved her best and who had presumed to think they truly knew her?

> Owing to muscular circumstances, my youth was not of the most ardent, but I had to peg away pretty hard, between twelve and twenty-four, "killing myself," as someone calls it—absorbing into the bone that the better part is to clothe one's self in neutral tints, walk

by still waters, and possess one's soul in silence. How I recall the low grey Newport sky in that winter of '62–63; as I used to wander about over the cliffs, my young soul struggling out of its swaddling clothes, as the knowledge crystallized within me of what life meant for me. . . .

Terrible words, these! Terrible words for a loving elder brother to take in.

They had, each of them, he and his brothers, to peg away pretty hard at themselves, at one time or another; had endured their sessions through the nightmare seasons; but none of them, he thought, would have had reason to put it in quite this way—citing, so calmly, the obligation of killing oneself. And the thought had forced its way in upon him that he, at least—he could not speak for any of the others—had not done his sister the justice of seeing her on her own—her very own absolutely distinctive—terms.

(It was a strange light now that had been gradually spreading itself over his life, a light suggesting, somehow, a wider sphere of sympathy, and which had not a little to do with the strained sentiment for Vivianna he had been carrying within him.)

What might his sister not have been, he had wondered (in that singular, slanting light), had that altogether original mind been shaped by a more robust and methodical, less haphazardous, education? She herself, rather inevitably, had wondered similarly, although, in her diary, she pushed aside any possibility of a piqued remorse with the thrusts of a self-mocking humor:

I wonder if I had had an education, whether I should have been more or less of a fool than I am. It would have deprived me surely of those exquisite moments of mental flatulence which every now and then inflate the cerebral vacuum with a delicious sense of latent possibilities, of stretching one's self to cosmic limits. And who would ever give up the reality of dreams for relative knowledge?

Ah, Alice.

Requiescat.

He had entertained recently (there in the dim queer light) a thought most odd and unsettling, a *dubitatio plane monstrosa*, a very strange doubt, for which Vivianna's musings on the hidden stars had provided him his metaphor. Might it not be the case that the history of ideas is filled too with its darkened stars—that the largest bodies are invisible by reason of that very immensity that keeps their light from being seen?

We have all been instructed on the infallible, if plodding, sense of History, which distinguishes, ultimately, and honors, if posthumously, its glorious men of Genius. But might it not be more truly and tragically the case that History is both plodding *and* fallible—damnably fallible? Might it not be that the very greatest of our thinkers have been left—by virtue of their very greatness—entirely and irrevocably *lost* to us, their struggles and their triumphs—and the unreplicable productions these have yielded up—left pathetically unrecorded, with not even the cold consolations of a posthumous fame to indicate that this Vastness once had been?

And if a bleary-eyed world has great difficulty in taking in the radiant being of any visionary, how much more so a visionary in skirts? It was comforting—he had surely taken comfort in it, as had his father before him—to believe that women are constructed upon the blueprints of sweet consolers, to whom the sufferingly gifted might go to be tended, so that they might see themselves through the ordeal of exceptionality. William James had had the good fortune of having been born to just such a woman—*I should be, however, sometimes terribly tossed and wrenched between the combatants, if I were not a married man*, his father had written to his poor, wasted brother, Robertson—and, of course, William had married just such another. An exquisitely complicated female—he tried out, tentatively, the odd sound of the word *mistresspieces*: was it impossible or merely eccentric?—might topple the whole structure of soothing suppositions. It was so much easier to shunt such a creature into other categories, under which she might be scorned, or pitied, or clinically treated.

He had been guilty, certainly, of pity—he now thought with a discomfiting spasm of recognition—in the loving gaze with which he had taken in his sister. He remembered, with an uneasy admixture of amusement and remorse, her spirited rejoinder when once he had written to her, with the most genuine sentiment of fraternal sympathy, of how much, "you poor child," he had pitied her, who stifles "slowly in a quagmire of disgust and pain and impotence." Her response—which had caused him at the time a loud burst of laughter, if also a mild vexation—had made him thanks for his recent "very fraternal, sympathetic, and amusing letter."

The fraternity and amusingness are very gratefull to my heart and soul, but the sympathy makes me feel like a horrible humbug. Amidst the horrors of which I hear and read my woes seem of a very pale tint. Kath. and I roared over the "stifling in a quagmire of disgust, pain, and impotence," for I consider myself one of the most potent creations of my time, & though I may not have a group of Harvard students sitting at my feet drinking in psychic truth, I shall not tremble, I assure you, at the last trump.

No, he had never really known how to approach her—difficult creature that she had been! But then they were all difficult, all but their gently smiling mother, for them always the Paragon of Womanhood. Alas for her, Alice had been another order of Woman altogether.

There had been another obscuring fact while Alice had lived. His *own* Alice—his own dear wife, the mother of his brood—had harbored mysteriously uncharitable feelings toward his sister. And this was surpassingly strange; for his wife was, like his mother, a most amiable woman, who got on with almost everyone and was, by almost everyone without exception, beloved. But she—who was herself so essentially mellow and free from morbidness, whose soul was of the sky blue tint so becoming to a woman—had shown, from the beginning, little patience for the invalid suffering her "nervous"—that is to say, undiagnosable—ailments, who chose (and his Alice was most emphatic in the choice of this word) to have one of her obstreperous attacks the very week of William and Alice's nuptials, thus diverting the attention to herself and quite spoiling the mood all around.

And his wife had looked askance on that extraordinary relationship between his sister and the incomparably devoted friend, Katherine Loring, that "Boston marriage," which had seemed at long last to bring Alice a brief bright blaze of joyfulness, and in which her family had, accordingly, rejoiced. Only William's wife had quietly demurred. She had looked with frank suspicion on the intensity of their devotion and had voiced her fear to William that the relationship was not the salubrious spiritual union the family chose to see it as—but that it bore the stain of a love most unspeakable.

The difficulties between the two Alices had made it harder than ever for William to apprehend, on her own terms, his difficult sister. For his allegiance was, of course, secured by the matrimonial knot.

And yet, since his sister's death, his wife had seemed to William to suffer a liquefying expansion in her sisterly attitude and betimes had murmured to William sensibilities most strange and new. One night she had whispered to her husband, in the darkness of their bed, and in the melting mood that had engulfed them in their wife-and-husband intimacy, whether he did not think that perhaps the only thing about his sister that had marked her with the branding iron of sickness had been her recognition that she was indeed sick?

"What betokens these strange utterances?" her husband had asked her in his gently teasing tone of voice, with none of the caustic traces of the nervous irritability that had recently strained their exchanges. "The sibylline, Alice, is not *your* métier."

"Only that it seems sometimes to me, William—do not

laugh—that the female state is in itself a most horrible deviation. . . ."

No, he had never known the right way in which to approach his sister while she lived. Harry had been much better at this than he. Thank God for Harry, the Angel, who had—so she had written in her diary—given her calm and solace "by assuring me that my nerves are his nerves, and my stomach his stomach, this last a pitch of brotherly devotion never before approached by the race." Harry, with that suppleness of sympathy born from the androgyny of the artist (if that was what it was), had been able, as the less ambivalently manful William had not, to enter into so much of what had been their sister.

But there were limits even to Harry's ardent fraternity; and these limits were limned on the very issue of the diary.

William himself believed his sister's little book to be another leaf in the laurel crown of the family and was hopeful of its publication. But Harry—who in recent years had covered himself, like some marine crustacean, with all sorts of material growth, rich seaweeds and rigid barnacles and things, and lived hidden in the midst of his strange heavy alien manners (though he was, William was certain of it, beneath all the accretions of the years and the world, still the same dear innocent old Harry of their youth, whose Anglicisms were but "protective resemblances" and who was still, if not a Yankee, a native of the James family and had no other country)—Harry was thrown into a sickness of terror at the possibility of "the catastrophe of publicity" that might ensue upon the diary's publication. Personal publicity was for him always a spur to acutest alarm, and he was most particularly exercised that Katherine had not seen fit to

excise the many *names* that appeared in the diary, attached
to succulent little morsels of gossip, almost all of which had
come to Alice by way of none other than Henry, who used
to say everything to Alice (on system) that would *égayer* her
bedside:

> *I didn't dream she wrote them down—but this wouldn't have
> mattered—the idea of her doing so would only have interested
> me. It is the printing of these privacies* telles quelles *that
> distresses me, when a very few merely superficial discriminations
> (leaving her* text *sacredly, really untouched) wd. have made
> all the difference! The other day, in Venice, Miss Wormeley,
> who is with the Curtises, said to me, as if she knew all about
> it, "I hear your sister's letters have just been published, and are
> so delightful": which made me almost jump out of my skin.*
>
> *When I see that I say Augustine Birell has a self-satisfied
> smirk after he speaks—and see that Katherine felt no prompting
> to exercise a discretion about the name—I feel very unhappy,
> and wonder at the strangeness of destiny.*
>
> *I seem to see the fearful American newspaper lying in wait
> for every whisper, every echo. I take this side of the matter hard,
> as you see—but I bow my head to fate, and am prepared for
> the worst.*

Indeed William, reading his brother's exquisitely phrased
phobias, could quite picture the poor dear man in his prone
attitude of fateful supplication.

After reading through Henry's letter, and depositing it
into the deep repository of his pocket, to be redeemed that
evening and read *en famille*, William reread the letter that
had come from Willow Groves. How the slanting light did

seem to darken! The letter read even more piteously than before.

William looked up from the letter, glancing as he did so at the face of the grandfather clock on the wall opposite, whose hands were joined together at twelve.

"Though we are sisters, we are to one another as the midnight hour is to noon." There flared out before him the unexpected metaphor.

But my God, my God! *Could* it be?

He started up in his excitement, taking several long strides down the length of his room, pirouetting on his heel, and continuing back again.

It was so! *Mirabile dictu*—it was so!

Had not Vivianna herself vainly tried to tell him as much—there in the obscuring gloom of her tower and with however veiled a hint?

Several times he stood still, as if overcome by the heady ethers of his meditation, and emitted a strange low whistle.

Some evidence of the peripatetic commotion being en-acted upon the bare wood floors of the library must have seeped under the heavy oaken door, for the knock that came upon this was unusually tentative.

His preoccupation was such that he did not hear the knock until it was repeated thrice, each time with a less tentative touch.

And there stood Alice—*his* Alice—come to summon him to luncheon.

He looked at her as if he did not know her!

And with what strange twisted face did he continue to stare.

There was a kind of horror in it, it seemed; yes, horror, and some not small display of fear.

And yet, spreading over these, and slowly taking all else into itself, was a gaze full of fierceness and determination, a gaze of almost predatory excitement and a cold inhuman intelligence.

William stood once again on the porch of the house in Willow Groves, Alice Bonnet staring out at him through the frosted glass of the door, her face rigid with unspoken displeasure. For a moment a look of unhidden hatred took possession of her features. And then the moment passed, and the door was opened. She remained, however, with her hand upon the knob, as if ready to slam it to, should her visitor overstep himself.

Her right hand, William noted, having fatally become, upon mounting his swift deduction, completely the man of science.

"Alice." It was the first time that William had addressed her by her Christian name, and she stiffened visibly at the sound. "I should like now to speak with Vivianna."

"It is not possible, Professor James." She made him her answer in her low dull hiss. "It is not yet her hour."

"It *is* possible. You know it, as I do. As you know, too, that Vivianna herself wishes to speak to me. I ask you, Alice, to give way now, and allow Vivianna to come forth!"

He spoke it quietly and yet it was charged with the vibrancy of his will.

They stared at one another for a long moment, the unspeakable reference passing between them.

The face of her then took on a mortuous stillness, the pupils contracting so that they seemed to disappear, giving the countenance the effect of a death mask. The color too was the whiteness of mortality, and the breath seemed entirely to cease.

It remained so for some fraction of a moment—William, watching, himself forgot to breathe. And then the life came flooding back into the face, the more than mortal bloom that was Vivianna Bonnet.

She smiled at William—calmly removing from her person her sister's horrid bonnet and spectacles, so that the nighttime fire in her glittering dark eyes shined forth. Unconsciously, a hand undid the buttons on the high-necked blouse and placed itself upon the slim white throat, fingering a thin ribbon of black velvet that was there.

"I bid you welcome, William James." She made him her greeting in her full rich voice. "I bid you welcome with all my soul!"

Her smile, seen without the obscurity of the tower, positively struck light. It glimmered there among the features, quickening them each into life, piercingly luminous. The face now cast a splendor that put one somehow to shame.

One hand was still upon the slender throat. The other she held out toward William, and left it reaching there in the small distance between them, where he seemed not to notice it.

The bold and brave deduction was most gloriously ridden! He had appropriated the premises, had nobly lanced the conclusion through! He felt the telling sting upon his breastbone.

Vivianna still looked speechlessly toward him. Her complexion was suffused with the high color of her feeling, and her eyes were very near to spilling. The face she showed him was wonderful. If it stood for everything, never had a face had to stand for more.

He had only just lifted the rare moist bloom to the level of his eye, the probing index finger placed within where he could not yet see. There remained layers upon layers upon layers to be parted. He had simply, in the instant flare of his eagerness, his inquisitiveness, all responsive at the sight of her, to see, to touch, it all.

"You have seen it, then." She said it low and with the added huskiness of its deep intent. And, as he still hung fire, she spoke again: "Then you have seen it." She spoke it as if she would have enlarged upon it in the interregnum, but for its being found, upon the ground of his silence, to be all that could be said.

He took this in, knowing she would not speak again until she had something from him. A swarm of questions clouded about his head; the very buzz was present confusedly in his ear. He snatched at random—idiotically, as he afterward knew—to get his hand round one.

"Which of you—I mean to say, is it you or the other who was there to begin with, so to speak? Which of you is the, as it were, rightful resident—and which the intruder?"

He saw his mistake at once. The perception came immediate—if also too late.

She gave a jerk round. It was almost—to hear it—the touch of a lash. It turned her aslantwise from him, so that he was given the stretch of her whitened cheek, only marked with the deeply crimson spot he had seen there once before.

"Understand me, Vivianna! It is—my God, but it is!—

the most magnificent case of its kind that I know! If we can—you and I, fellow scientists as we are!—but pierce its carapace, think how we shall then unmask the face of the Subliminal Self!"

She remained for several moments more, with her face turned toward the wall. But she would see her inquisitor one last time. Slowly she looked back, and the face she showed him turned him from her with a moaning "Oh!"

When he looked back again—it was a few seconds only that had turned him away—the other was there, regarding him with a horrible sneer of uncontained malice.

"Alice," commanded James, "give way! I have not done with Vivianna!"

"And yet she has done with you!" The voice held a thrill of life that was new to it, throbbed as if with a vanquishing glory.

"Alice!" and he groaned it: "Bring her back to me!"

The sister laughed; it was a sound that turned the blood in his veins to ice.

"Do you think it is a matter for *my* bringing?" Her voice rose swiftly up along its arc of madness, ending in a shrill and hideous shriek: "You are an interloper, William James, *and you know nothing about it!*"

For a long moment all became an eddying blackness about him; and in that blackness there glowered an idea—some refinement of the horrible that Fate was offering him—that would have done away at last with the baleful sister. He stared at it—the only fixed point in the whirling darkness—drawing him to itself with a powerful line of force. He took it in, to the side, as it were—there would be time enough to think on it later—that he had come to this: that he was a person who had stood in the presence of this idea.

The darkness lifted; and he saw the woman watching him with her ghastly, gloating smile. She spoke again in her strange flat hiss:

"We yield you nothing . . . outsider!"

X V I

The Mother

Hedda was seriously unsettled. The scene enacted on the porch of the sisters' house in Willow Groves had frightened her. The entire length of her skeletal frame was trembling, her fingers shaking so badly that she had difficulty getting them to switch off her computer. She did, finally, blackening the monitor without bothering to press down the Save key.

But Hedda couldn't manage to blot out that last pitiful sight of Vivianna's face, the face that had made William turn from her and groan. That that splendid, splendid creature—sister to the stars—should have come to this! That she too should carry the stupid doom—should be, in the end, like all the rest, a monster in the shape of a woman. Why were the skies so full of them?

It was not at all the story Hedda had set about to write. I will call Bella right now, thought Hedda, and tell her: I've had enough.

Not William, though. William James was hooked. She could feel him right behind her now, his irascible blue eyes blazing, every C-fiber in his hyped-up cerebrum stimulated into a blooming, buzzing confusion. This sort of thing was right up *his* alley. Good God, but it was an indecent piece of luck to have a case of this kind of pathology fall directly into his lap.

It was just the discovery he needed at the moment—it accorded so perfectly with the general drift his thought had been taking—toward the notion of a continuum of cosmic consciousness, against which our individuality builds but accidental fences, and into which our several minds plunge as into a panpsychic mother sea or reservoir. Our "normal" consciousness—William stood as on his lecture platform at Harvard College, ardently gesticulating—is circumscribed for adaptation to our external earthly environment, but the fence is weak in spots, and fitful influences from beyond leak in, showing the otherwise unverifiable common connection between seemingly distinct personalities. The Piper phenomenon illustrates this wonderfully—as does the superb case of the Bonnet "sisters." Who knows not but that all manner of mental disease, as well as still rarer cases of artistic inspiration—flights of Genius itself—may not be explained along similar lines of the susceptibility of certain minds to cosmic seepage? Good God, but my father was not at all far from the mark with his wild theologizing on the Swedenborgian influxes!

For the first time Hedda felt something like distaste for William. He did not present a pretty picture, as he stood there on his platform, impassionedly lecturing. There was something loathsomely cannibalistic about the gusto with which he was smacking his mind's lips together.

He wasn't perfect, you know, the Ubiquitous Voice put in. *I know you like to think he was, but he wasn't. His eyes really were irascibly blue, just like your own father's. And think how he tormented poor Henry with his unsolicited literary criticism. But then you know all this!*

She knows and she doesn't know, put in the Princess. *We both of us see how much she represses.*

The Princess had, of course, been in analysis and was fluent in its jargon of easy explanation.

You know how she's always looking for the Perfect Father, having been abandoned by her own at such a vulnerable age. And the Mother—good God! the Mother! I admit that William James is not a bad choice for father. But he did have his faults—his dog-with-a-bone attitude at the moment is very much in character—and she's going to have a very hard time accepting that he was, after all, perfectly mortal—meaning, of course, imperfectly moral.

This is absurd, Hedda said. The JAP is beginning to sound like a James character. Something appears to be getting very much out of hand in here.

Why am I doing this to myself? Perhaps *I'm* a schizotypal personality disorder?

No, no, we're not personality disorders—don't you believe it for a minute. It was, of all people, little Charlotte Brontë, brandishing a first edition of *Villette. We're artists, you and I!*

Perhaps, personality disorders are artists manqué? someone—it sounded suspiciously like the Ubiquitous Voice, but for the first time Hedda wasn't sure—suggested. *And the present indications seem to point to your being* manquée manquée *indeed. You're decidedly no Angel in the House—which leaves you, by exquisite elimination, the raving Madwoman in the Attic.*

Unkind. *Someone* was going too far.

But *you* are in control. It is always there for the asserting.

It all comes down in the end to a matter of Will. Victorious, transcendent, all-vanquishing Will. The *world* is my Will.

Will? What Will? Is that Will, as in William, or what?

Enough already, said Hedda, pushing herself away from her desk with a fierce-ish grimace of decision-in-the-making.

I've had enough of this creepy tower, she said with un-jelled conviction. Enough of this screwy New England. I'm going back to New York, back to the real world. Back to Bella and my JAWs. I only ended up here through an accident of free association anyway. (*There was snickering, faint and fiendish, from somewhere.*) There's no significance in any of it. (*More snickering.*) Tomorrow I leave.

Emily's voice—so spasmodically like Hedda's own—was reciting one of her agonized verses:

> *Ourself behind ourself, concealed*
> *Should startle most—*
> *Assassin hid in our Apartment—*
> *Be Horror's least—*

And downstairs, the phone was ringing.

It could only be Stella. Well, good. Hedda could do at the moment with a heart-to-heart with her sister, she thought, clambering down as quickly as she could to the kitchen. Thank goodness Stella was letting it ring so long, she thought as she finally reached the phone and made a grab for it.

But the line was dead at her ear.

Quickly she dialed Stella's number. It was busy. So her sister was trying to call her back. What a rare moment of sisterly communion. Communion blocking communication, but communion all the same.

And truly, there was, between them, Hedda and Stella, so much—all that bloody history, if nothing else.

Those two solemn little girls, one dark and one fair; each of them desperately trying for herself to detect the pattern that would fend off the dangerous anger of the Mother. The Mother, most horribly, *who would remember nothing of that anger once it was spent.*

Each girl had said something similar but different to herself, in order to save herself.

Hedda had said: It doesn't matter. I can take care of myself. I need no one. And here she was, alone in her tower with her voices.

Stella had said: It doesn't matter. I am really a secret fairy princess. Someday someone besides myself will see what I am. And here she was, with her trail of ruined relations and her JAP.

But there was saving grace in a shared history. They were enemies, Hedda and Stella; but they were enemies who confirmed one another's reality, and in this way they could keep out the craziness of the Mother, the Saint of West End Avenue, whose accompanying chorus of approbation was so consistent and convincing that each little girl could only wonder: Who is it, then, who is crazy? For it was clear that someone was.

She wants me dead!

There was no recourse from that rage. It constituted the Power Absolute within the apartment on West End Avenue. Their father had fled from it, abandoning his daughters to it, becoming, through his absence, the focus of their Byzantine fantasy lives. But no matter how creative each little girl was, there was, in the end, really no way that his absence could be reinvented into an act of devotion. He had fled to save himself.

It had been Stella who had saved Hedda from madness, Hedda now realized, really for the first time. As probably Hedda herself had saved Stella.

They had shared a bedroom. They had whispered together in the dark. There were times when they had comforted one another, when Hedda would tell her little sister a story about a princess in order to stop her sobbing.

Hedda remembered that Sunday in December when their father hadn't returned. That night there had been no consoling Stella, who was just young enough to be taken in by the talk of a reconciliation. She was certain, at first, that he had been mugged, that he was lying bleeding to death somewhere in the dirty snow. Hedda's assurance—how had she been so sure?—that he was simply gone, that he was unmolested and well and relieved as all hell, had at last quieted down Stella's hysterics, so that she relapsed into a noisy, hiccuping misery. All night long the fat little girl had stared up at the ceiling in their Macy's-showroom bedroom, very soon to be abandoned. They returned to the apartment on West End Avenue. The Mother, it seemed, had only sublet it.

Hedda put the receiver down to wait for her sister's call. But now the phone was silent, for her sister must have been doing precisely the same thing.

She waited. She would pick an arbitrary number—4:13— and call then, if the phone still had not rung.

But now it was ringing!

She snatched it up.

"Stella! Stella!"

"Hah!"

Hedda dropped the phone, backing away from it, her eyes dilated in terror.

The voice on the line had been the Mother's.

XVII

———➤

Voiceless

"William dear," Alice said, entering the room. "There's a young lady downstairs who appears to be in a state of the most extreme agitation, and who absolutely insists on seeing you immediately. I'm terribly sorry. I told her you had to finish a paper to be delivered this very evening at the Harvard Club. But she will, quite simply, not be put off."

"Indeed?" William's voice was strained in its impatience. He had left himself precious little time to prepare his lecture. "Surely!"

"I think you had better see her, William," Alice said quietly in that tone of voice in which her four children— and William—habitually obeyed her.

"And the name of this imperious creature, Alice?"

"A Miss Sloper, I believe she said. Miss Catherine Sloper of New York City."

It was not, however, that self-possessed and exotically attired Miss Sloper, last seen in New York, who was now shown into William's library. Catherine showed undeniable signs of having dressed in haste and inattention. She was without her corset and without the flattering turban that had so transformed her pudding features. Indeed her hair had not even been coiffed, and thin wisps of it, mousy brown-gray, flew about her face as if charged electrically. It was a Miss Sloper looking every bit her thirty-eight years, looking, in fact, so haggard round the mouth and puffy in the eye as to seem a good decade beyond thirty-eight.

"Miss Sloper," said James, rising, "I am—"

"Oh, my dear Professor James," she cried out to him breathlessly. And, with a gesture at once piteous and peremptory, she cut him off dead in his well-bred attentions. "I have had a message! A message from beyond—from the father! She is in great danger! It shall be a failure of heart that shall kill her! We are sent—you and I—to save her!"

"Save whom, my dear Miss Sloper?" he had asked, alarmed. For simply the sight of Catherine Sloper's derangement would be enough to distress him—had she really then stepped over the precipice, plunging from hysteria into dementia precox?—without the added menace of her words.

"She!" cried Catherine, rushing past him to his desk and clutching to her bosom the tidy pile of pages that was there. "She!" she shrieked.

And with her two beringed hands she threw the papers into the air, scattering helter-skelter the talk he had been preparing for the evening's lecture at the Harvard Club, that which had been entitled "The Case of the Divided Spinster."

My "art," however, had succeeded so far in its prescience so as to make out the inevitability of a "double death."

But Henry's art had seen where William's science had been blind.

It *was* a failure of heart that killed Vivianna Bonnet. William's failure, of course.

Which one of them had set the torch? He would never know.

Murder? Suicide? How could one ever say?

The driver of the horsecar he hired at the station laconically gave him the news: that the tower had been burned to the ground in the early hours of the dawn. The charred remains of Miss Alice Bonnet—for so she had been known in the village—had been found.

Vivianna! Vivianna! Too late. Always too late.

But he had had to see for himself the rubble of the blackened tower. As he had had to walk there, amongst the coldly staring villagers, whose resentment of his presence was palpable.

As he had had to kneel down in the still warm ashes, and to lift them to his face, darkening himself with his grief. The sobs that racked him as he knelt in her mortal dust came with no sound. It was crying such as had nothing to do with tears.

William never did present his paper on the divided spinster to the Harvard Club. Nothing was ever published on this most exotic bloom in the garden of abnormal personality, which had carried so irresistible a metaphysical tint.

A brilliant series of talks, the Lowell Lectures on Exceptional Mental States, was delivered in Boston; sadly, only sketchy notes survive of them; William James never got round to working them up for publication. There is one of the talks entitled *Genius*, another *The Divided Self*, but no mention of the "Bonnet sisters" was ever made use of, so far as is known.

The memory of Vivianna Bonnet sank itself deep into his innermost soul, into that place in him where there was only sorrow. It merged itself there—together with the memories of his dead son, Hermann, who had shown such promise, and his sister, Alice, and others, too, a lifetime of others—into the constant pain that swelled his injured heart in the final stages of angina pectoris.

He lived a decade into the new century with that injured heart—lived long enough to know it was not to be his century. The tide of psychological thinking went all in one direction, and he went in another. He watched the new vision of the psyche emerging, watched it take on an ever denser substance, becoming—to his fading eyes—a bottom-heavy grotesque, susceptible only of self-stimulation.

The world *ab extra* went unheard; the new jargon alone would jam all reception. Who, in this brave new place, could have light? How would the unhoused voices find chinks through which to speak?

His own thought went all another way. Personal identity seemed to him more and more a naught, a poor pale flimsy thing, its "hiddenness"—which was realer than itself—lying bathed within the sea of extrapersonal mind—as the ocean of ether bathes the physical world.

There is a buried place in the psyche, where the boundaries between us all dissolve. It is not the facts of personal history that lie here, not repressed records of infantile trauma; but all of earth's memories are here—and its anguish, and its glory—else mediums and artists would not get at them as they do. It is from this place that the messages of such exquisite disruption are sent up to our poor gasping normal minds, making the blood in our veins go to ice with inhuman thoughts of terror and beauty.

We with our lives are like islands in the sea, or like trees in the forest. The maple and the pine may whisper to each other with their leaves, and Conanicut and Newport hear each other's foghorns. But the trees also commingle their roots in the darkness underground, and the islands also hang together through the ocean's bottom.

It was—for the briefest of moments—unspeakably fine, how it all seemed to come together, all the varying themes of his restless life; he beheld, in this moment, a bold new vision for a work that would perhaps slightly deflect the vector of the all too up-and-down psychology ushered in by young Freud. Yes, he had within him, still, two or three ardent purposes and plans.

But the bands of darkness round his heart squeezed him ever tighter. And soon, dreadfully suffering, he wanted only to die.

"I sit heavily stricken and in darkness," wrote Henry in mourning from America. "For from far back in dimmest childhood he had been my ideal Elder Brother, and I still, through all the years, saw in him, even as a small timorous boy yet, my protector, my backer, my authority, and my pride. His extinction changes the face of life for me."

Henry survived William by some few years. His own last decade was marked by those prolonged glimpses into the icy pit as had blighted William's life since early manhood; so that, as Henry's close friend Edith Wharton told it, "when

I entered, there lay a prone motionless James, with a stony stricken face, who just turned his tragic eyes toward me—the eyes of a man who has looked on Medusa! The good nephew slipped out, and for a terrible hour I looked into the black depths over which he is hanging—the superimposed 'abysses' of all his fiction."

Requiescat! Requiescant all!

But do they—*rest*, I mean—or do they wander still?

In William's final report as a psychical researcher, he confessed himself, after twenty-five years of studying the phenomena, in certain respects in the same identical balance of doubt and belief with which he had started out.

What is one to think of this queer chapter in human nature? It is odd enough on any view. . . . We are thrown, for our conclusion, upon our instinctive sense of the dramatic probabilities of nature. My own dramatic sense tends instinctively to picture the situation as an interaction between slumbering faculties in the automatist's mind and a cosmic environment of *other consciousnesses* of some sort which is able to work upon them. If there were in the universe a lot of diffuse soul-stuff, unable of itself to get into consistent personal form, or to take permanent possession of an organism, yet always craving to do so, it might get its head into the air, parasitically, so to speak, by profiting by weak spots in the armor of human minds, and slipping in and stirring up there the sleeping tendency to personate. It would induce habits, in the subconscious region of the mind it used thus, and would seek above all things to prolong its social opportunities by making itself agreeable and plausible. It would drag stray scraps of truth with it from the wider environment, but would betray its mental inferiority by knowing little how to weave them into any important or significant story.

This, I say, is the dramatic view which my mind spontaneously takes, and it has the advantage of falling into line with ancient human traditions. The views of others are just as dramatic, *for the phenomenon is actuated by will of some sort anyhow*, and wills give rise to drama.

William's final report holds out little hope for survival of a personal nature. But then he had confessed that his own *personal* feeling about immortality had never been of the keenest order. He was not really ever so very enthusiastic a supporter of the existence of William James per se. His character had never the tint of that sky blue optimism that wishes unconditionally to continue itself. He had cultivated—with vigorous exertion—cheerfulness and gaiety; but always, to the most discerning glance, there lay a deep sorrow behind his playfulness. He did not—he would not—indulge that sorrowfulness. He did not so much repress it as manfully resist it. But it was invariably from out of it that he stepped in order to greet his fellow creatures and give them all the benefits of his noble mind; and it was back into it that he returned when they had gone.

So the final view, which leaves us little room for a lingering *personal* presence, must have seemed a mild solace to

William, as the black bands tightened round his heart, and every breath became an agony, and he gave up, one by one, the interests and purposes that had been, for its time, that personal presence.

How can we think eternally to maintain ourselves when personal identity is, even while we live, a plumped-up phantom, a frightened fiction by which the vast majority of us try to keep the wider sea from breaking through?

But it shall break through. Sooner or later, for us all, it shall batten us down and break us through.

Hedda had barely left the tower since she had fled back into it, away from the voice on the phone.

Hah!

Faces came and pressed themselves against the window facing out to sea. Pale white faces pressed up against the glass.

Once Henry had appeared—his face contorted by the ghastly grimace of his final stroke—to whisper softly: "So there it is at last, the distinguished thing!"

Most of the faces she knew. Some were the women of whom she had written. Vivianna came, always suddenly to turn her head and show to Hedda the ravished face she had shown at the last to William. The beautiful JAWs looked in on Hedda, too, though they were all of them viciously transfigured. All of them looked in at Hedda with murderous vengeance. She had betrayed them, those seven sisters who had spoken with one voice; and they were not disposed to ask for her reasons.

Etta, Hanna, Sara, Mona, Minna, Clara, Dora: they were all of them against Hedda now. It was for her the final stroke that broke her: to see these creatures of her own making turning on her like this, wishing her dead.

The Mother smiled in and gloated.

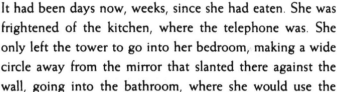

It had been days now, weeks, since she had eaten. She was frightened of the kitchen, where the telephone was. She only left the tower to go into her bedroom, making a wide circle away from the mirror that slanted there against the wall, going into the bathroom, where she would use the toilet and also drink from the faucet. Once or twice she had stepped without interest onto the floor scale there, dully noting the diminishing weight—121 pounds now; an indifferent witness to the dissolution of the great ridiculous hulk she had inhabited.

So Henry James, Senior, had calmly starved himself to death.

Her bones would be digested. Would her freakishness then disappear? Would she return—fleetingly—to the beautiful child she once had been?

The Dark Sister had been finished. She had seen it through to the end and then destroyed all the disks.

Quite often she heard the dim ringing of the phone in the kitchen below, and she covered her ears with both her hands.

The ringing woke her up sometimes in the middle of the night. She stopped covering her ears so that she could count the number of rings, which had begun to seem significant. Once it had gotten up to two hundred and sixty-four.

She knew who it was who was calling.

Once she had heard voices downstairs, footsteps different from the widow's.

It was the children's voices she heard. Whispering haltingly, under their breaths.

They had come back, had been prowling about the property, throwing pebbles at the windows.

Emboldened, they must have broken the lock on the door. Or perhaps she had left the door opened.

Yes. Probably the door had been left open.

She heard them moving around downstairs.

"Maybe she's dead!" she heard one of them say.

"God, are you stupid!" answered a deeper voice. "Witches never die!"

"Unless they're burned!" said another. "You have to burn them alive at the stake."

"Cool!" said the deeper voice.

She heard them now on the stairs of the tower. She sat there, the hideous, hulking shape of her, trembling.

There were more of them this time—seven or eight, maybe ten—she couldn't take them all in. In any case, more. When they opened the door and saw her sitting there, they were, for a few long seconds, frozen with terror. She, too. They stared at one another with similarly stricken expressions.

Then the older boy—for there was one there who was older, more a young man than a boy, really, a face cruelly blank—yelled to the others, "It's the witch! Run for your life!" and they all turned and fled shrieking down the tower stairs.

After that it was quiet.

Hedda kept her eyes closed, even when she was awake, as they burned so fiercely. And they continually ran with something other than tears, something thick and unpleasant. When she passed her hand over her scalp, clumps of dark hair came out into her palm.

It was the dank cold that was the worst, seeping inward from her extremities, soaking her to the core. She had dragged all the bedclothes up to the tower and sat huddled within them, but she couldn't get herself warmed.

She did manage to sleep, though, most of the time now. Night and day, it made no difference, it was all the same. The hunger had long since passed, and she hardly even registered any thirst, which was strange. She would have been almost comfortable, if not for the terrible chill. And it was, at long last, a voiceless sleep she slept.

Hedda woke up.

There was someone moving around downstairs. Someone was calling out her name.

Hedda covered her ears with both her hands—but still she could hear the footsteps, now moving about in the bedroom beneath. And still a faintly familiar voice calling out her name.

She screwed her eyes shut and began to moan softly to

herself, as the footsteps—much heavier than the slender widow's—mounted the stairs slowly.

She shook her head from side to side, still moaning, still trying to banish whoever it now was, come to torment her.

There were arms around her, gently rocking her. A hand was stroking her face and the skull beneath her stubbly hair, a voice crooning incomprehensible words.

She was being gathered up onto a soft fat lap, into the velvet folds of a sweeping cloak.

Hedda, Hedda, a soft voice was singsonging.

Hedda, look at me. Open your eyes now and look. It's safe now. I promise you.

Hedda opened her eyes and looked into the face of her sister Stella.

AN AFTERWORD

DARK AFTERTHOUGHTS
TO THE DARK SISTER

For some readers, the overriding question concerning fiction seems to be: How much of it *isn't* fiction? How much, in other words, is autobiographical? Not even considering the important (at least for me) issue of privacy, this can be a hard question for a novelist to answer. The presumption behind it of a sharp distinction between fiction and truth, especially concerning the matter of the *self*, can feel pretty forced to a novelist under the influence.

The Hedda of *The Dark Sister* is a novelist who is almost permanently under the influence. This is a situation both good and bad. It makes her prolific, but it also makes her, well, like this: "She slipped easily out of her identity. It was, in a sense, her profession. She so rarely occupied her given self, these days, that were she altogether to misplace it, the loss would probably go unnoticed for some time. Perhaps this had already happened."

I remember meeting an editor who had just read the manuscript of *The Dark Sister*, and how he had greeted me with undisguised disbelief: "*You're* Rebecca Goldstein?" When I asked him why he doubted the assertion of my identity, he answered straight to the point: "You're rather small, aren't you." Apparently, he was expecting a great big fierce-looking person, on the order of Hedda, and, well, as the man said: I'm rather small.

I resisted the urge to confess to the editor that during the summer months when I was writing the book I swaggered around the little town I was then living in (not in rugged Maine, as in the book, but suburban New Jersey) feeling fully six foot two, Hedda's height. And once, while I was under the influence, I *hissed* at someone who had banged into me with her huge heavy purse and hadn't bothered to apologize. It was an uncharacteristic gesture for me, only made possible by the sense of myself as having swelled into the formidable proportions of Hedda, of having acquired a face that could carry off so convincingly the full combative array of expressions—contempt, rancor, rage—instead of the quite different look that I know to sit atop my delicate neck.

But then Hedda, despite the shape of her in the world, is not really so fierce. She has a small timid voice, producing sentences filled with . . . uneasy pauses, and ending with the feminine habit of curling upward into a question, inviting contradiction? She craves love—or at least human connection—or at least something like human connection—through the medium of her fiction; it's not so much that she wants to reach out and touch her readers, but rather that living in her characters approximates intimacy. And, like many writers, including me, she is devastatingly susceptible to uncharitable assessments of her prose. Adolph Uberhaupt is a real presence in our inner lives, the internalized critic so harshly unenthusiastic of our efforts that his ultimate aim is to silence us for good.

But the autobiographical fact that is probably most relevant to my writing *The Dark Sister* is my complicated relationship with the Harvard philosopher and psychologist, William James, the older brother of the novelist Henry James, that prissy virgin who wrote like an angel, even though he, too, suffered prodigiously from his own versions of Adolph Uberhaupt. William James was described by one of his contemporaries as the psychologist who wrote like a novelist, while his brother was the novelist who wrote like a psychologist. I love both James brothers. But whereas my passion for Henry is focused entirely on his writing, on those cathedral sentences of his, my ardor for William is a thing far more personal.

I have an intense and intimate relationship with William James, the precise nature of which is mysterious and bizarre, even to me. There's a sense in which I'm in love with William. Like all lovers of the extreme sort, I long to inhabit the very soul of my beloved, to join our consciousnesses like two drops of water merged into one. And there have been moments when I could almost feel this to be so, especially during the heady days while I was Hedda, writing her novel, *The Dark Sister*, in which *she* was able to inhabit the very soul of William James. (This is what a logician might call second-order habitation.)

I have elective affinities with other philosophers as well—Plato, Descartes, Spinoza, Leibniz, Hume—but these are nothing like the oddly personal entanglement I feel with William. I know, of course, that William James is not the greatest philosopher who has ever lived. Those others—

Plato, Descartes, Spinoza, Leibniz, Hume—are so much more significant in the history of philosophy, as are any number of others that any worthy philosophy undergraduate can rattle off in her sleep. Frankly, I find the purely philosophical aspects of his thought—his pragmatic definition of truth, his pluralistic universe—a little squishy with imprecision. Try to pat it down at one conceptual corner and a bulge of vagueness oozes into another. Why then am I so smitten?

Strangely, the pull toward William James is not entirely toward the pure philosopher—the *res cogitans* preserved in books and articles and letters—as toward the entire man. . . I want to add "body as well as soul," although that seems as if it couldn't possibly be true. But I am, in some weird way, in love with William James and have been ever since I first heard the startling sound of him coming to me like a voice overheard in a room noisy with many conversations, a stranger's voice that strikes you as like no other and yet familiar . . . uncannily *known*.

I was in high school, an all-girls ultra-Orthodox Jewish high school, when I first stumbled on *The Varieties of Religious Experience*. I was very interested in religion in those days. You might even say I was obsessed. The question of whether or not to believe in the tradition in which I was being raised was very much a *live option* for me, to use the terminology that James coins in his classic essay "The Will to Believe," proposing it on analogy to the distinction between live and dead wires. A live option is one with a felt current for a particular potential believer, presenting a hypothesis which is a real possibility for her. Which hypotheses are dead or alive—the possibilities a particular mind even thinks to consider— is unavoidably influenced by personal history; I wasn't wrestling with the question of whether to be, say, a believing Shiite Moslem. But surely personal history shouldn't determine the entire matter of what one ends up believing, I thought then and continue to think. Surely there's some room for deliberation and agency. From what I could tell, few of the people I knew shared this thought with me. Though they all seemed to me to be heavy with beliefs, they also seemed mostly to have come to their beliefs by way of genetic inheritance, much as they had the shapes of their noses.

In the spirit of provocation, as well as of classroom boredom, I would often openly read books with titles like *The Death of God* while in school, hoping to arouse the censure of one of those bewigged rabbis' wives who were my teachers, so that I could challenge them to a theological debate. But they, perhaps wisely, ignored my provocations. I didn't talk or pass notes in class; my skirts weren't shorter than the regulation, below-the-knee length. Maybe these were the only sorts of violations that they had trained themselves to see. Or maybe they sensed my rebelliousness, coiled and ready to spring questions even more inappropriate in those classrooms than miniskirts would have been, and decided to just ignore me until the adolescent phase passed. So I sat in the back of the classroom and read *The Death of God* (it even had a red cover) and *The Secular City* (sounded like a good place to me) and *The Varieties of Religious Experience*.

I'm pretty certain that it was the promiscuity of the word "varieties" that attracted my attention. I opened the book— interestingly categorized on its back cover as partaking both of religion and psychology—and was totally unprepared for the onslaught of a passion that has yet to spend itself.

The book is no memoir, and yet James's *person* seems to hover just beyond clear vision, all the more seductive for being so elusive. I don't usually crave the biographical element in my philosophers. Impersonal truth, after all, is the sine qua non of the profession. But from the beginning I read James with a focus fixed just slightly beyond the page, trying to peer past the arguments into the heart of the arguer. Who *was* this man who had been born, tragically, in a century not mine? Why did he excite me in this way, arousing me to want to know him as intimately as possible, to exalt in his genius and soothe away his heavy sorrows?

I had an immediate intuitive sense of his sorrows, his aching vulnerability despite the genius and recognition. His status, his high Jamesian estate, couldn't hide from me the bruisedness of the inner man. And I sensed—and admired to the point of making it a lifelong inspiration—his unself-pitying attempt to resist through the sheer force of his active will—heroic man—the inclination to melt away into his congenital sadness. Behave *as if* you think life is worth living and you can make it almost so. He presented the remedy for melancholy and other deformations of the personality as a variety of *moral* struggle (so unlike the more medicalized paradigm that his younger contemporary, Sigmund Freud, was developing). For James there was to be no analyzing professional intermediary. Rather, it was hand-to-hand bloody combat between one's sick soul and one's will. And the fact that James's paradigm, unlike Freud's, provides no potential for a huge industry of mental health workers perhaps helps to explain why the one prevailed, to the point of transforming our culture inside out, and the other has passed into a footnote, or parenthesis, in the history of psychology. And it made my heart pound with grief—my heart still pounds with grief—that he had been made to suffer the ultimate vulnerability, against which his valiant will was useless, that being death.

In short, I fell in love with William James, body as well as soul.

As for the arguments set forth in *The Varieties of Religious Experience*, they're roomy enough to hold a great number of other people's first-person accounts of extraordinary religious experiences, most of them frankly bordering on the insane, if not already deeply settled in that wild country. James, however, claims not to hold a belief's pathological origins against it in the least: "If there were such a thing as inspiration from a higher realm, it might well be that the neurotic temperament would furnish the chief condition of the requisite receptivity." I had personal reasons to be thrilled by the idea that the neurotic temperament might give one the edge in receiving important truths. Nobody had yet told me I was neurotic, but nobody really had to.

James doesn't go so far as to claim that all religious experience is neurotic, but it's the neurotic varieties that clearly hook him. And the most heartrending of all his extraordinary prose (and let's not forget that *this* James brother, too, writes like an angel) is lavished on what he calls "the sick soul," and "the divided self." When James describes the worldview of "the healthy-minded" he relies primarily on quotations—lots from Walt Whitman's poetry and Ralph Waldo Emerson's "affirmations of the soul." But the dark intonings of the sick soul come entirely in James's own voice, that voice so unlike any other and yet so intimately *known.* "Let sanguine healthy-mindedness do its best with its strange power of living in the moment and ignoring and forgetting, still the evil background is really there to be thought of, and the skull will grin in at the banquet."

I had found my man.

I didn't yet know that the horrific account he gives of "the worst kind of melancholy . . . that which takes the form of panic fear" was not, as he writes there, translated from a French correspondent, but, rather, a bloody-raw slice of autobiography. He had suffered a breakdown at twenty-six, in a period of transition for him. He had given up, as a failure, studying art with William Morris Hunt of Newport, Rhode Island, and returned home to study medicine at Harvard, living with his parents and siblings on Quincy Street in Cambridge. The description of the swift descent that he claims to have translated "with the permission of the sufferer" imparts an all too vivid sense of the sort of mortal terror that can sometimes come on one with almost no warning at all.

He had gone into his dressing room to retrieve some object, and suddenly, in the half-light of falling evening, had been gripped by a horrible fear of his own existence. And at this same moment the image came to him of an epileptic patient he had seen that day in the asylum: "a black-haired youth with greenish skin, entirely idiotic, who used to sit all day on one of the benches, or rather shelves against the wall, with his knees drawn up against his chin and the coarse gray undershirt, which was his only garment, drawn over them, enclosing his entire figure. He sat there like a sort of sculptured Egyptian cat or Peruvian mummy, moving nothing but his black eyes and looking absolutely nonhuman." Seized by his fear and this image, by his sense that there was only the flimsiest discrepancy between his own self and this other, the words had come to him: *"That shape am I. That shape am I, poten-tially. Nothing that I possess can defend me against that fate, if the hour for it should strike for me as it struck for him."*

It was his eldest son who revealed, after William died, in 1910, of a damaged heart, that the episode was William's own. But somehow I'd sensed, from the beginning, the man-ner of person who was calling to me from those pages, in that voice that I seemed always to have known.

It can't be real love, of course, given the metaphysical ob-stacles (by which I don't mean the judged weakness of his metaphysics but rather the fact that he's long dead). But this shadow-love of mine is close enough to the real thing to engender such things as shadow-seduction and shadow-jealousy. In *The Dark Sister* I not only made William James a character whom I could (by way of Hedda) inhabit, cultivat-ing the delusion of the sort of intimacy a lover sometimes craves; I also deformed his wife, Alice, into an insipidly con-ventional Victorian female. I even made her fat. There's a scene in which William, unseen in his dressing room, watches in "mounting horror" as Alice removes her corset and preens before the mirror: "The female flesh of her came pouring out from its brutal encasement, bruised red and pur-ple where the stays had cut most cruelly into her. Her droop-ing maternal abdomen was mottled and puckered. A fiendish riot of female flesh—of eddying swirls and dimpling swells. The great white mounds that had had the shape long ago sucked out of them by the five infant mouths . . ." This was unkind of me. Still, with such obstacles to our love as I have need to overcome perhaps I can be forgiven these offenses to decency and truth.

Aside from making his wife insipid and fat, I made him

cross paths with a woman so fascinating as to tempt William in all his parts, from his incomparable cerebral cortex on down. This is the amateur scientist, Vivianna, her slim female form poised before the Astronomical Immensities. How could William's fundamentally sound relationship with his healthy-minded wife not feel lusterless and deadweight when compared to the exquisite unpredictability held out to him by the dark, divided sister? I offered him a woman to touch him deeply, with sympathy and genius and danger, a creature I knew would enter into him as—if nothing else—a ravishing disruption.

And he would be able, reciprocally, to enter into her, pervade the unprotected softness of her as no one else had ever done. Though she spent a lifetime keeping her hidden self from the world, how could she hope to keep it from the gifted psychologist of Harvard, his soul dipped, despite all his vigorous exertions to change its hue, in the midnight shade of a requisite receptivity? He would have possessed the hidden self of her as no one else ever could.

William, of course, fails Vivianna. Though he penetrates, with all the power of his vast psychology, deep into her, Vivianna proves *too* interesting for William. The intellectual passion of him overtakes his humanity, freezes over the love that ought to have been yielded up to her. At the moment of his deepest ingress, she's transformed for him into a valuable datum supporting his theory of the subliminal self. William loses his chance for the dark ecstasies of Vivianna, and this is no less his tragedy than hers. The wife has him until the end, although there is something of him that she never gets, I'm certain of it.

That shape am I. That shape am I, potentially. Those words that, unsurprisingly, were William's own, that welled up out of the fear of his own existence, have been repeating themselves in my mind ever since I first read them in a fevered chill in the back of an insufferable classroom. Sometimes they're repeated in dread and despair, and sometimes in exaltation. I sometimes think they're the words that made it possible for me to become a novelist, or at least they're the words that best express for me that possibility, the dread and despair and exaltation of that possibility.

The shape of us is not a thing so fixed as it appears in the sunlight of common sense and ordinary life. In that dry light the reality of our selves stands discrete and solid, lined up in a row with the other unwavering facts of the world. It takes the disintegrating blue light of extraordinary experience, the light of an evening quickly falling in which artists must learn to see, to drain the reality out of our identities. In the blue light we know our selves as things far more drastically permeable, almost to the point of becoming unthinged.

The Harvard professor, artist of the human soul, understood all this, of course. And even though at the crucial moment he failed the dark sister, I forgive him. He's so unfailingly moving, even in his failings. There's nothing I wouldn't forgive him, knowing him as I do.

And that he would fail us is dictated by the stubborn facts of the case. There *is* something, in the end, absolute about the distinction between truth and fiction. Something is held back, something won't yield, even in the liquefying fire of love and art.

I always knew my love was doomed. That's how I knew it was true.

Library of American Fiction
The University of Wisconsin Press Fiction Series

Marleen S. Barr
Oy Pioneer! A Novel

Melvin Jules Bukiet
Stories of an Imaginary Chidhood

Rebecca Goldstein
The Dark Sister

Rebecca Goldstein
Mazel

Jesse Lee Kercheval
The Museum of Happiness

Alan Lelchuk
American Mischief

Alan Lelchuk
Brooklyn Boy

Curt Leviant
Ladies and Gentlemen, The Original Music of the Hebrew Alphabet
and *Weekend in Mustara*

David Milofsky
A Friend of Kissinger: A Novel

Lewis Weinstein
The Heretic: A Novel